LORD EDGINGTON

BOOK 15

THE CHRISTMAS CANDLE MURDERS

A 1920s MYSTERY

BENEDICT BROWN

COPYRIGHT

For my father, Kevin,
I hope you would have liked this book an awful lot.

A typical winter scene on the frozen river at Kilston Down, at the foot of the Surrey Hills.

READER'S NOTE

My Christmas books are always standalone mysteries, which means that they don't give away any secrets from the rest of the series. All you need to know to enjoy this one is that an eccentric aristocratic detective and his now adult grandson have spent the last three years solving mysteries together.

At the back of the book, you will find a list of characters, a glossary of unusual words, and information on what inspired me to write this novel. I hope you love it!

Competition

This story contains a lot of hidden references to popular Christmas films, books, and songs. There are at least seventeen, plus a few I've probably forgotten. These include direct quotes or allusions to famous scenes, and this year about half of them are influenced by the beautiful short story "A Child's Christmas in Wales" by Dylan Thomas. You can read it online for free, and I can't recommend it highly enough.

If you find a good number of references, e-mail me at **bb@benedictbrown.net**. The person with the most correct answers by the end of 2024 will win either a signed book sent anywhere in the world, or your name included in a future story – admittedly, some names are more suitable than others, and I can't imagine Lord Edgington crossing paths with a Mandy or Skip. (No offence meant to anyone named Mandy or Skip!) If there's another prize you fancy, I'm open to ideas. Last year I had some interesting answers, and I'm excited to see what you come up with this time!

PROLOGUE

Maude Evans had long since forgotten the attraction of Christmas. She just couldn't see why people should behave differently for one week every December. She did her very best to be sour and rude twelve months a year and certainly wouldn't take time off just because there were decorations hanging from the lampposts outside her cottage.

Really! she thought as, swaddled in a thick woollen scarf and ankle-length coat, she bustled through the village with her shopping. *Some people simply never grow up.* It was only the first day of Advent and the inhabitants of Kilston Down were already getting into the Christmas spirit. It seemed to happen earlier every year, and Maude could not abide it. There was barely a half inch of snow on the ground, and yet the young hoodlum who had just moved to the village was throwing a party as if it were already Christmas Eve.

Loud, *modern* music blasted from the house opposite hers and someone had hung a "Happy Christmas" sign from the bare willow tree on the front lawn. *Happy Christmas? More like miserable three and a half weeks to go.* To her horror, she even spied a couple leaning against the side of the house talking close together. Such behaviour was common at number three Bitterly Close, and she turned her eyes away in case she were to catch them kissing one another like… like… Well, to be quite honest, Maude had no desire to think what they were like, but it certainly wasn't respectable, and so she hurried along the pavement, up the garden path and into her tiny house all the quicker.

Admittedly, she could still remember a time when the mere mention of that holiest of seasons had lit a candle within her. As a child, she'd longed for December to arrive, but that was when she'd had a family with whom to celebrate, and aunts and uncles – her parents never went in for such things – who were generous enough to scrape together their meagre savings in order to buy her and her sister a small toy, or perhaps even a book.

Those days were long gone. There was no one to welcome her that freezing night as she placed her two heavy bags on her dining room table and went to make a cup of tea. Maude lived a frugal life, but she was so cold that she decided to brew a fresh pot for the good it would do her. With great relish, she unscrewed the lid on the tin of Assam that she'd just bought from Mr Tibbs the grocer, and then stood beside the stove as the water first sparkled, then bubbled, then boiled.

She was not one of those people who say that you shouldn't watch a pot. She knew full well that it takes the same length of time whether you're standing next to it or not. It also offers the benefit of warming your hands at no added cost. The ice in her veins had begun to thaw and, though the house was as cold as a parson's nose – and she tended not to light a fire until the winter had started in earnest – she felt a touch less critical of her neighbours' jollification.

She could just about concede that it was natural for young people to want to spend time together. When she was a girl, she might well have gone across the road with a plate of biscuits and hoped for an invitation. But that was back when her fellow villagers were simple, down-to-earth folk, not the Bohemian types who had taken over the place recently. It made her sick to her stomach to think of old Mr Cranston, who was born and died in the house opposite, making way for such ingrates.

And so, as she spooned the loose tea leaves into the pot and cursed the wailing saxophone of the no-doubt American music that sounded as though it were being piped in through her letterbox, her comprehension faded. She had no sympathy whatsoever for people who thought only of themselves. With her hands wrapped around her mug, she went to sit down at the small dining table, which was barely big enough for one.

Her cat Snowfall came to rub against her leg, but Maude hissed and scared him away. She would not be distracted. She had a job to do and, unlocking her near-scalded fingers, she selected a piece of paper from the pile and dipped her pen into the well that she made sure to keep full to the brim.

"Dear Mayor Perkins," she said aloud as she wrote. "This is the third letter I have penned on the topic of Gareth Heywood, the newest arrival to Kilston Down, who unhappily resides just feet from my own humble dwelling. I believe that I have already informed you of his antisocial habits, but the events of the first of December truly took things too far."

The letter continued in such a manner for three pages, and Maude had the zealous look in her eyes which told Snowfall that his owner would be occupied for some time. Aware that he would get no supper until she had finished, he languidly wandered to the bedroom at the back of the house and chose a spot for himself on the bed that was hard, narrow, but marginally more comfortable than any of the chairs his mistress possessed.

Maude was composing a particularly wonderful sentence on the wickedness of the modern world, when the music across the road changed and her pen fell from her fingers. Strains of a Christmas carol filled her miser's cottage. The young chap who had bought number three was a musician of some sort. His friends were musicians, too, and they liked nothing better than to deafen their neighbours with awful, discordant noise that no one in their right minds would ever want to hear.

But this time, the music was different. She wandered to the front door and peered through the frosty window at the glow of the house opposite.

> **"All poor men and humble,**
> **All lame men who stumble**
> **Come haste ye, nor feel ye afraid."**

The words meant nothing to her, but the tune sent her shooting back to her childhood. She'd never before felt so disconnected from the world around her or the present moment – she felt detached even from her own body. A sense of joy ran through her, and she might well have run out into the street as the snow fell, but all she could do was listen.

> **"For Jesus our treasure,**
> **With love past all measure,**
> **In lowly poor manger was laid."**

For the first time in decades, she remembered the excitement of the season. Had some full-bodied, bushy-bearded gentlemen come down her chimney with a bag full of presents, she might even have cracked a smile.

But then the music faded away, and she felt the cold of her gloomy house and remembered that there would be no jolly man coming to visit her, nor a present at the end of her bed. As that uniquely uplifting sensation died, she almost wanted to cry. She looked back along the corridor to the kitchen but couldn't face returning to her letter. And that was when she saw it. There was a small parcel placed on the table by the sitting room door. Her sister must have brought it inside when she came to clean.

With much of the spirit of a child on Christmas morning, she travelled across the room on her seventy-two-year-old feet, which she blamed for many of her woes. She seized the small present and held it up to the light. In her hands was a red candle wrapped in gauzy white tissue paper. There was a string tied around it with a paper label which said,

To Miss Evans,

May this candle brighten the coming month.

From your neighbour,

Gareth Heywood

And it was at this moment that Maude decided to put a log on the fire after all. Once she'd prepared and eaten her dinner, she lit the candle and placed it on the windowsill in the sitting room that she normally only used when the vicar paid a visit – not that she approved of the man. And there she sat with a Welsh quilt over her knees, the fire blazing and that pretty candle sending its magical light about the place. The flame danced in the draft that poked its way in through a crack in the window, and as she sipped a second cup of tea, Maude thought to herself, *Perhaps Christmas isn't so terrible after all.*

Well, I imagine that's how her last night on earth played out. I can't say for certain as there was no one there with her. All we know is that, when her sister came to see her the next morning, Maude Evans was sitting in the only armchair in that tiny room, and she was stone-cold dead.

CHAPTER ONE

I've never understood people who don't understand the attraction of Christmas. It would take a truly hard-hearted, myopic sort not to see the wonders of that most charitable time of year. I, for one, am not ashamed to say that I love every moment of it. From the first of December to Twelfth Night, I am a child once more. Having spent the last few years training to become an assistant-detective to my famous grandfather and attempting, as much as possible, to be more mature, this might sound like a backwards step, but the older I get, the more I enjoy this pleasant contrast.

At Christmastime, it is more than acceptable to run about with a gigantic smile across one's face. Adults are free to play the games of their childhood without fear of judgement, while those who do, indeed, judge them can be denounced as the Scrooges that they are. And that, more than presents and snowmen and chubby men in green outfits, is the true wonder of Christmas: it is the time of the year when human kindness – which should be an eternal presence in our lives – can be seen more clearly.

Admittedly, our last three Christmases were spent investigating grisly murders, which rather undermines every last thing I've just said, but I was determined that Christmas 1928 would be different. While it is true that the odd splash of scarlet is indubitably festive, I was looking forward to a crime-free holiday. And how could I be so sure of myself? Well, for one thing, I would be spending a week with my parents, brother and a string of irritating relatives at home in Kilston Down. I had spent the first eight years of my life at the modest manor house on the South Downs, but since going away to boarding school, then living with my grandfather, my visits had become less frequent before drying up altogether.

It had been four years since I'd last celebrated Christmas with my whole family, and I was anxious to see them. I stood outside in the snow to watch my grandfather's servants packing the cars. They all seemed so jolly as they loaded crates of wine and fine food, though a few of them stopped to tell me how sorry they were that I was going away.

"I'm sure you'll have a wonderful time without me," I told each of them in turn, and O'Mahony, the youngest of the gardeners, replied with a knowing look.

"That we will, Master Christopher." He even winked. "That we will!"

I couldn't imagine to what he referred, but he was a jolly Irishman and, as my infinitely disapproving grandmother would have me believe, jolly Irishmen always have something up their sleeves.

It was the twenty-second of December, and it had already snowed for six days and six nights, which is a positive eternity in the short life of a Christmas. Regardless of the piles of snow around Cranley Hall, the cold did not deter me from my watch. I could think of nothing more enjoyable than seeing our much-appreciated staff working away so joyfully like sandboys. Our not-so-very-old-after-all dog, Delilah, was dashing after each person who arrived, unsure whether the smells that the packages gave off might spell treats for her.

"If you're just going to stand there, Christopher," my grandfather's voice boomed down to me from the terrace at the side of the immense property, "then you might consider helping."

He had a point, but that didn't mean I had to agree with him. "I'm savouring these final moments before we set off on holiday."

Our factotum, Todd, was passing and, as our most senior employee, he was permitted to rib me (ever so lightly). "I believe that Cook has a rather large turkey that needs carrying from the kitchen if you would like to savour these moments whilst lending a hand, sir."

"You tell him, Todd," Grandfather called down. He had the ears of a fawn and could hear effortlessly over long distances. "There's nothing quite so Christmassy as everyone coming together to get a job done."

I could hardly disagree (again), so I walked through the corridors below stairs to reach the kitchen.

"Do you have any idea how many of Grandfather's regular attendees will be coming to Kilston Down with us?" I put to our retainer. Todd is one of the sharpest fellows around and usually knows of his master's plans before I do.

"I couldn't possibly say, sir." He was also a keeper of the old lord's secrets, and I didn't trust him one bit. "But I can tell you that I am happy to be one of them."

14

"Your family won't miss you?" It often strikes me that the life of a servant in a grand house rather limits the private life he can have.

"My mother is going to visit her brother in Oxford, and my sisters have families of their own. I'd much rather set off on another adventure with you and your grandfather than be stuck here." His eyes lit up when he said this, and I knew just what he was thinking.

"I'm afraid we might have to disappoint you there, old friend." The smell of mincemeat and homemade orange marmalade had led us by the nostrils, and we reached the large, airy kitchen, where several maids and footmen were hard at work. "I've set my heart on a Christmas that is one hundred per cent free from crime."

Todd didn't smirk or grin, but I could tell that he thought this an unlikely outcome. He leaned in to whisper in a confidential tone. "Yes, of course, Master Christopher. We are very unlikely to come across a dead body in the village where you grew up." He tapped his nose with one finger, and I believe I tutted in response.

"Really, Todd. I mean it. I want nothing more than a quiet holiday with no stressful investigations, no chasing after suspects, and certainly no murders."

To be fair to the man, he nodded and accepted this point most humbly. It was his colleagues who burst out laughing.

"Oh, I am sorry, sir," our normally sober footman, Halfpenny, told me. "It's not that I don't believe you for one second." His podgy grey face became a little rounder as he smiled. "It's just that murder goes together with you and your grandfather the way that gravy goes with beef and potatoes."

"Precisely." Our cook, Henrietta, was rolling pastry, but she paused her work to contribute to the discussion. "If the pair of you were to go on holiday somewhere and there wasn't at least a jewel robbery, though preferably a series of dreadful murders, that's when I would think that something was wrong."

"I just want the sort of Christmas I had when I was a child. No one was ever murdered back then. Is it really so difficult to return to those innocent, carefree times?"

Rather than answering my heartfelt question, they all found something with which to occupy themselves, and I realised that there was nothing left for me to carry out to the cars.

"Don't look so glum, Master Christopher," our skinny cook called to me, as, apparently, I was looking glum. "Come and help me fill the mince pies. I'm hurrying to do one last batch before we leave."

I tried my best to continue to feel hard done by, though I couldn't quite remember why, and the sight of all that delicious food was too tempting not to give in. There must have been another batch already cooking; the whole room smelt so good I was tempted to take a bite out of the nearest wall.

"So you're coming with us, too?" I said as I washed my hands. "Don't you have family to see?"

"Your family are my family, Master Christopher." She stopped what she was doing and gave a truly warm smile. When I was a child, the often-stern cook had scared me no end, and so I was amazed that she would make such a generous comment. "I have a sister with a large family in Wokingham. She doesn't want me bothering her when she's busy, and you and your brother are the only children I've ever seen grow from babies to men."

This was all very sweet, of course, but I was trying to work out what game Grandfather was playing. He always insisted on taking far too many servants with us on holiday, but he would be staying at my house this time. We had staff of our own, and they were perfectly adequate. It also presented another potential point of conflict.

"You haven't met our cook Maggie, have you?" I asked as I spooned the sweet and spicy mincemeat into the cases.

"No, but I imagine we'll have a lot in common." Henrietta took a circle of pastry and placed it over each filled pie before cutting a small hole in the centre with a sharp knife and then fluting the edge all the way round. "What's she like?"

I didn't know what to say because there was no very nice way of answering. "I'm sure we'll have a lovely Christmas together."

I've never been a good liar, and Henrietta eyed me as though I'd just dribbled on the pies. As it happens, I thought I'd done a rather good job and hardly spilt any of the filling on the blackened metal baking tray, though I did have to lick my fingers a few times when that happened.

Once the pies were in the oven, I went upstairs, and every member of staff I passed had a similar message for me.

"I'm looking forward to Christmas at your house, Master Christopher." Our maid Alice waved her feather duster rather affectionately.

"Not long to go now, M'lordship's grandson," her oversized colleague Dorie yelled down the hallway at me – Grandfather did not choose staff based on their decorum or even their domestic skills so much as their ability when it came to eavesdropping on suspicious characters, operating within a network of spies, and, in the case of ex-convict Dorie and her sister, the lightness of their fingers. "I love a holiday, does I!"

Timothy the page boy, the youngest of our servants, was all smiles and answered my question without my uttering a word. "My folks live in Essex, sir. Lord Edgington said it was a shame for me to stay here without any family about, so I'm coming with you. And if there's anything you need while we're there, I will be only too happy to help." He bowed, pulled on his shirt sleeves and scampered off into one of the salons to do... whatever it is page boys do in a modern household.

By the time I'd found my grandfather in his sitting room, I'd counted seven different members of staff who would be coming to my family manor house fifteen miles away. The comparatively minute home had only fifteen bedrooms and some extra servants' quarters, so Christmas would be something of a squeeze.

"Don't look at me like that, please, Christopher," Grandfather told me without turning around to see my expression.

I searched the room for a mirror to see how he'd achieved this feat, but there wasn't one. "How do you know how I was looking at you if you weren't looking at me?"

He was tying up a small parcel with coarse red string and took a moment to finish a large and elaborate bow. "I could hear it in the way you climbed the stairs. Clearly something has upset you, and you've come to complain."

I pretended this was not true, which only made me more upset. "Fine, you're right, I do have a bone to pick with you. Did the heaviness or otherwise of my steps tell you what that might be?"

His moustaches twitched for a moment, and I thought he might sneeze, but he really wasn't that kind of person. "No, but I can hazard a guess." He set the present aside and spun on the ball of his foot to look at me. "Either you've eaten too little or too much food, you're feeling insecure about your skills as a detective, or you are shocked by the number of employees who will be accompanying me to your house for Christmas."

I kept my expression expressionless. I didn't want him to know that, essentially, all three of these things were true. I was annoyed that we would be travelling to my family home at lunch time and might miss the chance to eat. I rarely went a day without wondering that my detective's apprenticeship might only prepare me for the unemployment line and, yes, I had failed to fathom why he required so many staff.

"The problem is not that our trusted servants don't deserve a holiday," I told him as I approached his writing desk. "I'm simply worried where they will all sleep when there are so many members of my father's family staying."

"There's plenty of room for us all!" He sighed as though we'd had this conversation many times before, which we had. "Let me ask you this, Christopher. How many people did I bring with us on our recent trip to Silent Pool?"

I had to think back a few months. "One."

"And to London in the summer?"

"Four."

"That's right. I took but four servants with me, even though we were there for two whole months. I believe I have been incredibly reasonable this year."

I was far from convinced by his argument but decided not to contradict him. "Very well, but does Mother know that you're about to land on her doorstep with two-thirds of a rugby team?"

As I'm no expert on team sports (or mathematics), I could tell that he would have liked to correct me in some way, but he concentrated on the more pressing issue. "It is Christmastime. How could she possibly object?" As a senior police officer, my heroic grandfather had apprehended savage killers and hunted down violent gangs. He was scared of no man, but his own daughter certainly made him quiver. "Although, if she happens to ask, it might be best to say that Dorie, Timothy, Alice and Driscoll are there to attend you."

"Driscoll is coming?" My voice instantly rose higher. "What possible use might I have for a gardener when the ground is covered in snow?"

He ignored my question and looked pleased with himself as he peered out of the window. "Four servants per person sounds far more reasonable than eight between the two of us, don't you agree? Now, you had better look lively. It is almost time to depart."

CHAPTER TWO

Is there anything quite so thrilling as a homecoming at Christmas? I had dreamed of that day since my grandfather had first suggested that we spend the holiday at Kilston Down – though I was now coming to wonder whether he had planned all this solely to be able to take so many members of staff with him. He really was a strange man.

The ten of us piled into four overstuffed cars like rag and bone men leaving a scrapheap. Grandfather would have no doubt enjoyed picking one of his sportier models to transport us over the Surrey Hills to my homestead, but we needed four larger vehicles to transport all the people, presents and the p… the p… Oh, bother! I don't know a word beginning with P that means food.

We slowly rolled off the estate, not only because of the ice on the road, but because the cars were so laden that even the motor of Grandfather's grandest Daimler struggled. There was a real nip in the air and—

Provisions! I should have said provisions. The cars were packed with people, presents and provisions! I knew it would come to me.

Anyway, our convoy set off at a stately pace, and, five minutes later, we came to a complete standstill as a cart filled with parsnips had got stuck in the snow in the middle of St Mary-under-Twine. To pass the time, we all started singing Christmas songs. In each of the cars, a different carol was sung. It was rather difficult to concentrate on 'Past Three o'Clock' as I wished, when Dorie's loud voice in the car behind ours was singing 'Ding Dong Merrily on High' and Cook and our head footman were holloing 'We Three Kings' in front. I found myself losing my place on a number of occasions, and the songs became muddled together.

> **"Past three o'clock;**
> **And a cold frosty morning,**
> **Past three o'clock;**
> **In heav'n the bells are ringing**
> **Ding, dong! verily the sky**
> **Is riv'n with angel singing.**
> **Field and fountain,**

> Moor and mountain,
> Following yonder Star."

By the end, every last one of us was singing "Glor-or-or-or-or-or, or-or-or-or-or, or-or-or-or-or-ria" because that song is simply too ear-catching. Grandfather whistled along with the melody, and even Delilah accompanied us with a howl, though she didn't quite have the tonal range. For perhaps the first time that year, I felt that unmistakable thrill. It was a mix between a pleasant tingle and a painful stab: between nostalgia for Christmases past, and anticipation of what was to come. I was perhaps less spirited after waiting ten minutes for the cart to be cleared, but then we were finally free to keep driving.

"Of course, if someone were to be murdered, I hope you wouldn't be too disappointed," Grandfather told me when the singing – in our car, at least – had come to an end.

Evidently, someone from the kitchen had told him of the conversation I'd had with the staff. As I've already mentioned, they were excellent spies.

"There's no time for a murder. I have too many plans for our week. First, I will go with my mother to buy our Christmas tree – that tradition dates back many years. Then I will make mulled wine in the kitchen with our cook, (if she's in a good mood). And afterwards I'll…"

The list of my programmed activities took no short time to recite. Thanks to the worm's pace at which Halfpenny drove at the front of the convoy, the normally forty-minute journey was twice as long. By the time we were approaching the wonderfully named hamlet of Friday Street, on the other side of Leith Hill, and I could see my village beyond the trees, I was practically shaking with excitement.

We drove through the streets, and I looked for small differences that jarred with the picture in my head, but there weren't any to find. Kilston Down was not the sort of village that went in for change. In the twenty years since I'd been born there, the most dramatic thing to happen was when the clock on the clocktower became rusty and they had to replace the hands. There was something of an uproar after it was announced that the finished timepiece would now have black pointers instead of the copper ones it had previously had. The Evans sisters, in particular, were furious.

Despite or perhaps because of the old-fashioned air to the place, it was the perfect spot to spend Christmas. The half-timbered Tudor buildings on the main road wore hats of white and had fang-like icicles hanging from their gables. Houses ran in rows up the hills on either side of us and the glow of candles from within each made the whole scene all the prettier. I felt quite wonderful to be home again and was even more thrilled to know that I was just seconds away from seeing my family.

We drove through the town square and then the road curved around between lines of trees that were impossible to identify in their winter outfits. A left turn gave me my first glimpse of our estate and, when the house came into view, I was quite breathless. We rolled to a stop on the drive while the servants parked their cars behind the house.

I had expected a welcoming party to rush out to greet us, but no one appeared.

"Your family must be busy with something more important," Grandfather explained when we'd been sitting there for a minute and there was still no sign of anyone.

"That doesn't make me feel any better. You're essentially saying that our visit is less significant than whatever they're currently doing."

"Precisely."

Delilah was so eager to escape from the Daimler that she had climbed onto his lap, and so her master gave in to her demands. I followed them out of the car, still hoping that the sound of my well-slammed door would cause my loved ones to come running out to me. This did not happen. In fact, not even our butler was there to open the door to us.

Despite this cold welcome, I was happy to see our lovely old house again. It had been nine months since I'd last visited for a family lunch, and years since I'd seen it decked out in snow. It brought back so many memories of my early childhood and the Christmases I had spent there. Though small by my grandfather's standards, it was a well-proportioned Georgian manor house with steeped gables at either end and a semi-circular porch furnished with columns. The dear old place seemed to will me to walk inside – which is exactly what I did.

"Oh, hello," Father called from the drawing room between puffs on his pipe. "Is it today you're coming? I hadn't realised."

He at least stood up to shake his father-in-law's hands before returning to his newspaper. He had never been the most effusive person, but I thought he might at least offer a "Happy Christmas" and tell me how glad he was that we would be spending the week together.

"I'm glad you'll be spending the week here, son," he said, as though he'd gone fishing in my head and reeled in the very words he found there. "Everyone else will be out tomorrow. The staff have the morning off for Christmas shopping, and I'm expecting a package to be delivered. I don't know what I would have done if you hadn't been here."

"I missed you too, Father," I began quite spontaneously before the reality of what he'd just said penetrated my mind. "I beg your pardon?"

He folded up his copy of The Times, but only to read the reverse of it. "That's right. Some important papers will be delivered. It's bad enough that the office is closed for days. If I can't at least get some work done while I'm here, it will be catastrophic."

My father is not one of those men who are obsessed with money, but he is one of those men who are obsessed with the money market. Almost everything in his life revolves around his job in the City.

"It's nice to know we can be of service," Grandfather told him in a voice which very much suggested he didn't believe what he was saying. Father was oblivious to sarcasm and would have nodded his agreement had we not been interrupted by a psssting from the entrance hall.

It went, *Pssst!* as my paternal grandmother peeked through the crack in the door. "Are they here yet?"

"Are who here yet?" her favourite adversary enquired, and she slipped through to shake Grandfather's hand.

"My brothers, their broods and other assorted leeches. Have they arrived?"

I looked around the well-appointed room. There was a handsome walnut drinks cabinet in one corner, an illuminated globe showing the continents and what have you in another, but no sign of our relatives.

"I don't believe they are here yet," I told her, which seemed to make her both happier and more exasperated at the same time.

"Ahhhh," she groaned to express her anguish. "There are no two people on this earth who are more vexing than Thomas and Terry. And as for their offspring…" She collapsed beside her son as though the very thought of these people had drained her life-force. "I managed to avoid them last year, but if I try anything like that again, I'll have civil war on my hands."

"I still don't understand why you didn't tell them you wished to

24

have a smaller celebration in order to avoid all this fuss." Her son, my father (and Lord Edgington's son-in-law if we're being precise) looked quite bemused.

"Don't you think that I tried that?" My grandmother had softened somewhat over the last few years – presumably because I'd grown up enough for her no longer to describe me as an under-developed nitwit – but she was still a certified eccentric and wafted her hand through the air as though trying to get rid of a bad smell. "I called them to make up an excuse and before I knew it, I'd offered to host them all here."

We caught the sound of voices out in the corridor, and she immediately seized Father's newspaper and hid behind it in case the dreaded guests had arrived. Far from that familiar, life-sapping drone of my great-uncles' voices, a busy, bustling noise reached us.

"Mind where you're going, Albert," a woman's voice said. I don't wish to keep you in suspense any longer than necessary and can confirm that it was undoubtedly my mother's.

"Then don't push like that. I came very close to knocking a vase off the bureau." This was my brother's usual whine. He sounded as though he were rebuking her for some great crime.

The door soon opened and in they came, carrying – to my horror – a Christmas tree.

"But…" I said, as I couldn't believe my eyes. "But, Mother, it's our tradition to choose the tree together. Albert has never been interested before."

She was obscured by the enormous thing for a short while longer. It was only when her elder son had guided her to the wide bank of windows, and they'd put down their burden on the carpet, that she was free to reply. "It's lovely to see you too, Chrissy."

To ensure that I wouldn't complain again, she opened her arms for a hug. As soon as I reached her, I knew what had been missing. She had always been the centre of the family, and as much as I love my father, coming home to find her absent was like waking up one morning with only the left side of my body.

"Happy Christmas, little brother," Albert told me as he ruffled my hair.

Mother must have gestured to her emotionally limited husband, as he dutifully came to put one hand on my arm in what, for him, was the peak of physical affection. Soon, even Grandfather was at it. He went to greet his daughter whilst my grandmother looked on with a dubious expression and announced, "I'm sorry, everybody. I do not believe in hugging."

Perhaps to show that he wasn't quite as bad as his dear old mummy, Father squeezed my arm a little tighter.

"My apologies that we couldn't wait for you, old stick," my brother said once the embracing was over. "I have important plans this Christmas, and I need the tree in place from the very start."

"Important plans?" I asked with a touch of apprehension.

Mother saw the fear on my face and explained. "Albert is determined to make up for missed opportunities in past years and decorate the house."

A little voice deep inside me, that sounded really quite similar to my nine-year-old self, said, *But that's my job!*

My brother was already eyeing the tree. "I've taken three whole days off work before Christmas to dress every last room." He marched from one corner of the salon to the other, taking large strides as he went, and I concluded that he was measuring the space for the garlands he planned to hang. "Every... last... room!"

Father sent a look over to me that said, *Please do your best to discover what's got into him. We have been trying to work it out for some time and are still none the wiser.*

For the last year, the two of them had been working together at the stock exchange. This had helped Albert recover from a broken heart after his wedding was called off at the last moment in somewhat disastrous circumstances. So, while I would normally have explained that I didn't trust him to decorate the upstairs cloakroom, let alone the whole house, I chose a kinder approach.

"And I will be here to help you." I tried to smile but might have gritted my teeth just a touch.

"Wonderful!" he clapped his hands together and ran from the room. "I'll find our old decorations from when we were children and meet you back here in a moment."

I was about to ask my mother whether she had any theories as to why he was acting like a loon, but then I heard the crunch of tyres on the path outside the house. The heart of every person in that room immediately sank; our extended family had arrived.

CHAPTER THREE

"More tea, anyone?" Granny asked for the seventh time as we sat waiting for the meal to be over.

"None for me, dear sister." Uncle Terry's voice was like a funeral dirge.

"Nor me." His brother Thomas's breathy whisper was the kind you might use at a wake.

Silence returned to the dining room. It was only broken by the sound of the two cooks occasionally shouting insults at one another in the kitchen below stairs. There was a small shaft with a dish lift, so we could hear much of what was said quite clearly.

Distributed around the table were a selection of my very worst second cousins. Gerald had devoured double portions of everything that was on offer but was staring hungrily at the unfinished orange mousse on his mother's plate as though he hadn't eaten in days. Next to him sat Midshipman Peter in full uniform. He wasn't actually in the navy, but his mad father referred to him and his brothers by naval ranks because, as I have already mentioned, he was mad.

On the other side of the table from that undelightful assortment of humans was my father's cousin Philippa and her husband Paul. Philippa called people who came from beyond the south of England "foreigners" and Paul, perhaps fortunately, didn't appear to have the power of speech. Their daughter Pauline had married ("of all things") a Dutchman to irritate her family. She soon realised that she was just as close-minded as they were and deserted him. Disappointingly, she could not attend this year.

In short, there was a reason that my grandmother was not looking forward to Christmas: her side of the family was awful! The only thing worse than the awkward silences that were a feature of our meals together were the moments when someone actually spoke.

"I can't stand all this modern rubbish," Terry's son Aldrich announced, as though we had been talking about John Logie Baird's recent experiments in sending televisual signals from London to New York, which, now that I've raised the topic, sounds jolly interesting to me. Just imagine: a telephone for the eyes!

"Quite!" Thomas always agreed with whatever his brother was (or in this case, wasn't) saying. "There's nothing worse than change in my book. I said the very same thing when they first introduced the safety pen. I remember thinking, what's so good about a pen that doesn't leak everywhere? Perhaps I like getting ink on my clothes, hands and everything I touch. Did the meddlers who invented it stop for one moment to consider that?"

Everyone deferred to the senior members of the family, and so we inevitably waited to hear what Terry, the older but livelier of the two brothers, had to say on the matter.

"If I had my way, I would take us all back to 1878. I was twenty-eight years old. The Second Anglo-Afghan War was getting started, the Great Game was afoot, and I'd just fallen in love with the most beautiful girl in the village. I'd never seen such a pair of—"

"Wasn't the orange mousse delicious?" my father interrupted, just to be on the safe side.

"Scrumptious! Now, what was I saying?" Terry looked about in a manner which suggested that he'd never before seen the people there and couldn't ascertain why we were intruding on his lunch.

My brother bravely stood up from the table with one finger raised momentously, as though he were about to rush off to join the army or save a fair maiden from danger. "I have a Christmas tree to decorate!"

"Sit down, boy," Thomas bellowed, and Albert did exactly as he'd been told. "The meal isn't over until everyone has left the table."

Grandfather was clearly puzzling over how this might be achieved if no one was allowed to stand up, but he said nothing. For once, our dog Delilah wasn't sitting at my side looking sad that no one had offered her any scraps (even though I normally had). She'd stayed in the drawing room to escape from the torture we were enduring.

Through the course of the meal, my mother – who was related to the cavalcade of horrors by marriage alone and could hold on to the idea that she might still get a divorce one day – had tried to steer the conversation with little success. She was apparently only now capable of repeating bland sentiments in the hope that the time might pass a little more quickly. "Yes, the orange mousse was very tasty."

Timothy the page boy was standing stone-faced beside the door like a servant from the fifteenth century. His presence there must have alerted Mother to Grandfather's usual scheme.

"I hope you didn't bring too many of your entourage with you, Father," she told the old detective, who still looked confused.

"No, no," he reassured her. "*I* only brought four essential aides with me."

She looked relieved until Grandfather gently kicked me under the table to prompt me to say more.

"But *I* also brought four people," I reluctantly mumbled. "Among others, I thought that it would be useful to have our head gardener here so that…" I tried to think of a plausible end to this sentence. "…so that he can help us identify what type of Christmas tree you bought."

She now looked just as confounded as her father, but don't worry, Uncle Thomas soon thought of a distraction.

"Women have a lot to answer for!"

"Hear, hear, Father!" eternally bee-bonneted Philippa encouraged him. "I've always said that, without women, there would be no sin in the world."

I felt one of the more principled people at the table would stand up and find an excuse not to have to listen to this bilge. Mother was a dyed-in-the-wool suffragette who had fought for equal franchise for all, and my money was on her to speak first. In the end, though, it was my Granny who did the honours.

"You know, I'd forgotten what a jolly time we have together. I can't wait for dinner! However, I'm feeling somewhat dozy after all that stimulation and simply must sleep for six or seven hours."

"You are a wise woman, Loelia!" the most decrepit of her brothers announced. "A woman's place is in—"

"I must go to the ironmonger's," my father interrupted, again just to be on the safe side, and I didn't hesitate to hurry from the room after him.

"What do you need from the ironmonger's?" I whispered as our dear old butler Jessop fetched our coats and hats, and several family members I actually liked appeared from behind us.

"I haven't a clue, but I'm sure I'll think of something."

Grandfather came out of the dining room at a wondrous pace. "Let's go, everyone. Let's go quickly. One of them just told a story about the romantic feelings he had the first time he saw a woman milking a cow. It will haunt me for the rest of my life – which will hopefully not be too long."

"Why did you think it would be a good idea to come back here for Christmas?" I asked him, all aflutter. "Those people are insane!"

"Why didn't you warn me that they're like this?" he retorted. "Those people are insane."

"They get worse every year," Granny added, already pulling a hat over her ears to hurry outside. "I blame our parents."

My brother was the only one brave enough to remain in the house. He was still set on decorating non-stop until Christmas Day, but my parents, unrelated grandparents and our golden retriever bundled up to skip towards the village. Well, the dog didn't put on any extra clothing, but she did have a nice all-weather coat that would do the job.

My grandmother put her arm through mine and gripped me with her talons. "I am sorry that we're related to such monsters, Christopher," she said rather kindly before instantly undermining the sentiment. "If I'd never had your father, you wouldn't have to suffer like this."

I tried to ignore her own jagged edges. "You know, Granny, considering what your brothers are like, it's impressive that you're as kind-hearted and cordial as you are."

"How dare you, boy!" Her voice was so loud that it shook the snow from the trees along the drive. "If anyone hears such things about me, I'll lose my standing in the community."

Granny was very good at keeping her face serious when making a joke. She was so good at it that I sometimes questioned whether she was actually joking. In a similar vein, I was yet to decide whether she was terribly nice but tried to hide the evidence, or she was as mean and cantankerous as she wanted everyone to believe.

The further we got from the house, the jollier we all became and, in my case at least, the guiltier I felt for leaving our staff with those living vampires.

Evidently my mother was having similar thoughts. "Jessop is a capable butler and will know how to deal with the situation," she said to reassure herself. "And think of the fun we can have in the village as a family." She smiled at me from beyond the fur collar of her coat. "It's been too long since you were here for Christmas, Chrissy. I'm so glad you've come."

She let go of Father to muscle her mother-in-law out of the way, and I no longer noticed the cold.

"The problem is that we can't keep finding excuses to leave the house," Father said in his usual restrained voice.

"Who says we can't?" his mother loudly demanded. "I've spent the best part of my life avoiding my brothers. Why should anything change just because I accidentally invited them to stay?"

"We'll have to be in our own home on Christmas Day, at least." I believe that my words came out a little too needily, but I was longing to recreate all my childhood memories and couldn't stand the thought of only making rare appearances in the place where I grew up.

As our ice-bound boots went crunch crunch crunch along the drive and onto the main road, we all fell silent to consider our unique and uniquely horrible situation.

"We'll have to bring in food by the wagonload," Mother said in a mournful voice. "They're like a plague of locusts, and you didn't help by bringing so many of your servants, Father."

The august Marquess of Edgington raised one finger self-importantly. "Four members of staff for a whole week away from home is hardly indulgent. I don't even have a valet. Most men of my status have a valet." He was convincing no one, and this speech merely left me with the impression that he would soon hire his own valet.

"What we need," Granny pronounced each word ever so carefully as she debated how to broach the topic that would evidently offend several of us. "…is a murder!"

"Oh, please no," I begged. "I'm supposed to be on holiday. Can't someone be murdered next week instead?"

"Now, now, boy." Her haughty tone was perfectly pitched to put me in my place as she seized her son's arm to navigate a slippery patch of ice. "I'm not saying that I wish for anyone to die. Although now that I come to think of it, were my intolerable nephew or perhaps my niece's husband to be killed—"

"Thank you, Mother," her son interrupted. "But this time of year is about birth and hope, not death and darkness."

Neither my grandmother nor the detective who had investigated a total of eight suspicious deaths over the previous three Christmases could hold in their laughter at this claim.

My grandfather was surprisingly receptive to Granny's idea. "Of course, a fake investigation would work just as well as a real one."

I had to untie my tongue before responding. "Are you seriously suggesting that we pretend to investigate a murder just to have a reason not to spend time with my great-uncles and their families?"

"Yes." Grandfather's moustaches had gone even whiter with the tiny crystals that had gathered on them, but they weren't entirely frozen as they perked up considerably at this moment. "Has anyone died in the village recently?"

"Really, Grandfather. I thought better of you."

"Old Miss Evans!" Mother proclaimed almost jubilantly. "She died in her sleep a few weeks ago."

"How suspicious," Granny said, though we all knew that old Miss Evans (as opposed to her sister, young Miss Evans) had been on her last legs for a decade or longer. The woman was always complaining about one malady or another.

I could see that my grandfather's brain was ticking away with possibilities. "Was there anything unusual about the way in which she died?"

"Nothing whatsoever!" Mother's smile was bright enough to illuminate a Christmas tree, or at least a large nativity scene.

Grandfather clapped his leather-mittened hands together. "Wonderful. That will make it all the easier to invent a far-fetched story around her demise." I believe I must have tutted then, as he turned to me with a frown. "Do you have a better idea, boy?"

I was hoping to think of an alternative to pretending to do the job that I don't get paid to do the rest of the year, but we had reached the village square, and he was distracted by the scene before us. The little place was truly aglow. Each shop had boughs of holly hanging in the window, and Dotty's Teahouse had a garland of electric Christmas lights, the like of which I'd only seen in department stores on Oxford Street.

What I wanted to do more than anything else was to run over there with my family and warm our bellies with mugs of hot chocolate. I'd recently read a story in the newspaper of a biscuit van which overturned and caught fire somewhere in Essex. The people who went to help the driver had to navigate streams of liquid chocolate that came flowing out towards them. Once the man was safe, all of those kind-hearted people dipped their hands in and made the most of the sweet, warm treat. I could think of nothing so lovely as that.

"I still have some presents to buy," Mother said to disappoint me. "I'll join you a little later."

Even more disappointing than her leaving was the fact that she was walking in the direction of the cobbler's. I had the distinct impression that she was about to buy me a pair of slippers. People are forever buying me slippers. I must have fifteen pairs of them under my bed at Cranley Hall, and I certainly don't need any more.

"I must go to the post office to confirm tomorrow's delivery." Father was walking away as he said this, and I could tell from his distracted tone that he was already thinking about business.

"What about you, Granny?" I asked. "Should we treat ourselves to something sweet in Dotty's?"

She initially looked receptive to the idea, then made a face as though she were chewing on horseradish. "Come, come, Christopher. You've made such good progress over the last year. We don't want you turning into a Christmas pudding." I was fairly confident she was only teasing. She walked away laughing in the direction of Mr Tibbs's grocery shop.

"So it's just the two of us," I said to my grandfather, and Delilah gave me a thwack with her tail. "Would you like—"

Before I could put my previous plan to him, he interrupted. "Where did she live?"

"Where did who live?"

"The dead woman?"

I let out a long, slow breath to show him how uninterested I was in the whole affair. "You don't really intend to poke about in the life of a woman who was well into her eighth decade of existence and almost certainly died of natural causes?"

He stood up taller as though I'd offended him, which, of course, I had. "I'm in my eighth decade of existence. If I die tomorrow, will you just assume that there is nothing suspicious about it?"

"No, Grandfather. If you die tomorrow, I will be certain someone has murdered you for two reasons. Number one, you are fitter than a weight-lifting flea, and number two, there are approximately seven hundred people on this earth who would be ever so happy to see you dead."

He huffed at this. "Only seven hundred? I very much doubt it."

An apple-cheeked family of shoppers bustled past us along the pavement, so I had to pause before replying. "My point is that Maude Evans was a very different case, and we have no reason to believe that anyone murdered her."

"Someone murdered Old Miss Evans?" a familiar voice said from behind us, and there stood Ethel Perkins, the mayor's wife. She was one of the town's most dedicated gossips, and I knew that this apparent revelation would instantly spread around Kilston Down.

"No... I wouldn't say... There's really nothing to—"

"Just wait until the reverend hears this!" The gaudily dressed woman tottered off along the snow-caked pavement. The heeled shoes she was wearing were quite unsuitable for the conditions underfoot, and I half expected her to go sliding off them.

"There you go." Grandfather hadn't stopped smiling. "It's practically official. Now we'll simply have to investigate."

"You're still not listening." I started walking towards the place that I most wanted to visit (after the teahouse, at least). "Maude Evans was not murdered."

"How can you be so certain? Was she a wonderful person whom everyone adored?"

"No, she was a terrible person whom everyone despised." I clamped one gloved hand over my mouth then. Not only did I feel guilty for speaking ill of the dead, I had no wish to provide him with the impetus to justify his fool's errand.

"Then it won't hurt to have a quick peek at the scene of the murder, now, will it?"

I stopped walking and wanted to shout, *There was no murder and you know it,* but I decided to be diplomatic. "Fine. But then we're going to the river and we're going to build a snowman."

Yes, I did march away from him angrily as I said this. And, yes, I did sound very immature indeed.

CHAPTER FOUR

Bitterly Close was a small cul-de-sac that led off the southern end of the square. It was the kind of place you could live a hundred yards from your whole life and have no reason ever to visit. I noticed some children Thomasing from door to door , but even if Old Miss Evans had been alive, she was not the sort to give to charity.

There were six cottages arranged in a horseshoe, with one larger dwelling at the end of the road. Maude Evans's miniscule cottage was more like a shoebox than a house. It sat back from the road as though trying not to impose on the buildings around it. With its cape of snow, it looked even more like it was hiding.

Before I could point it out to my grandfather, a man called to us from the house opposite.

"Lord Edgington!"

Grandfather was used to people he'd never met knowing his name, but I was still unaccustomed to fame.

"And Christopher Prentiss, if I'm not mistaken." He was a young man of perhaps twenty-five with hair swept to one side in a very modern style. He had a thin, friendly face and, judging by the saxophone he was holding, I was willing to assume that he was a musician. "Where are my manners? My name is Gareth Heywood."

He'd been some yards away when he first called to us but had descended the path of his rather messy front garden and now held his bare hand out to my mentor.

"It's a pleasure to meet you, Mr Heywood," Grandfather replied in the amiable manner, which I was certain concealed his suspicions that we had already found the old lady who wasn't murdered's killer.

"Please, call me Gareth, or Gary if you're short of time." He shook his head as though he couldn't quite believe who was standing before him. "I don't suppose you're here on a case, are you?"

We both responded at the same time.

"No, my parents live in the manor house on the outskirts of the village," I answered quite rationally.

"Yes, what do you know about Maude Evans?" the madman at my side enquired.

"Old Miss Evans?" The young fellow ran his hand through his floppy hair. "I can tell you that she didn't like me. She would bang on my door at all hours to tell us that we were making too much noise with our instruments."

"Us?" Grandfather had already turned the pleasant conversation into an interrogation. "Do you live here with other people?"

Gareth must have noticed this, as he smiled at the question. "No, but I often have friends staying. I'm a saxophonist," he revealed, and I thought, *Well, done, Chrissy. We'll make a detective out of you yet!* "I moved down here from London at the beginning of the year."

"You were looking to escape the racket and clatter of the city, I suppose?" Grandfather suggested, thus going against (one of) the foremost rules in a detective's notebook: never answer a question which you yourself are asking.

"I do appreciate the peace in this part of the world, even if I'm guilty of spoiling it from time to time. Did you know that Miss Evans wrote letters to the mayor complaining about me?"

"I didn't, but that is very interesting." Grandfather actually nudged me then. He fully nudged me with his elbow, and I pretended I hadn't noticed.

"I never saw them myself, but apparently she recommended throwing me out of the town for being a public nuisance. I really don't think it was warranted. Aside from the odd party, I'm not exactly a troublemaker."

"So you're better off now that she's gone?" Grandfather's voice was flat, and Gareth immediately adopted a suspicious attitude.

"Exactly. And that's why I murdered her! The old monster got what she deserved." He let out a truly wicked cackle, and Grandfather stepped backwards into a heap of snow that was piled on the pavement behind us.

"You..." He couldn't form a response.

"He's teasing you, Grandfather," I told him, and our new friend became apologetic.

"I didn't mean to upset you, Lord Edgington. I'm terribly—"

It was grandfather's turn to laugh. He moved closer to jab one lambskin-covered finger into the man's chest. "Two can play that game, *Gary*, but I would still like you to tell me the last time you saw

36

Miss Evans before she died."

They both smiled as the potential culprit of a non-existent crime thought about the question. "I believe it was on the day she died. My friends and I were busy celebrating the start of Advent."

"How very pious of you."

"Not really. I simply can't ignore any excuse for a party. We'll be having another one tomorrow evening if you're interested in coming along. A good time will be had by all."

"Will there be mulled wine?" I had to ask, because... Well, there was no pressing reason other than the fact that very few of my Christmas traditions looked as though they would reach fruition, and I thought I might at least enjoy a cup of that delectable winter beverage.

"I can go one better than that." He dropped his voice to reveal his surprise. "We have homemade elderberry wine, which I'm sure can be heated to your taste."

"Exceptional!" Elderberry wine was something of a local speciality, and it made the perfect festive treat.

"You should bring your family, too, Christopher. The more the merrier."

"Please, call me Chris," I said for the first time in my life. I hadn't meant to rechristen myself (if you'll excuse the pun), but Christopher sounded a touch formal, and I've been wondering recently whether I'm too grown up for Chrissy, even if I still like it.

"Then I hope to see you at six tomorrow." He turned to look back over his shoulder to point at the two-storey building behind him. "You can't miss the place; it will be alive with music, and the walls may well be shaking."

"That sounds lovely," Grandfather replied, his face (and moustache) quite straight.

Gareth Heywood seemed uncertain how to interpret this final comment, and I don't believe he was the sort of person to be caught out by such things. His eyes were sharp and his manner confident and energetic. He had gone nose to nose with the unrufflable Lord Edgington and held his own.

Aware that the conversation had reached its natural conclusion, he bowed to us in the extravagant way that I imagine Italian counts greet everybody, then sauntered back to his porch to return to practising his instrument. It was only as he left that I realised he had been standing there the whole time in soft grey moccasins. As if having lots of them wasn't bad enough, this only reminded me of their inadequacy when it came to popping outside. Whoever invented slippers has a lot to answer for.

"Shall we?" Grandfather asked, pointing to Old Miss Evans's house.

"I doubt I have a choice in the matter."

He did not wait for me. "You don't."

The path up to the house looked as though someone had salted it, despite the fact there was presumably no one living there anymore. There were no lights or candles lit inside, but I noticed some movement through the hazy, mottled glass.

"Perhaps there will be a key hidden in one of these flowerpots." Grandfather peered down at the stones beneath our feet and moved around some leaves and the pots themselves with the toe of his boot. He was happier than he had been in weeks and, not for the first time, I had to wonder whether the part he liked most about being a detective was nosing through other people's lives. I knew he didn't really believe that Maude Evans had been murdered, but he evidently relished the opportunity to play the detective.

Whilst he wasted his time, I took the direct approach and knocked on the window.

"Who are you?" he asked, as though the woman who had just opened the door was trespassing in our home.

"Lillibet Evans. Who are you?"

"I'm the Marquess of Edgington." Grandfather looked shocked not just by the bluntness of her tone but that she should have to ask in the first place. Perhaps he was confused as to what Miss Evans was doing back from the dead.

Young Miss Evans, the deceased woman's sister, was not impressed. "Oooh, are you now? Well I'm the queen of Shepherd's Bush, but you don't hear me crowing about it."

I felt that I should step in to ensure that no punches were thrown. "Grandfather, Miss Lillibet Evans is Maude Evans's sister."

The tetchy woman dressed all in brown wool with sallow sunken cheeks stopped looking at the overdramatic lord and turned to me. "Little Chrissy Prentiss? Is that really you? I haven't seen you in years, boy." She grabbed me by the shoulder and gave me a shake, as though wishing to make sure I was there in corporeal form. "There's not as much of you as there was when you went off to that posh school of yours. Don't misunderstand me. You're definitely taller, but what you've gained in height, you appear to have lost in width."

"Hello Miss Evans, it's nice to see you."

Grandfather had evidently got her number and increased the smarm and charm in his voice. "Madam, it is a pleasure to make your acquaintance. I knew your sister in my youth."

"Did you?" she replied, and I echoed that very question.

"Did you?"

"I did indeed. Our acquaintance was only fleeting, but it left its mark upon me, which is why I wanted to come here to pay my respects."

"Oh, you're the one, are you?" Her gaunt face became a touch rounder, and she protruded her false teeth from her mouth to show that she was not impressed. "She told me all about you, and I know exactly the mark your *fleeting acquaintance* left on my sister, you swine."

Grandfather's subterfuge had clearly backfired, but he tried his luck nonetheless. "Does that mean we can't come inside?"

"As far as I'm concerned you can walk south thirty miles to Shoreham Beach and keep walking when your feet get wet." With a huff, she turned and disappeared down the hallway. Rather helpfully for the investigation that we weren't conducting, she left the door open so that we could traipse inside.

"I wonder why she's in here when her sister's been dead for weeks," I said in low tones. This annoyed me as it meant that my grandfather's inflated suspicions had already invaded my brain.

"I know poor Maude is dead," Lillibet called from a room at the back of the house, "but I still come in here from time to time to clean and look after the cat. I'd been doing it for her for years, and it's hard to change my routine."

"How kind." Grandfather was still trying to sound charming. "It is certainly very clean."

I was worried for a moment that the acoustics of the place had amplified my previous comment, and she'd heard what I said. Just to be careful, I tried to drop my voice even lower and pronounced,

"Kent are a much better cricket team than Surrey." When she didn't immediately scream at me for being a traitor to my home county, I knew that I was safe.

"Where did she die?" Grandfather asked, and I pointed to the tiny, but ever so neat parlour at the front of the house.

I was tempted to ask him how he knew that I knew where she'd died. In response, I'm sure he would have told me that, in a small town like Kilston Down, everyone knows everything, and everyone tells everyone everything, which would practically guarantee that my mother had told me the details of the woman's demise. As it happens, he would have been right.

"Mother told me on the telephone a couple of weeks ago," I confessed. "She said that the postman spotted Maude through the window and got the key from the sister. From what Mother heard from Mr Tibbs, the grocer, who heard it from Mrs Gimbel, the farmer, who had it directly from the postman, she was sitting there in her armchair looking out at the falling snow."

Grandfather was poking about (literally, I hasten to add) with a poker in the grate of the fire. "Was the chimney in use when she died?"

"Funnily enough, it was." I went over to see what he had found. "Why? Are you hoping to discover a burnt piece of paper with the remnants of a message written on it, the meaning of which will at first elude us before finally becoming clear, thus enabling us to solve the case when all seems lost?"

He stopped his task and turned his head ever so slowly to look at me. "No, Christopher, I am not." He tutted and went back to his poking. "That is the kind of thing that happens in sensational mystery novels... and, admittedly, one of the cases we have investigated together. I was more interested in whether something could have fallen into the fire which led to noxious fumes filling the room while she was asleep."

"Very good, and what have you found?"

He fell silent and kneeled down to take a closer look. "It appears to be... a small piece of paper with writing on it."

I was almost too excited for words. "What does it say?"

He flattened out the charred scrap with the tips of his fingers. "'Cow and Gate milk food. Babies Love It.'"

"Well, either the killer was a young parent, or that has nothing to do with Miss Evans's death."

"It must be an advert from a newspaper. There's more text on the back. She probably used it as a spill to light the fire."

"So we won't have to go through the neighbourhood asking every family which brand of baby milk they prefer?"

He said nothing to this, and we both moved on about the room. It was a clean but meagre space, which perfectly represented the lady who had previously resided there. My only memories of Miss Evans the older were of her telling me off for imagined offences. She once complained that I walked too loudly past her house on my way to see a friend, which, now that I think of it, is the kind of thing that my grandfather often says. Unlike my generally sanguine forebear, however, the former resident of number two Bitterly Close was best known for her negativity.

"You know, Maude Evans took exception to everything when she was alive," I decided to explain aloud rather than just in my head. "I believe she considered herself something of a moral police officer. She was forever wandering about the village looking for people and things to criticise. (Her sister Lillibet is just as bad)." I muttered this last sentence in little more than a whisper.

Grandfather didn't have a great deal to say in response, but hmmmed, and we continued to inspect the little room.

The decoration was almost non-existent, but it really was spick and span in there. There was a painting of two cats ignoring one another above the mantelpiece, and a brick fireplace with the mortar crumbling away. It was just as cold as outside, though knowing Old Miss Evans's miserly ways, I very much doubt it had been any different when she lived there.

I noticed that, on the windowsill, there was a small piece of card tied to a red ribbon. It was attached to some once-white tissue paper which, judging by the message I read, had previously contained a candle. I leaned closer to see the greasy red residue and drops of wax that remained.

Grandfather had appeared at my side as I was reading and finally found something to excite him. "I wonder why our new friend across the road would be sending his cantankerous neighbour a present."

"It is Christmas," I unhelpfully pointed out. "Perhaps he sent them to everyone on the street."

"Perhaps." Whatever spark of curiosity he had found had already died. "I'm afraid to say that I think you were right, Christopher. There is little here to interest us. I will ask the lady's sister a few of the usual questions, just in case."

As he spoke, a small white cat slipped into the room and began to make a fuss of my ankles. "And I will stay here to stroke this moggy."

CHAPTER FIVE

After a good length of time spoiling Lord Kittington, as I decided the creature should be called, Grandfather finished his interview, and we both returned to see our dog, whom we'd forgotten was waiting for us outside. At the very least, my human companion was now up to date on all the gossip he could ever need about the various characters within the village.

Delilah wasn't happy with me when she smelt the cat on my hands, and Grandfather wasn't happy to have found so little evidence at the scene of the imaginary murder.

"So, what did you discover?" I asked, though his glum expression told me all I needed to know.

"I discovered that Maude Evans was an unhappy old lady with any number of ailments. I also learnt that it is best not pretend to be a former sweetheart in order to extract information from the family of the deceased." He winced then, and I could tell that his conversation with Lillibet had not been a pleasant one. "I had to listen to her poor opinion of practically every person in this town. She claims that the vicar is a drunk, the grocer is having an affair with the mayor's wife, who is known as a something of a man-eater, and that the presence of licentious young men like Gareth Heywood has turned this village into a pit of immorality."

"At least she didn't recognise you." I quickly had to follow this statement with another, as I knew he would fail to see the advantage. "You successfully maintained your disguise."

Before he could answer, I heard someone calling my name from along the road.

"Christopher Prentiss, is that you?"

Delilah evidently liked the sound of the lady's voice as she went bounding off through the snow for some attention. They'd never met before, but our dog is a good judge of character.

"Mrs Steele." I'm sure I sounded quite amazed to see my old teacher, though I knew she lived nearby.

She reached the dead woman's cottage and stood marvelling at the sight of me. "It must be five years since I last saw you. I won't

43

tell you that you've grown because it's blindingly obvious. I barely recognised you."

I must have turned as red as a post box, but at least I remembered my manners.

"This is my grandfather," I told her, and she stepped forward to shake his hand.

"It's a pleasure to meet you, Lord Edgington. I've heard so much about you. I was Christopher's teacher when he was very young. My name is Alisha Steele."

"Mrs Steele is the best teacher I've ever had," I said a little too gushingly. "She lives in the big house at the top of the road." I pointed up the hill to the address in question, and something finally caught my grandfather's imagination.

"Oh, how interesting. I don't suppose you've recently received a gift from young Gareth Heywood, have you?"

She took a step back, as if the question had offended her. "Why would I have? I barely know the man."

"Allow me to explain, madam." He tipped his head forward to apologise. "I'm merely making some enquiries into the death of Maude Evans. She was sent a candle by Mr Heywood, and I was curious whether there was any connection between the two of them, or he was similarly generous with everyone in the street."

"Oh… Oh, I see. Well, I can't help you, I'm afraid. All I know is that she didn't particularly like our new neighbour. Whenever I saw her about the village, she would keep me talking for some minutes in order to list the many faults she saw in his behaviour and personality."

"I know the very type!" Grandfather said a little melodramatically, and I decided that he would have been a good actor in a bawdy comedy, always on hand with a quip. "Do you remember the last time you saw her?"

Alisha looked up at the sky that was clouding over in preparation for another frosty downfall. "It was the evening she died. I spotted her coming home from the shops and going into her cottage."

"Did you speak to her?" I asked.

"No, no. I was… Well, I was in my living room, and she was… she was out here." Her uncertainty vanished, and she became more cheerful again. There were tiny lines that appeared around her eyes and

44

on her forehead, and it was as if she could smile with every muscle in her body. "I may have a teacher's voice, Christopher, but even I can't hold a conversation over such a distance."

"Thank you for taking the time to talk to us," Grandfather said very formally, and Alisha bent once more to stroke our equally smiley dog. "I wish you a very Happy Christmas."

"And you." She really was a nice lady and even issued an invitation. "Oh, Christopher, you must come to the river with Rodrick and me tomorrow. It's spectacular down there with all the children off school and the trees gripped with snow."

"I would love to come, Miss."

She laughed and extracted her free hand from the thick muff that hung on a cord around her neck to pat me on the shoulder. "You are funny, Christopher. But you're an adult now and must call me Alisha."

I didn't know what to say to this, so I nodded, and she continued on towards her house with a few last words called back to us. "We'll see you there at nine in the morning. It was lovely to meet you, Lord Edgington."

With her brown fur stole and long bustling skirts, she looked as though she'd stepped out of a Victorian Christmas card.

Grandfather said (almost) exactly what I was thinking. "What an attractive woman. I'm sure she was a superb teacher." Most comments he makes have a hidden purpose, and this one was no different.

"She really is." Without meaning to, I found myself confessing the deepest feelings of Christopher Prentiss, aged five to eight. "I was madly in love with her when I was at school. It may not be common for boys of such an age to know true love, but I found it with Mrs Steele. When my parents sent me away to Oakton Academy, I thought that I would never recover from the loss."

"Christopher, you have always been a very strange individual." He didn't say anything more for a moment. "I heartily approve."

I was still peering after Alisha Steele. Although she was around thirty years older than me and married to a very handsome doctor, I found her just as charming as ever. I believe I emitted a doleful and romantic sigh as she disappeared behind the hedge that obscured much of her house.

"Come along, you lovesick pup." He was talking to me, not the dog. "Let us search this cesspool of human iniquity for some serviceable refreshment to warm our cockles."

The old genius had read my mind again. I would put off my trip to the river until the morning. This would provide more time to stare longingly at my former teacher, whenever her very nice husband Dr Steele wasn't looking. But for now, what I needed more than anything was hot chocolate.

Dotty's Teahouse may sound like a sedate sort of establishment, but it was the throbbing centre of the village and the hub of gossip for much of the region. The more loquacious members of our community could often be found there chattering away to their hearts' content on a number of topics, many of which were based on hearsay and speculation.

"You know who must have done it," Dotty herself said. She was a nineteen-stone, former champion weightlifter (at the summer fête in Guildford at least) but her voice was even stronger than her immense arms. "That sister of hers!"

"I fear you may be correct," our vicar Reverend Deacon agreed. "I have often told the pair of them that he who is without sin etc etc." The rotund, mole-like individual wasn't a very good vicar, but he was popular with a certain crowd. "They judged one another even more fiercely than they did the rest of us."

"Oh, yes!" The mayor's wife batted her heavily mascaraed eyelashes. "They were always bickering. It's amazing that Maude survived as long as she did."

"That is such a wise and succinct reflection on the matter," Mr Tibbs the grocer said as he stared at the woman with whom, or so we had heard, he was engaged in an illicit affair.

"Here he is. The man of the hour!" Dotty boomed when she saw us. "Lord Edgington. What is it to be?"

"I'll have a hot chocolate please, Dotty!" I yelled back at almost the same volume.

"I would like a cup of Earl Grey," Grandfather added rather curtly, as though the very idea of hot chocolate didn't agree with him. "And a mince pie, if you have any."

The teahouse was full to bursting, and we had to take spare chairs from other tables to occupy the one free spot in the corner. A few people I had known my whole life (without ever learning their names) waved at me as the conversation continued above the heads of the customers.

"It's a good thing you're here, Lord Edgington." Mr Tibbs was a puffy-cheeked man with no hair and a perfectly egg-shaped head. He was vain, and I'd always found him rather stupid, not that I would have said any such thing to his face. "It does make you wonder how many injustices are left unrighted in this world. After all, even great men like you can't be in all places at all times."

As much as Grandfather enjoyed the praise of his adoring public, even he wouldn't accept compliments when they were not due. "That is kind of you to say, but after a brief investigation, I've come to the conclusion that Miss Evans most likely died of natural causes."

There was an audible groan that travelled around the café. It was interesting just how much my fellow Kilston Downians were hungry for a murder in which to sink their teeth. Perhaps they were looking for a reason not to spend time with their families, too.

"Oh, that is a shame," Ethel Perkins said absentmindedly, even as she winked at her apparent paramour across the room.

The village had always been home to a lot of curious characters, but I'm afraid that I had to agree with Lillibet Evans when she said that things had changed. I'd never seen two married people carry on so openly with one another before. Perhaps even worse than that was the fact that Mr Tibbs had abandoned his wife in their shop on one of the busiest days of the year while he filled his tummy with Eccles cakes and cups of coffee.

The noise of babble and clinking teaspoons died for a moment as the villagers came to terms with the fact that there would be no Christmas mystery to keep us all entertained. This hush was soon interrupted by the vicar who had more thoughts on the matter.

"Of course, we can't rule out the possibility that Old Mr Marley is to blame." As he spoke, he peered out of the tinselled window at the man dressed in a long black leather coat who was salting the pavement around the clocktower. "There's always been something unseemly about him. He lives entirely alone in the forest, and we only ever see him when it snows."

I shuddered a little, and I believe that several others in the teahouse did the same, before the whole place erupted once more in speculation.

"You know," Grandfather sat back in his chair to think. "It's rather a shame that no one has been murdered. There are certainly plenty of suspects from whom to choose."

Dotty served our drinks, and I proceeded to burn my tongue because I couldn't wait for mine to cool. I then burnt it three more times, as I never learn my lesson, and we were just finishing our mince pies when the door burst open as though a gale-force wind had battered the façade of the shop.

"Nigel Tibbs!" Mrs Tibbs shouted as the cold rushed in around her. "You were only supposed to come here for a quick drink. You get back to the shop this instant or I won't cook your Christmas dinner this year." Though the message was meant for her husband, she glared at her love rival the whole time she stood there.

"Yes, my darling, Nora," the simpering rat responded. "Of course, my precious." He was up on his feet faster than a snowball through the air but was apparently stunned when his wife sat down at his now empty table and banged her fist on top of it.

"Dotty," she said in a firm but quiet voice. "I'd like a hot cider and a large piece of ice cake."

She watched as her husband took one last look at the scene, and everyone there stared back at him. It felt as if we had all taken Mrs Tibbs's side, and I think he knew it. He shot outside and into the cold, just as the sky opened and it began to snow once more.

After a minute or two, Ethel Perkins paid her bill and made her excuses to leave. "It was nice to see you," she told Nora Tibbs in as sincere a voice as she could muster. "I hope you have a lovely Christmas."

When she left, the vicar and Dotty fell oddly quiet. What talk there was turned to presents for in-laws and predictions of a forthcoming thaw.

"Christmas isn't Christmas without a healthy dose of spectacle!" Grandfather said with a wink, then he raised his cup of tea to Mrs Tibbs and smiled.

CHAPTER SIX

While the village had no shortage of drama, there was plenty going on at home, too. The last of my father's relatives had arrived, and their occupation of the communal areas of the house was nearly complete. To call it an invasion would be an understatement. In the drawing room, Uncle Thomas was boring his side of the family by describing the marvellous time he had during the Anglo-Zulu War. Meanwhile, in the rear salon, where we always put our Christmas tree and celebrate the most important parts of the holiday, his brother Terry had stationed himself to criticise my parents' taste in furniture.

"Uncles!" Albert despaired as he hung decoration after decoration on the tree. "There are always uncles at Christmas, but what are they actually good for?" He did not need to whisper as, though Terry was not hard of hearing, he never listened to what anyone around him actually said.

I was standing on a chair next to my brother, passing up golden angel after apple-red robin after silver star. He had practically hidden any hint of green from the branches underneath with cotton wool snowballs and toffee bonbons wrapped in shiny paper.

"It's only for three more days," I promised him. "We can survive for three days. I'm sure we can."

He didn't respond but threaded the decorations onto the end of the branches with even more determination than before. There was something indescribably intense about him that week that was quite different from his usual manner. It was as if he was trying to prove himself. He'd acted just as manically when he'd started working with our father. Perhaps he imagined that if he could decorate the house to the specifications he had set for himself, it would make our holiday perfect. Perhaps he thought that a house that was suitably garlanded and decked out to the nines would be enough to make us forget the horrible people who were staying there. I very much doubted that it would do the job.

My mother and father hadn't returned from the village, and I retreated to the kitchen so as not to have to see any of my cousins. Sadly, there was just as little peace on earth below stairs as above.

"I know how to make a cinnamon roulade, thank you very much," Maggie, the Kilston Down cook, assured her opposite number from Cranley Hall.

"I wasn't saying that you didn't." Henrietta at least tried to remain calm. "I just thought that it would be a good idea to include raisins."

"Raisins?" Maggie's eyes were small and dark like two... well... like two very dark sultanas. "Raisins? Do I look like the kind of person who would put raisins in a cinnamon roulade?"

Henrietta clearly didn't know how to respond and turned to her colleagues, who were grouped together at the other end of the kitchen. A footman, three maids, a gardener, a page boy and the head of household kept mum, though Halfpenny did help himself to a strawberry tart from the plate in front of him.

"If you know so much about cinnamon roulades," Maggie yelped when no one said anything, "then perhaps you should be the one to make it."

She'd been aggressively kneading pastry until now and seized the immense ball she'd been working in both hands. She slapped it down on the work surface in front of Henrietta before leaving the room.

"What's been going on here?" I asked the whole lot of them as the silence spiralled around us like smoke.

"It's not Henrietta's fault, sir," Todd was quick to explain. "Maggie hasn't exactly welcomed us into her kitchen."

"I can see that," I said, with a touch more discretion than my previous blunt question. "And I'm very sorry if that is the case. I can only think that the stress of the occasion is too much for her. But that doesn't explain why you're sitting there like spectators at a Punch and Judy show."

There was another brief pause, punctuated only by the sound of our head footman nibbling on his treat.

"Well, sir." Timothy, the youngest of the bunch, stepped forward to say what the others were too frightened to admit. "The truth is that we're hiding."

There was a groan from big Dorie. "Don't tell him the truth, little man! I've spent the last two years teaching you to lie, and you've let me down!"

"I appreciate your honesty, Timothy, but from what or, more likely, whom are you hiding?"

Heads turned and waves of whispering floated around the kitchen as they tried to pick another spokesperson. It didn't entirely surprise me that brave and bright Alice, our Irish maid, would be the one to accept the role.

"I'm afraid to tell you that t's your father's family, sir," she said most delicately. "They're all completely mad," she said less delicately.

"Ah, I see…"

"One of your cousins keeps trying to get me to dance," she continued.

"I am so sorry. It wasn't Midshipman Peter, was it? He is quite a strange one."

Alice's husband, Driscoll, put his arm around her and answered when she couldn't. "No, sir. It wasn't. It was that brute Philippa. She spent five minutes complaining about the Irish and then suggested a swift two-step."

"That's terrible," I began, but there were more complaints to be issued.

"And as for your father's cousin, Aldrich…" creaky old Halfpenny exclaimed with a shake of his head. "He keeps telling me that I'm not fit for the navy. He says I should have retired years ago."

For the first time in my life, I felt a modicum of sympathy for the bunch of coots upstairs. I really don't know why. "Perhaps I should explain. You see, Aldrich thinks that he's an admiral or some such. He's never set foot aboard a ship, but…" I stopped talking then as I couldn't think of anything that might explain such bizarre behaviour.

It was at this moment that, still squashed against the wall, to get as far from my relatives as possible, the whole gang of servants broke into discussion.

Little Timothy was waving his arms around as he described Thomas's claims that Charlie Chaplin had stolen his idea for a tramp-like comedy character. Todd was discussing the impropriety of someone (other than his master) ordering him around like a lazy donkey. Cook was detailing her ongoing problems working alongside Maggie, and I believe that Dorie and her sister Connie had forgotten why everyone else was so annoyed as they went to help themselves to some leftover mousse.

I was about to call them to order when the door flew open and my family's butler, Jessop, came into the room and almost collapsed.

"The horror!" he exclaimed, and Todd was quick with a chair to catch him. He stared into space and mumbled a few words that soon became a chant. "It's only once a year," he said. "It's only once a year. It's only once a year."

I tried to think of something that might aid the situation and clapped my hands together to get their attention. "Ladies and gentlemen, I am well aware that my father's side of the family are the least tolerable people you are likely to come across. I have honestly met several murderers with whom I would prefer to spend Christmas. In fact, I'm tempted to invite a few of them here to—"

I must have been rambling as Todd gave a short, *Ahem,* to return me to the matter at hand.

"And with all that in mind, may I make the suggestion that, as none of us can avoid them entirely, when required to wait on them, you do so in pairs." There was a murmur of approval at the idea, so I moved on to my second spark of inspiration. "With that said, there really is no better way to 'soothe a savage Breast, to soften Rocks, or bend a knotted Oak' than through music. I was thinking that those of you who previously sang in the Cranley Hall choir might—"

This proved less popular, and Cook was the first to refuse. "No."

Halfpenny was next. "No." Then Timothy, Dorie, Todd, Connie, Alice... well, none of them liked my suggestion. Even Jessop disagreed with it, and he had been fifteen miles away, working in a totally different house at the time of our choral performances.

"No, Master Christopher," the normally discreet servant began. "That lot don't deserve it."

CHAPTER SEVEN

Something quite inexplicable happened that night. My whole family must have come down with some kind of illness, as not one of us was hungry enough for dinner. Admittedly, I found my grandmother hiding in an airing cupboard, eating a chicken leg that she'd pilfered from the kitchen, but I'm sure she had her reasons. As for the rest of us, we were all in bed by seven o'clock... except for my brother, who had run out of Christmas decorations and decided to stay up half the night cutting, sticking and sewing new ones. I didn't like to ask why.

The good thing about heading to the land of nod so early was that it meant the time would go swiftly before I could take my old sledge down to one of my favourite places in the world. The bad thing about going to bed early was that I ended up waking at five the next morning, and not just because Delilah had climbed onto my bed and was whipping me with her tail as she dozed.

I couldn't fall back asleep, though she managed it without any problem, and so I opened the curtains to let the last of the moonlight shine into the room. I was planning to read, but the sight of all the books on my shelves sent me into such nostalgic reverie that I simply had to sit on the carpet in the middle of the room to enjoy my childhood sanctuary.

Our perception of what makes a perfect Christmas is surely defined in our early years, and so it was hardly surprising that I should enjoy taking in the scene there in such detail after so long away from home. My gaze hungrily tripped across the titles of books that I hadn't read since I was tiny. Adventurous novels like 'The Swiss Family Robinson' and 'The Count of Monte Cristo' were mixed in with the darker tales of Arthur Conan Doyle and Edgar Allan Poe. Certain titles stood out like electric lamps on an otherwise dark street. I'm fairly certain that I can recite favourites like 'The Railway Children', 'Kidnapped' and 'The Jungle Book' even now.

But it wasn't just my books with which I was happy to be reunited. My parents had never thrown away the stuffed toys who had been my firm friends throughout my infancy. There was a train set on top of my wardrobe, and I remembered being so excited to receive it for the

Christmas of 1915, when I was just seven, that I went to bed with a carriage in either hand. There were even pictures in frames on the wall that my brother and I had drawn together. Imaginary scenes of castles surrounded by dragons in front of mountains topped with snow hung alongside a sketch of the four members of my family skipping along together. I could no longer be sure which of the messily drawn people was my father and which was Mother, but I was glad it was still there.

It was a thrill to travel back in time like that, but it only took me four minutes, and I still had three hours and fifty-six minutes to fill. Perhaps inevitably, as I hadn't read it in almost twelve months, I took my extremely battered copy of Dickens's 'A Christmas Carol' and managed to get through the whole, admittedly short, book and still have time for a nap before sunrise.

It struck me as I read just how sad a character Mr Scrooge is. I mean, it's all very well that he learns his lesson, and everyone goes for a nice lunch and "a Christmas bowl of smoking bishop" (whatever that might be), but when you think of his tragic life, it rather changes the feel of the story. I cannot say whether this new interpretation was down to my advanced years or the glimpse I'd had of Maude Evans's solitary existence the day before, but I felt bad for old Ebenezer, who is surely one of literature's loneliest beasts. He wandered through my dreams, like the Ghost of Christmas Yet To Come, and my rest was a restless one.

I somehow still managed to oversleep, and I'm sure that, had it not been for Delilah coming to lick my face, I would have missed my appointment entirely. To make up for my tardiness, I grabbed the first clothes I could find and pulled them on as I ran from the room. This meant that I was wearing a fluffy pink jumper that my mother's Aunt Clara had knitted for me as a Christmas present, but it was too late to choose anything else. I just about managed to avoid falling down the stairs as I pulled my thick galoshes over my trousers. Albert was sleeping on the hall carpet, surrounded by scraps of paper and fabric, but there was no time to worry about him.

Delilah thought it was all such a game and barked enough to wake up the house. She followed me out to the stable where we don't have any horses, but we do keep lots of bits and pieces that no one uses anymore. I was surprised how happy she was to be in the snow with me, but I suppose the alternative was to spend more time with the great-uncles and that would never do. To thank her for her company, I put her on top of my sledge and found a rope to pull her all the way to the river.

She sat with her tongue hanging out and her tail wagging. I had to believe that, as she glanced about at the wondrous scenery, she was thinking the very same thing that I was. *Magic!* That's the only real explanation for what was before us. Just like in a fantastical novel, the world had changed colour from the greys, browns and khaki green of a week earlier to this pure, white wonderland. It was all beauty, and we hadn't yet left our driveway.

The first traders were opening their shops as Lady Delilah was pulled through the square by her hardworking driver. Mr Brown the butcher and Mrs Lamb the baker waved to us as they cleared the snow from their front step, but the previously bustling teahouse remained dark.

"Lovely morning, Christopher," Reverend Deacon called to me from the other side of the square before losing his footing and falling with a bump on his bottom. Other villagers rushed to help him, so I think he was fine.

I wouldn't allow any such interruptions to slow me down. I'd been waiting for this moment ever since we made our plans for Christmas months before. There's nothing quite so special in my town as the river when it freezes. Even though the few local friends I'd once had were now making their way in the world, and it must have looked odd for a twenty-year-old and his dog to be heading off to play on a Sunday morning, I was determined to relive this one Christmas memory if no other.

By the time I arrived, there were already plenty of families playing on the frozen surface. I could see no sign of my teacher or her husband, but various couples were skating arm in arm, their eyes locked on to one another's (somewhat dangerously, if you ask me). Young children were sliding about on their tummies and a man of about my age was rolling up large snowballs and putting them in a wheelbarrow. I stopped just next to him to catch my breath before I embarked on the climb to the top of the sledging hill.

"I know you," he stated in a taunting voice, and I already didn't like him before I realised who he was.

Rather than coolly respond as my grandfather would have, I simply stared. He had a fleshy face that was so red it had presumably just been slapped, and the dark craters on either side of his nose were surely still haunted by the ghosts of black eyes past. Two of his front teeth were chipped and, after five long seconds, I realised that I was looking at Dean Henderson: my least favourite person from the time I was five until I went to boarding school three years later.

"Don't ya remember me? I once gave you a haircut with Mrs Steele's scissors." He paused to see whether this would be enough. "I was the one who swapped your reading glasses for Mr Henry's so that you thought you were going blind." He sounded quite disappointed, and it was tempting to pretend that none of this jogged my memory. "Oh, come on. You must know me; I was the funniest boy in school."

"Yes, Dean. I remember." I considered explaining that his definition of funny and mine were a thousand miles apart, but instead I changed the topic. "Why are you making all those snowballs?"

He smiled his chipped-tooth grin. "I'm going to take them back to my garden in town and throw them at the neighbour's cats. I hate those cats."

I should have known not to ask. "That sounds…" I couldn't think of a word to finish this sentence, though I was reminded once more of my grandfather's comment that there were plenty of good suspects in Kilston Down, and all we were missing was a murder. "Why don't you just make snowballs in your own garden?"

"Are you stupid or somethin'? The snow here is much better!" His piggy nose crumpled, and his sharp eyes drilled into me.

I *really* should have known not to ask. Luckily, my friends arrived at this moment, and I didn't have to say anything more.

"Christopher, it's so nice to see you again," the doctor told me, and my lovely former teacher smiled. Tall, handsome Rodrick Steele (with his silver-wire hair and the jawline of a matinee idol) noticed my unappreciated companion. "Ahh, Dean. You're also here."

The odd creature glared at the doctor and pushed his wheelbarrow away. It was tough going as the wheel kept sinking into the snow. He eventually made it to the beaten track, and glanced over his shoulder as if to say, *See, I knew I could do it.*

"What a strange young man," the doctor said in a bemused tone as Alisha made a fuss of Delilah, who was still sitting prettily on the sledge. "I wonder what he's going to do with all those snowballs."

I considered telling him, but that would only have led to more questions I couldn't answer.

"I don't know about you two," the dear lady said, and I suddenly realised why I fall in love with every pretty girl I meet. I'm clearly trying to make up for my first heartbreak when this vision of charm and sophistication had decided not to divorce her lovely husband to set up home with a small chubby boy in short trousers.

Anyway, what was I saying?

"I don't know about you two, but I'm ready to go skating." Alisha turned to look at the wide bend in the river, which was shallow enough to freeze every year, but deep enough to last through the season despite hundreds of locals making use of its slippery surface. It was a lovely sight, and it reminded me of a pencil drawing of the wintertime. Everyone there was dressed in uncheering black and, against the white background, even the trunks of trees looked as though they'd been shaded with a dark lead.

"I have something else to do first," I told them, already eyeing the peak. "If I achieve nothing else this Christmas, I'm going to sledge from the highest point up by the treeline all the way to the other side of the river." I climbed the hill with my eyes alone, and the very thought of it excited me.

"Jolly good, old man," the doctor said with a nod of appreciation. "We'll be down here when you're ready for us."

I didn't like to tell him that I hadn't brought my skates, so would only be pushing myself around on the ice like a toddler. I said goodbye and began the climb. The truth is that I'd never had the courage to go up there on my own before. The only time I'd actually descended the famous hill was with my mother steering the sledge. The further truth that I've never told anyone is that I had my eyes closed the whole way down and was afraid that I might die of fright before the ride was over. I've heard people say that, were you to jump from somewhere high like the Eiffel Tower or the Matterhorn, you would have a heart attack before you hit the ground, which certainly sounds preferable to the alternative.

It was hard going to reach the top, especially with Delilah weighing the sledge down, but I knew there was a bigger challenge ahead. I half imagined myself getting up there, losing my nerve and refusing to come back down again. There'd be a terrible scene, and the only solution would be to send for my mother, who would gently convince me that everything was all right before leading me to safe ground as everyone from the village stood laughing at me.

I shook the image from my mind and tried to remember that I'm nearly an adult and not an eleven-year-old boy. When I'd pushed on through the snow and got to the very top of the hill, I looked back down at that old familiar sight, which so exemplified the winters of my childhood. It turned out that it really wasn't so high after all.

"I always thought this place was a mountain," I told Delilah, but the boy who had just reached the top in front of us looked at me as though I was very odd indeed. "Oh, I mean... after you, please."

He was at least two feet shorter than I, but he threw himself down the hill, head first, on nothing but the lid of a rubbish bin. I would say that his bravery offered me hope, but it was too late for that. I was no longer scared of what I was about to do. I was more confident than I'd ever been and spun the sledge around to sit behind Delilah. I made sure that I was perfectly positioned to steer, held on tightly to the rope (and my dog) with both hands, and pushed myself off down the hill.

The wind whipped my cheeks, and there were tiny flakes of snow in the air that stung my skin, but I didn't mind. I didn't even dig my heels into the snow to slow us down. The speed that we achieved was like nothing else. We positively shot down the hillside, and even lifted into the air for a moment as we went over a bump.

I wasn't frightened; I was exhilarated. My knuckles had turned blue in the cold, and I'm sure my face was quite pink, but we reached the frozen river and, despite my normal poor luck in such potentially calamitous situations, I didn't go crashing through the ice or flip the sledge; I turned at just the right moment, so that our journey could continue.

I saw Todd coming at pace along the path to the river and even managed to give him a wave, but he was looking about the scene and didn't notice. He clearly had other things on his mind, and I was enjoying myself too much to mind.

The runners below the sledge made a whistling sound as we glided along the ice ever so smoothly. Delilah had her tongue out and was clearly having just as much fun as I was. I didn't want it to end, but weaving in and out of skaters and onlookers, I could already see the bank of snow that curved slightly upwards to mark the finish line.

I took the curve as wide as possible to extend the journey, but the surface was rougher now, and I was already slowing down when I reached the far side of the river.

Delilah let out a happy bark, and I jumped from our chariot, full of the joys of winter. I immediately wanted to climb back up and do it again, but before I could, I spotted Dr Steele talking to Todd. They both looked so serious that I involuntarily started walking towards them as Delilah ran along at my side.

"I don't know all the circumstances, sir," our factotum was saying as I arrived. "I was in town to buy presents, and the mayor asked me to fetch you at once."

"I'm sorry, Alisha," the doctor said, turning to speak to his wife as Gareth Heywood lurked nearby to listen. "I'll have to go."

"You too, Master Christopher," Todd added. "We must get back to town."

Todd had brought the Daimler and there was room in the back of the immense vehicle for the sledge, our dog, the three of us and perhaps a football team or two. We were back at the town square in seconds and, for some reason, it didn't surprise me that Todd stopped the car in front of the house that belonged to Mr and Mrs Tibbs, the grocers.

"You must come quickly, Doctor," Dotty was standing in the doorway as we hurried out of the car. Even Delilah came, though she was soon distracted by a wall she needed to sniff.

"What can you tell me?" Dr Steele demanded as the proprietor of the teahouse ushered us inside.

"Miss Evans found him when she came to clean. He's quite under the weather."

We entered the Tudor building, which had a first floor that overhung the snow-covered garden. There was a small entrance hall barely wide enough for two people to walk through it at the same time, and rather than turning off into the lounge, we followed Dotty into the back parlour. The house was rich with the smell of wood smoke, and when we entered the room where Mr Tibbs was, I noticed a fire still smouldering, along with a number of expired candles on the hearth and a cold kettle sitting next to them.

Nigel Tibbs was in an easy chair just next to the fireplace. His eyes were closed, his head was tipped back, and he looked perfectly comfortable as the doctor knelt to take his pulse.

"He's not just under the weather," he explained, looking back over his shoulder at us. "He's dead."

CHAPTER EIGHT

Grandfather soon arrived to stake his claim to the case. It felt peculiar to be more informed than he was, and I did my best to explain anything that wasn't apparent to him at first glance.

"The grocer's wife, Nora Tibbs, can't have come in here this morning when she left to open the shop. The body was found by their cleaner, Lillibet Evans, who's in the kitchen talking to Sergeant Keel. She's in quite a state, but I have to wonder whether it's all an act and she's the—"

"Let me stop you there, Christopher." He held one hand up to get my attention and closed his eyes as if this would be such a strain that he needed to steel himself. "Are you suggesting that the cleaning lady is the likely killer because she happens to have been the sister to one of the deceased and found the body of another, the first of whom we have no reason to believe was murdered?"

"I am," I said resolutely, before adding more evidence. "Of course, there is also the fact that the corpses were discovered in very similar states and..." I sought another connection and took a wild guess. "And I imagine that both of them drank tea before they died." I pointed at the kettle to support this assertion.

"Tea?" He didn't actually roll his eyes, but he might as well have. "I'm not sure that the presence of tea at the scene of two murders is enough to suggest a pattern. In actual fact, I'm fairly confident that, should you wish to look for any so obvious a factor, the vast majority of domestic killings are carried out with the paraphernalia for making that fortifying beverage close at hand."

I believe he would have continued to point out the limitations of my theory had he not taken a moment to reflect upon the wonders of that most British of Far Eastern drinks.

"Very well, not the tea," I eventually had to interrupt. "But you must admit there are similarities."

"Judging by the colour of the deceased's skin and, no doubt were I to take the time to touch him, his temperature, it seems fair to conclude that Mr Tibbs has been dead for some time."

"The doctor believes that he died late last night, or first thing this morning."

"I see." It turned out that he hadn't finished criticising my idea after all. "So presumably you are suggesting that the man's cleaner came here before bedtime to give him a poisoned brew, as she had done for her sister several weeks ago, and then popped back this morning to find his body."

"When you put it like that," I muttered, then seamlessly changed tack. "More importantly, what killed him?"

He'd needled me long enough and placed one hand on my back to show he didn't mean anything by it. "It is difficult to say so long after the event, but he does appear to have evacuated his stomach before death. If we can rule out natural causes, I think it's fair to imagine that— Well… I'm jumping ahead of myself. We will have to speak to his doctor and hope that the local coroner can take a look at the body before Christmas."

"But?"

"But what?" He looked so innocent then that we might have been discussing how pretty snow was or what to buy my mother for Christmas.

"You were about to reveal your theory of what killed him."

"I do not wish to speak precipitously." He put one finger across his lips as he considered the circumstances one last time. "However, there is a high probability that this man was murdered. If, as you imagined, the substance was hidden in his tea—"

I had to grit my teeth to stop from shouting. "You just said that it couldn't possibly have been the tea that poisoned him. You told me I was wrong approximately seven times."

He moved closer to the body then, and I waited for him to say something clever that would infuriate me even more. "It was not the method of delivery to which I objected. It was your assumption that the connection between the two cases was anything more than coincidental."

I still wasn't clear on one small point. "So you *do* think that the poison was in his tea?"

"We can't possibly know any such thing until we investigate further."

I considered biting my hand in infuriation, but he moved us on to his next point. "It is still possible that his demise was natural or accidental, but we investigated one such death just yesterday, and the chances of us finding two so close together are surely very low." He injected neither humour nor sarcasm into this statement, though I

62

imagine he was only making it to see whether I would react.

I would not.

Instead, I looked around the cosy parlour in which Nigel Tibbs had breathed his last. It was so small that it might more accurately have been called a nook. I noticed an empty glass on the floor by his side, and there was a recently popular book on his lap, though from the reviews I'd read, the slice-of-life literary novel 'Bad Girl', subtitle: 'Banned in Boston' would not have offered the titillation for which a man like Tibbs may have been searching.

I had the feeling, based on the other similarly titled books on a small shelf on the wall and the line of unremoved empty beer bottles near the door, that this was very much *his* room. A den, of sorts, for him to enjoy himself without fear of interruption. It was certainly less clean than the rest of the house. The floor was black with soot from the fire, and there was even the body of a dead mouse peeking out of a hole in the skirting board behind the door. It was quite the opposite of the perfectly clean space in which Maude had died, which made me wonder why her sister hadn't cleaned in here.

The only other thing that I noticed was a piece of string protruding from the top of the book. I carefully prised it open to see whether the passage he had been reading might offer some clue as to how he had died, but it was merely a scene of a young girl caring for her baby and told me very little.

When our inspection of the scene was complete, we followed the sound of the doctor's voice to the dining room. He was sitting at a table with Lillibet Evans and my old friend Sergeant Keel. The three of them wore matching frowns.

"Ah, Lord Edgington, I'm glad you could come," the doctor said as he and the officer rose. "It's a perplexing situation. I really don't know what to make of it."

Before he'd finished speaking, the stone-hearted, judgemental lady did something that I, for one, had not been expecting. She burst into tears. "Death is following me! First my sister, now Nigel. It's too much, it really is."

The middle-aged sergeant put his arm around her shoulder and, seeing that it would do us good to have a moment alone, he led her to the kitchen with a mention of gingersnaps and lemonade.

"Do you think there's anything in it?" Grandfather asked when the door had shut behind them.

As the doctor considered his answer, a bitter wind came down the chimney above the unlit hearth. Despite its relative cleanliness, the room was less inviting than the previous one. The chairs were hard, the flagstones were as cold as a hairless cat in the snow, and the table was so old that it was scarred a thousand times over by kitchen knives.

"I'm afraid that I do." Dr Steele appeared hesitant to say what he was really thinking. "Tibbs was a healthy enough man. He had no history of heart disease or anything of the sort. He was also fairly moderate in his appetites compared to many of my patients, and he was on his feet enough to remain active well beyond the age of forty-nine."

"Perhaps it was when he was off his feet that the trouble came," I said by way of a pithy quip, but Grandfather did not like my lewdness and offered a well-directed tut.

"Yes, that may turn out to be the explanation." The dashing doctor flicked his fringe from his eyes and conceded my point. "It seems you know the gossip just as well as I do."

Grandfather was having none of it. "I'm more interested in what you think killed him than conjecture on who could be responsible."

"Yes, of course, Lord Edgington." Unlike me these days, Doctor Steele was apparently a little frightened of my domineering grandfather. "I cannot eliminate the possibility that there was something wrong with Nigel that had not previously manifested itself, but the coroner is better placed to do such a thing. Presumably what you'd like to know is whether he was poisoned."

"Well?" I said because I'm impatient. "Was he?"

The doctor's eyes travelled between us, and he bit his lip. I could tell that he had a big decision to make, and I didn't blame him for taking his time. "The fact is that, beyond the sickness he evidently endured before death, there is nothing to tell us conclusively. There is noticeable discolouration to his cheeks, and his pupils were certainly dilated when he died, but until a post-mortem is conducted, we cannot say whether he was poisoned."

He said all this in a tone that suggested there would be a caveat, and he swiftly provided it. "Of course, his lack of symptoms alarms me a little, too."

"In what sense?" I asked, just as my grandfather mumbled, "Arsenic!"

The doctor began to speak more quickly. "I'm only telling you this to provide a full answer but, yes, it is not beyond the realm of possibility that he was poisoned with arsenic, as you so smartly concluded, Lord Edgington." He was no sycophant but clearly wished to give credit where due. "Arsenic leaves little immediate trace on a body. That's why they call it the king of poisons. You have to cut the victim open to find out what was happening inside. If you're there at the time of death, you may notice clamminess of the skin, and the victim may suffer vertigo and nausea in addition to gastroenteritis, but there is nothing definitive. Even in this enlightened age, it can go undetected when there are no suspicious circumstances to catch a detective's or loved one's attention."

Grandfather shuddered just a little then, and I wondered whether it was the idea of a crime going unpunished that upset him. "Could that have happened in the case of Maude Evans?"

It was a bold question, but then I expected nothing less of him.

Dr Steele, on the other hand, was not ready for such a query. "Old Miss Evans? Do you really think that she could have been..." As he spoke, the possibility must have settled in his brain as the muscles in his face tightened somewhat. "I do see the connection. Even the timing of their deaths is similar." He drummed his fingers on the table, and for a moment the only other sound was the wind whistling down the chimney and a mouse or two scuttering in the walls.

"What should we do next?" I asked when neither of them said anything more.

My words served to jog the doctor back to the here and now. "The coroner is already on his way. Whether he'll be able to give us any answers soon is another matter. It really isn't the best time of year to investigate a murder."

I was tempted to question whether this was the reason that killers so often picked Christmas as their season of choice, but Grandfather spoke before I could.

"In a way, it is irrelevant what actually killed them. The fact is that we must treat their deaths as suspicious." He paused and straightened his back to make an announcement. "We are on the hunt for a killer, whether he exists or not."

CHAPTER NINE

Grandfather found a new sense of urgency that he hadn't possessed for some time. It was always tempting to think that his age had finally caught up with him but, considering the fact that we would spend the new year on a grand tour of Europe, he clearly still had plenty of living left to do. As I followed him around that day in search of a ghost, the retired police superintendent had all the vitality of a new recruit.

We left the doctor to wait for the coroner and went to speak once more to Miss Evans, the younger. On our last meeting, we had treated her as little more than a bystander. But whether my grandfather would admit it or not, her closeness to two different murders made her a genuine suspect.

"You didn't like Mr Tibbs very much, did you, Miss Evans?" Grandfather started the interview as he meant to continue. He was cold, hard and just a little bit rude. This was perfect, as Lillibet Evans was ten times worse.

"I don't like anyone." She had a rather jaundiced face, like the poor young ladies who had worked in armament factories during the war. Her eyes were large but dark and lifeless and the lines around her mouth were forever pointing downwards to the white pinafore apron that she wore.

"That may well be true, but we only spent a few minutes in your presence yesterday and you couldn't resist telling me of his rumoured infidelity."

Her expression immediately betrayed her confusion. "There's nothing rumoured about it. He and that Perkins woman made no effort to hide it. They were carrying on like wild animals." She nodded a few times, then reconsidered this comparison. "Actually, they were worse than that, because wild animals don't know no better. Those two were flouncing around the town like… like…"

When she couldn't finish her sentence, Grandfather put another point to her. "Tell us again what happened when the postman found your sister."

Lillibet was too preoccupied to respond. "…Like wild animals! No, wait, I already said that. My point is that they didn't even conceal their indiscretions from their spouses. They were a disgrace, but I still cleaned this house to help poor Nora." She dropped her voice to a grumble then, and the question I wished to ask was instantly answered. "I refused to clean in his room, though. I have my principles!"

As she had ignored him the first time, Grandfather simply repeated his previous demand. "Your sister, Miss Evans, will you remind us how her body was discovered?"

She scratched at a mole on her chin and looked up at the bare beams overhead. "I gave the postie the key. He went in ahead of me, and there she was, dead in her chair. The fire had died down but was still warm, so she couldn't have frozen to death, if that's what you were thinking."

I was tempted to ask whether there was a cup of tea present, but I didn't want to seem fixated on an insignificant detail. Instead, there was a pause as Grandfather decided where to take the interview next.

"Did you notice anything else that felt significant?"

She cast her mind back to that day. "Snowfall, her cat, was scratching at the door to get in to the parlour. Maude had a cup of tea beside her chair." I managed to contain my joy at this moment. "And... Well, that was it, really."

"Do you know who the last people to visit your sister were before she died?"

Young Miss Evans was standing beside the sink, with a tiny window that gave onto the garden just behind her. She was silhouetted by the bright white of the snow, but I could still make out her reaction. It told me just how little she thought of the questions we were asking.

"No, I do not. I have never been one of those people who stand on their doorsteps watching the world go by. Maude had her life, and I have mine."

"But you did clean her house?" Grandfather reminded her. "And you continue to do so?"

She turned her head so that I could only see half of it. "Wait one minute. What's any of this got to do with you, Lord Nosy? Just because you led my sister on all those years ago, it doesn't mean that you get to rifle through her business now."

"I'm afraid I lied." It cheered my grandfather to know that his ruse had worked so effectively, but then Lillibet Evans was no match for him. "I never met your sister when she was alive. I am a detective and, with the help of my grandson, I am investigating the possibility that your sister and Nigel Tibbs were murdered."

Miss Evans raised one hand to her mouth. She hadn't shown much love for her sister in life or death, but this apparently shocked her. "Murdered? You mean they were killed by someone from our village?"

"It's too early to say, but in most instances the killer is known to the victim."

She had to lean back against the sink as the idea hit her. "My big sister, murdered? We may never have got on like some siblings do, but we fitted together in our own way. To think that someone…"

I had never seen either of the Evans sisters lost for words. They were part of the constant background chatter of life in Kilston Down. They were rude and judgemental, but people tolerated them, saying, *Poor old dears, they've had a hard life and deserve a little sympathy,* even as they railed at the world around them. I'd never imagined that I would see Lillibet Evans reduced to stuttering sobs.

"Can you think of anything that might connect the two victims (other than tea and the fact you cleaned both their houses)?" I didn't say these last eleven words because I didn't want my grandfather to look witheringly at me.

"I… I…" She put her hand on the draining board for support but finally managed to summon the strength to answer. "It's hard to say. I mean, we've known the Tibbs ever since they moved here twenty years ago. But then everyone knows everyone in the village. That's hardly enough of a connection for someone to murder them."

"What about friends they might have shared?" Grandfather asked, perhaps considering the possibility there had been a falling out between them.

"Maude didn't have any friends. She had me, her cat and the people she didn't like."

I knew from my own experience that this was a perfectly accurate description.

"She was a very holy woman, my sister. Not in terms of going to church or doing good deeds or anything like that, but she lived her life as I do: soberly, correctly and free from sin. I can't think of a single thing that she did in the last five decades which could have upset anybody."

I could think of many things that Maude and her sister had done to upset people. They were the most judgemental souls in Kilston Down. Their brand of piety was based on the idea that they were perfect and every single other person in the village was the devil, but that didn't tie Maude to the grocer, and I didn't see that the remaining Miss Evans would have much more to tell us.

That didn't stop her from talking. "If you ask me, Tibbs was killed by the mayor for his indiscretions. However, I suppose Nora might be to blame. Heaven knows that woman put up with a lot. Perhaps she finally snapped and did her husband in. He was an abominable man. Can anyone really say he didn't deserve it?"

"Thank you for your time," Grandfather told her, but she was just getting into her stride.

"An abominable man who did not respect the sanctity of marriage or the decorum that should be a prerequisite of village life." I believe she must have realised that she was speaking poorly of a murder victim in his own home, as her voice dipped a fraction, though her spite and invective only increased. "I genuinely loathed having anything to do with him. And as for the woman he carried on with! That Ethel Perkins is a succubus if ever there was one."

"Thank you, Miss Evans."

A pall came over her face at this moment as she pieced together a potential motive for the killings. "Perhaps that's what happened! Perhaps that evil woman killed my sister and then Nigel Tibbs."

Grandfather had tired of her speculation and sighed before asking his next obligatory question. "Why would she do any such thing?"

It had often been said that Lillibet was the cleverer of the two sisters. Had her parents not required her to go into service at a young age, she might well have taken up a profession like a school teacher or nurse. That had not been her lot in life, but I did see a brief flash of intelligence behind her eyes as she went through a process with which my grandfather and I were only too familiar.

She even walked across the room to stimulate thought as she replied. "Perhaps Maude saw something she shouldn't have."

"You said that Mr Tibbs and Mrs Perkins's liaison was an open secret." I chose my words carefully, as I've learnt that it's best to be discreet when it comes to sensitive topics.

"I didn't say that she saw the two of 'em together. Maybe Ethel was carrying on with another young man." Everyone was young compared to the Evans sisters. "Maybe it was that new fella – the musician who moved to the village this year. Maybe she wanted to get rid of Tibbs and take up with Hartwood."

"Heywood," I corrected her a little impatiently. "His name is Gareth Heywood."

Sadly, she took this as encouragement and, wiping her hands on her starched white apron, as though to clean away the sin she was discussing, she continued her imaginative tale. "That's it! Maude must have seen Heywood and Ethel together. She killed my sister to hide her secret and, when Ethel tired of her dalliance with the grocer, she killed him too."

I was about to make our excuses and leave when Grandfather stepped closer to our mad witness. "What a fascinating theory. I don't mind admitting that I'm impressed by your capacity to connect seemingly disparate fragments of evidence. Not everyone could come to such conclusions so quickly."

I had never seen the woman blush before. I'd always assumed that she lacked the blood in her veins for any such thing, but that's what happened. She looked up at the flattering lord as though he were the king coming to make her a dame.

"You are too kind, sir. I've often been told I have a head for puzzles and the like. I suppose it's similar to that." She glanced down at the floor with all the coyness of a schoolgirl.

"I will certainly give your idea some consideration." I like to think that I can tell when my grandfather is speaking disingenuously, and this wasn't the voice he normally used. "In the meantime, if you think of anything else that could be important, you must let me know. I always have time for people like you who observe your surroundings and are capable of quick thinking."

"Yes, M'lord." I had never seen her so thrilled. "Of course, M'lord."

He bowed and put on his top hat so that he could tip it to her. He was a jolly old gent just then, and I was a little baffled.

When we got to the front door, I stopped to talk to him. "Did you really mean everything you just said?"

I could see how much he enjoyed the fact he had surprised me. "I did indeed. A woman like Miss Evans could be a useful ally, and she has already put me in mind of a curious possibility."

"But she's the town gossip." My tone was quite incredulous. "Well, one of the many town gossips. If anything, gossip is Kilston Downs' main produce and currency."

He moved his head closer to my ear as though he were about to reveal a secret. "Perhaps I have never told you this, Christopher, but during my early days as a constable of the Metropolitan Police, the acquaintance of people like Lillibet Evans was essential when it came to keeping the area I patrolled under surveillance. I developed a network of such loquacious individuals and, as such, I was often aware of criminals' plans before they had completed them. Had it not been for the help of these inquisitive citizens, I might never have advanced in my career."

He pulled away again and nodded resolutely.

"You can't honestly—" I began, but he had already opened the door.

I followed him out to the tiny scrap of a garden in front of Nigel and Nora Tibbs's cottage. Delilah was there waiting for us, and before I could say anything more, I took in the sight of approximately half the population of the village. They had gathered in the square to wait for news.

CHAPTER TEN

It felt rather like a dream I occasionally have in which I get out of bed and go downstairs in my pyjamas, only to find that approximately half the population of Kilston Down are there waiting for me. My subsequent response changes from night to night, but the most common one is that, not knowing what they want, I start to dance.

I'm usually quite nervous at first but, as the seconds roll by, I find myself growing in confidence and ability until, by the end of the performance, I am jumping about the drawing room with all the grace of a *danseur noble* in a Russian ballet troupe. Sadly, even after this show of athleticism, the villagers remain unimpressed and boo me. All I can do is keep dancing in the hope I'll win them around, but the longer I dance, the louder they protest, and it is at that moment I usually wake up.

You will be happy to know that I did not prance about the square on the morning that the second body was discovered. I stepped forward to address the crowd.

"I imagine that you're waiting for news of Mr Tibbs," I began, and I was just as surprised by my apparent courage as my grandfather looked. Of course, there really wasn't anything so brave about it. I knew every last person there and had for most of my life. I spotted Mayor Perkins standing by the clocktower. My old teacher Alisha Steele was next to him, comforting the dead man's paramour. Dotty stood just beyond the garden gate, and even Reverend Deacon was lurking at the edge of the congregation, though for once he wasn't leading it.

"What do you know, boy?" the barrel-chested mayor demanded, and I had the definite feeling from the way he kept looking at the Tibbs's house that Miss Evans was peering through the front window behind me.

"It is not our place to inform the public of police business," I responded in my grandfather's voice. "But I believe we are at liberty to reveal that Mr Tibbs died in the night."

There was a rustle of voices as neighbours whispered to one another. I caught snatches of "See! I told you, Margaret," and "What is the world coming to?" but a hush soon recaptured the scene.

Were it not for the time and date, I might well have mistaken the gathering for the village's Christmas Eve celebration, to which I was very much looking forward. A glance at the faces of those present, however, showed that this was not a moment to celebrate.

The hush was broken by the sound of a simple question ringing out around the square. I couldn't quite catch it at first, but then it finally reached me.

"What about Mrs Tibbs?" Sir Joseph, an elderly eccentric who spent most of his time in the pub, asked no one in particular.

Miss Tring, who previously worked in the cobbler's, raised her hand for attention. "Yes! Where is she?"

When no one could answer, all eyes turned to Lord Edgington. My parents never publicised their connection to the famous detective, but evidently plenty of people had recognised him.

"Has anyone told her the bad news?" he asked, and the lack of any clear response suggested that they hadn't. "Has anyone been in her shop this morning?"

The look of doubt on all those faces had turned to one of shame. As word of Nigel's death had spread about the town, no one had found the courage to tell the man's wife.

I saw my mother arriving from along the road, and she already looked worried. Perhaps she saw all those gloomy people and thought that I was in trouble for some reason. Or perhaps she noticed her father, checked the date in her head and thought, *Ah, that'll be another murder then.*

Wrapped in a heavy black coat, with large Admiral-Nelson-style boots on his feet, the mayor took this opportunity to approach Lord Edgington and stand between us. There was something false in his gesture, and I could tell that he wanted everyone to think that we were on the same side.

"Now, listen, all of you. Obviously, it is a great tragedy that Nigel has died in such a manner," he began, and I had to question how he knew in which manner this was. "We must give the police and Lord Edgington our support. I am sure that all of us here in Kilston Down will co-operate as best we can."

Grandfather had been unusually quiet as this scene unfolded. Normally on our cases, he walked into a grand house or what have you, and the place was instantly his. But as Mayor Perkins talked about civic responsibility, and the hope of a cheery festive season,

Lord Edgington seemed to fade into the snowy background, just as a soldier uses camouflage to disappear from the enemy's sight.

He motioned to the shop and moved to leave even before the man had finished speaking. It was clear to me that this was no accident. He did not wish to be a puppet for the leader of a small Surrey village, especially when that very man was a suspect in the murder of his wife's lover.

Grandfather wasn't the only one to tire of the mayor's speechifying. With no more secrets set to be revealed, the crowd had started to disperse about the square. The talk continued, but with Perkins's voice getting ever faster to ensure that he could say all he wanted before there was no one left to hear it.

"And a very Happy Christmas," he said to finish, then bustled after us as we arrived at the well-stocked shop.

Grandfather reached out to open the half-glass door but stopped himself. "I think I have a clear picture of the different scandals that have divided this town over the last few years. Is there anything else I should know before we speak to the man's widow?"

I tried to think, but nothing of great importance sprang to mind. "Beyond rivalries over tall trees between neighbours' gardens and a particularly antagonistic disagreement over who makes the best Victoria sponge, very little has happened here in my lifetime."

He smiled and pushed the door open, but not before the mayor could call after us.

"Lord Edgington, young Master Prentiss!" He was a large man with a tiny head, and he was already out of breath by the time he reached us. I don't know whether the size of his head had anything to do with this. Perhaps a small mouth limits the intake of— Actually, never mind.

"Mayor Perkins." Grandfather nodded, but there was no warmth in the greeting. I felt that he had a good sense of the man's character from the start.

"I just wanted to tell you that if there is anything you need…" He paused to inhale every few seconds and his eyes strayed towards the shop. "…you have my full co-operation."

Grandfather looked quite unimpressed but, as he offered no rude response of his own, it fell to me to do so.

"You already mentioned that in your speech, Mayor. Now, we

have to see to some important business." I pulled on my hat – which was not the kind for tipping as it was blue and red and had a large woollen bobble on the top – and then we turned to enter the grocer's.

"I'll be easy to find," the apparently desperate character continued to blather even as the shop bell rang above our heads, and we slipped inside. "Night or day!"

CHAPTER ELEVEN

'Tibbs and Tibbs the Grocer' had always smelt of sawdust for some reason, and it was no different that frozen winter's morning. It sold all types of food from dried prunes to garlic, but the overriding smell was much the same as a carpenter's workshop, and I had never been able to understand why.

It didn't just sell food, of course. It had a little of everything, and I'd long since noticed the owners' ability to cram so many wares and goods into such a small space. There were no specific Christmas decorations of which to speak, though a line of three red candles burnt in the window in a small space between a large box of Bird's custard and a stacked pyramid of Robertson's bramble jelly. The sole living owner of the shop didn't react to our entrance, as she was busy with another customer.

My brother was reeling off a list of demands. "Glue – as many bottles as you have. And crepe paper, of course. And then if you have anything shiny."

Mrs Tibbs looked quite confused by the excitable young man in front of her. "We have some cutlery on sale. Was that what you had in mind?"

"No, no. I need to produce a large quantity of Christmas decorations. I'm trying to spruce up the manor house." He leaned in to speak to her over the shop counter and the expression he wore suggested he had a plea of the utmost importance to make. "Mrs Tibbs, you simply must help me, or I will never manage it."

"Christmas decorations? Well, why didn't you say, boy?" With a wide smile on her even wider face, Nora Tibbs disappeared through the doorway behind her and reappeared a few moments later with boxes under either arm. "Not only do I have every last item you might need to create your very own decorations, I have plenty of tinsel, beads and braiding. My sapheaded husband bought far too much. I didn't think we'd have a chance in Devon of selling it, but—"

"Give me every scrap you have!"

I hadn't seen my brother's eyes grow so large since the last time he was in love, which, now that I thought of it, was rather a long time ago.

He previously became enamoured with a new young lady every other month, and I still found it difficult to believe that he had poured all his energy into his job in the City or, as it now turned out, decorating for Christmas. Something was clearly not right with him, but he was too busy handing over his money and ferrying his purchases to his tiny, open-top car to stop and talk.

"Sorry, both," he called to us en route. "I'm rather occupied. It looks as if I'll have to make several trips."

"We'll let you off this time, Albert," Grandfather spoke in a confused tone, but this strange scene was soon forgotten as it was our turn to be served.

"How may I help you gentlemen this chilly morning?" Nora Tibbs was from somewhere far away in the countryside where, I could only assume, children are given a piece of straw to put in their mouths at birth, and the only drink is cider. By which I mean to say, she had a very strong rural accent.

She had asked this question in such a hearty manner, that it left both me and my grandfather searching for a response. It felt mean to put our questions to her without first breaking the news of her husband's death, but that was what the job required.

"Good morning, madam. Perhaps you know me. My name is—"

"Lord Edgington! Yes, of course I do."

"That's right." He winced a little, as though her shining positivity made it painful to continue. "In which case you may know that I am—"

"A master sleuth. Yes, sir. I certainly do. I read every article I can find about you in the papers. I loves a good mystery me, and you're the greatest detective that this country has seen in forty year or more."

For a moment, he became stuck, and I had to give him a nudge to get him working again. "That is very kind of you to say, madam." His mouth hung open, and he glanced at me. I could tell that he was reluctant to move the conversation on to our real purpose, and so, as Albert picked up the final box of decorations and muttered to himself about his tasks for the day, I reluctantly changed the topic.

"Mrs Tibbs, would you mind telling us what time you left your house this morning?" I almost called her madam, but it would have felt very wrong.

"I don't mind at all, young Christopher. I always arrive here at a quarter to nine to open the shop on the hour. My useless layabout of a husband is supposed to be here with me, of course, but he was sent a bottle of whisky by his brother in Oxted, and I imagine he's still sleeping off the effects."

Grandfather's eyebrows flicked upwards for a moment at the mention of the whisky, but he gave no other reaction.

"When was the last time you saw Mr Tibbs?" I asked, though I was certain that she could work out every last detail from this simple question.

She put her large, calloused hands on the counter to support her weight. "Well, it's like I said. He settled in the nook last night with the bottle of whisky from his brother and, as he'd been a pain for most of the day and he were in my bad books, I poked my head around the door to snap at him before I went to bed at ten o'clock."

She clucked her tongue like a disapproving hen. "He looked very comfortable in there. I can tell you. He was sitting in his easy chair with a blanket wrapped around him, the fire blazing and a book on his lap. To be quite honest, I've never known him to get through more than a chapter without falling asleep, and the acrid smell of that alc'ol hit me like a seal's flipper. Of course, I've never been a drinker and don't appreciate that sort of thing come summer or winter."

She had a unique turn of phrase that I'd always appreciated. It took me back to trips to buy sweets there in my childhood. Even as I thought of this, my eye was turned by the selection of confectionery on the counter. I saw horehound candy, Welsh butter fudge, chocolate cracknel, French almonds and marzipan of every colour.

Sadly, she was about to drag me from this pleasant digression and back to the present day.

"'Ere, why are you askin' so many questions about Nigel?"

Grandfather and I looked at one another, and it was clear that the time had come. I left it to the professional to do the undesired honours.

"I'm afraid we are the bearers of bad news," he said with downturned eyes. "When she went into your house to clean this morning, Miss Evans found your husband dead in the very same position that you described."

Nora Tibbs just stared. The revelation had touched her so profoundly that she didn't have the co-ordination to let her jaw drop or bow her head in sorrow. She stopped moving altogether and looked as though some wicked person had injected her with embalming fluid.

"My Nigel?" she finally said.

"Yes, madam, I'm afraid it's true."

"Dead?" she asked again, and I decided that I would tackle her question this time.

"That's correct, Nora." It sounded wrong to say her Christian name, but this was not the moment for formality. "I'm afraid to tell you that we believe he may have been murdered."

This was what really sparked a response. Her face scrunched together to display a mix of dread and sorrow. "Who would murder that foolish man except for me?"

This was a difficult subject to discuss, and one, I had to imagine, that would occupy us for some time.

"It is too early to draw any conclusions," Grandfather replied in a calm, comforting tone, whereas the voice in my head had suddenly got a lot louder as it shouted, *She knows that she's a suspect! She essentially admitted that she is the only one with any reason to kill her husband. The case is closed.* Luckily, I have learnt not to listen too closely to that voice and made no rash judgements.

"In fact, we were hoping that you might be able to answer that very question. Isn't it possible that Nigel upset someone in your circle of acquaintances?"

She had to lean against the high shelves that covered the wall behind her. As she did so, she upset a jar of mint humbugs, but didn't seem to notice as a cascade of black and white sweets fell to the floor at her feet.

"I suppose…"

I would be the one to prompt her for more. "Anything you know may turn out to be of great importance to the investigation."

"Well, I suppose that the mayor is the only other person who might have grown tired of my husband's foolery." She already looked exhausted, but I noticed that she was yet to cry. "Nigel Tibbs was smart as a dead rabbit and persistent as a flea. I was long past caring what he got up to when I weren't looking, but John Perkins may have been less forgiving."

I was still puzzling over her use of simile when Grandfather raised another point. "I'm sorry to be gauche, but are you saying that your husband was engaged in some sort of romantic liaison with

80

Ethel Perkins?"

"Hadn't you 'eard? They were carrying on like two stoats in a nest. Not that I really minded. It was nice to have him out of the house. Nigel had spent the last ten years hanging about there, moaning about the weather or his lumpy chair or his shoes being too tight. If anything, Ethel was doing me a favour."

Grandfather was knocked speechless by this comment, and so I took up the slack. "And what about the mayor?"

Whatever sadness I'd previously spied on her face was now replaced with confusion. "What about the mayor?"

"Did he object to his wife running around with your husband?"

For the first time since we'd entered the shop, Mrs Tibbs's demeanour was less than obliging. "I couldn't possibly tell you."

"You've never discussed the fact that your respective spouses were having an affair?" I didn't like to speak so plainly, but sometimes it is necessary.

"The tongues in this village wag enough without either of us getting involved. What could I gain from a cosy chat with John Perkins?"

There was something contradictory in her account and I was about to point it out when, always one to ten steps ahead, Grandfather beat me to it. "Madam, we were in the teahouse yesterday when you came to retrieve your husband. You certainly didn't seem so blasé about his spending time with Mrs Perkins then."

Nora Tibbs was one of the kindest people in Kilston Down. As she'd rightly mentioned, she was nothing like the many gossips who inhabited the place; she had a soft word and a smile for almost everyone. However, when riled, she was quite a different proposition.

She pulled up the sleeves on her muscular arms and curled her fingers into a fist. For a moment, the image formed in my head of her punching us back out into the snow one after the other. "Are you saying that I killed the silly beggar just because he was an unfaithful mole?"

I really should have considered a response to this question, but I found myself wondering about the mating habits of animals in the talpa genus.

"No, of course not, Mrs Tibbs." I believe that even Grandfather suffered under her furious gaze. "We merely wish to find out what occurred in the final hours of your husband's life."

This seemed to appease her a little. "Well, in that case, I wasn't angry because he was with that irritating woman. I was angry because he left me here in the shop to serve customers, stock shelves and then go home to make his dinner." She took a great gulp of breath as she'd been speaking so fast. "And before you point out that I don't sound too sad that he's gone, let me tell you that you're right. He was a pain in the neck and a worthless husband. And yet I'll still leave here this afternoon and, as I stand in front of a stove cooking his favourite turnips, I'm sure that I'll shed a tear for the wastrel I was married to for the last twenty-five years."

She crossed her arms in front of her chest, and I admit that I'd become distracted once more. I don't mean to sound unprofessional, but really! Whose favourite food is turnips?

"I appreciate your candour, madam." Grandfather's usual extra-polite tone had returned. "Perhaps you can tell us something more about your husband. Were his people from this part of the world?"

"His people?" She still hadn't calmed down since our previous insinuations. "He didn't have any people. Or at least, none that he knew. He and his older brother Michael were orphans. They never knew what happened to their parents. The only attention they ever received was the back of the matron's hand in the orphanage where their mother left 'em."

She had become quite agitated, and I felt that she was as angry on behalf of the abandoned infants from five decades earlier as she was for her murdered husband now.

"How terrible," I replied quite sincerely. "The world can be very cruel."

There was a tall stool in front of the mechanical till, and she pulled it closer to crash down on top of it. "He weren't all bad, my Nigel. He'd had a hard life before we met, which is probably why I was always easy on him. He could be as friendly as a robin when he wanted." This was the first comparison she had made that I felt was self-explanatory. "Perhaps if I'd been tougher – like the nagging wife he needed – perhaps then he wouldn't have met such a sticky end."

She pulled a handkerchief from inside her blouse and proceeded to blow into it, though I still didn't notice a single tear.

"Thank you for sharing your thoughts with us, Mrs Tibbs."

Grandfather bowed once more. I believe that he liked to put across an old-fashioned, gentlemanly attitude to our suspects. It lent an extra air of mystery to a thoroughly enigmatic man.

"You're welcome, Lord Edgington." She had another brief blow and put the cotton hanky back in her bosom where it belonged. "Now, what can I get you?"

She stood up and looked hopeful that we would make a big order. Grandfather has a soft heart and pointed at whatever was in front of him on the other side of the glass. "I'll have one of those for my dog, please."

"Your dog likes Stilton cheese?" Her voice rose in surprise.

He winced but maintained the unlikely story. "Only at the weekend. A pound of Stilton should be plenty."

It occurred to me as we were leaving that she hadn't asked how her husband had—

"I'm sorry, Lord Edgington," her voice carried across the shop to us just before we stepped outside. "I must ask. How did my Nigel die?"

Grandfather paused and looked back over his shoulder. "It is too early to say for certain, but initial evidence suggests that he was poisoned."

I expected another wave of emotion to hit her, but she merely blinked a few times and replied in a cold, calm voice. "I see. Thank you for your honesty." And then we wandered back out into the snow.

CHAPTER TWELVE

It occurred to me that this wasn't like one of our normal cases. If we charted a path between Maude Evans and Nigel Tibbs, it did not take in a neat line of suspects. Almost anyone in the village could have wanted them dead. I glanced around the square, and it wasn't just the coating of white that made it different from the picture that I often viewed in my head. I no longer saw Kilston Down as the peaceful, innocent place that I'd always imagined it to be.

Something had changed, and what was most disconcerting was that I couldn't say whether it was my own perception, now that I had grown up and seen something of the world, or the village itself. Had a channel of evil always been there – lurking under the floorboards of all those pretty Tudor cottages? Or had the village just recently gone to seed?

I wasn't the only one with a conundrum to solve. Grandfather stood looking at the candles in the window of the shop as the flames moved seemingly of their own accord.

"It is a puzzle," he muttered, sounding far from optimistic. "It truly is."

"Do you think that she could be involved in her husband's death?" I asked without expecting a clear answer.

As usual, he found a way to surprise me. "Experience tells me that it is unlikely. For one thing, if she was the killer and wished to hide her guilt, she went about it in the wrong way. She made no effort to play the grieving widow and underlined her own credentials as a suspect. While this very attitude might normally fool a detective, it is a dangerous game to play and, as she is familiar with our work, I believe it would take a truly great liar to achieve such aims. So, to answer the question more succinctly: nothing is impossible."

"That matches my own feelings on the matter to a tittle. Of course, you said it better than I ever could."

He laughed, and the conversation would have continued had Delilah not barked at us from a spot on the nearby pavement. That brute Dean Henderson was standing beside her and looked just as angry as when I tripped him up at school aged seven. I promise that it was only an accident, but he didn't see it that way.

"Hey!" this was him speaking, not the dog. "What do you think you're doing leaving your poor mutt out here in the cold?"

"We haven't been introduced." Grandfather held out his hand to impress the young man when Henderson grunted some more.

"That's inhumane, that is."

He was still pushing the wheelbarrow that I'd seen him with beside the lake, and I felt I had to point out a flaw in his argument. "Aren't those the snowballs that you made to throw at some cats? How is that better than leaving Delilah to be spoilt by our neighbours for half an hour while we were busy?"

"Cats aren't people!" He just glared at us. "Why should I care what happens to them?"

With this unanswerable question delivered, he stomped off across the square with his barrow leading the way. Delilah watched him go with all the bemusement on her silky face that Grandfather and I felt. She didn't appear to object to the cold and, judging by how wet her fur was, had presumably been rolling about on the ground while we were working.

"Lord Edgington," a voice called from further along that side of the square, and there was the handsome doctor, exiting the dead man's garden, "I was hoping to catch you before you disappeared."

"Hello, Dr Steele," I called back. "Have you discovered anything useful?"

"Nothing to tell us for certain what happened to Tibbs, but I have taken another look at the body." He spoke in the same tone that my grandfather adopts when discussing the "careful methodology" he uses to investigate a crime. "I believe that an eye for detail is a doctor's greatest tool."

"Much like a detective's." Grandfather frowned and nodded his head in that special way he has whenever something unexpectedly impresses him.

"I don't like leaving things to chance and, to that end, I recommended to the sergeant on duty that the bottle of whisky I found in the kitchen be sent for testing; I believe Tibbs had been drinking it before he died. I also found a used teacup in the sink and suggested the same thing."

I was tempted to shout *You see, Grandfather! I knew he'd had some tea!* But I doubt that either of them would have thought me sane, so I kept my thoughts to myself.

Grandfather held his hand out, and the two men spoke at the very same moment. "I believe that careful methodology is the watchword of a good detective."

Very well, they didn't use the exact same words, and Rodrick Steele obviously said "doctor" not "detective", but apart from that, it was very close indeed. For a moment, I contemplated whether Grandfather had found a long-lost son whom he'd never known before.

"The best news we have so far is that the coroner expects to file his report by the end of the day."

Grandfather shook the man's hand a little more eagerly. "That is excellent."

"I would love to stand here all day talking," the doctor said, and I believed him, "but I must meet Alisha again. I don't know where she could have gone."

"Will we see you at Gareth's party later?" Grandfather clearly wished to continue the discussion.

"I beg your pardon?"

"The musician who lives on your road invited us to his house this evening. I wondered whether you would be there."

Steele looked a trifle wounded, as though Grandfather had stomped on his little toe. "Oh, Heywood. I'm afraid I barely know the man. I pray you'll have a pleasant time, though."

Grandfather tipped his top hat, and I pulled my woollen head-hugger even further down over my eyes. I was curious as to where our investigation might now take us but, before I could ask, we were interrupted by yet more acquaintances. Well, that's probably not the right word for them. You see my mother stepped out of the post office just as my father and grandmother appeared in the square.

"Please tell me that you need our help to find a killer!" Granny begged. "I can't stand being in that house a moment longer. Why my parents had more than one child is beyond my understanding."

"Have you heard about Mr Tibbs, then?" I foolishly asked.

"No, should I have?" She didn't wait for an answer but came to her own conclusions. "If he has been murdered, I'd like to list the reasons why I would be the best person to aid you in your investigation."

"Really, Loelia," her daughter-in-law interrupted. "A man has died, and all you care about is finding an excuse not to be at home with your own family. Of course my father doesn't require your help." Despite her disapproving tone, I waited for the inevitable continuation. "Not least because I'm the one with the knowledge and experience required to catch the killer. I assisted on any number of cases when I was younger, and I know this village better than any of you."

I half expected my father to put forward his candidature due to his ability to focus on boring details and the fact he was in possession of a deerstalker hat. He did not, but only because our attention was drawn at this moment to a group of new arrivals. My two great-uncles and their numerous followers were bustling along the road like a party of tourists. Uncle Terry was at the front, pointing out beloved sights from his youth that were no longer there.

"This very corner is where the local magistrate's wife first noticed what a wonderful speaking voice I had and suggested I become a judge or a politician. She's long dead, of course, and her house was knocked down to put up the schoolhouse, but I will never forget that day. Over to the left is the spot where I kissed my first wench. She told me that I had lips like two moist balloons." It was amusing to see this bizarre flock shuffling along. Terry could only walk at the speed of an average snail and his relatives already looked terribly bored. "Straight ahead we can see…"

I have no doubt that he continued talking of himself in glowing terms for some time longer, but I stopped paying attention because my parents and grandmother were keen to effect a quick escape.

"I should return to the house to help Albert decorate." Mother didn't even look at us as she imparted this message.

"And I completely forgot that I have that package coming this morning," Father was quick to add, before his mother explained her own (far more honest) thinking.

"And I'm doing all that I can to avoid the monstrous people who just arrived here." Granny placed a cold hand on mine. "Have you considered the possibility that the grocer killed himself to avoid having to listen to my brothers blathering on for hours on end?"

She didn't wait for an answer but hurried along the icy pavement before any of my cousins, aunts or uncles could spot her.

Grandfather, Delilah and I stayed right where we were. I would have liked to put aside these distractions to focus on the details of a case which we were yet to grasp with both hands. Sadly, I was too distracted by my Uncle Thomas, who spoke at a loud enough volume for shoppers on the other side of the square to hear.

"I don't approve of public houses, or balloons for that matter. And as for wenches... well, they're all right, I suppose, but only in moderation."

CHAPTER THIRTEEN

"So, Christopher, what should we do next?"

I looked back at my grandfather quite aghast. It was my job to ask him such questions. If he didn't know what we should do, the investigation would surely fall to pieces.

"Well, next…" I began, before my voice trailed off.

The problem was that we had no core from which to work outwards. I could see no clear connection between our two victims, if that is what they were. The village felt bigger than it ever had before with its population of two hundred locals now transformed into a multitude of potential murderers. This certainly wasn't the homecoming which I'd been craving.

Perhaps it would have made more sense to focus solely on Nigel Tibbs and dismiss Miss Evans's death as an unfortunate case of food poisoning or some such. But before I could utter another word, Grandfather answered his own question.

"I agree, Christopher."

"But I didn't say anything."

"Yes, but I'm sure that some part of your mind was thinking that it was time for a late breakfast."

I couldn't deny this entirely, though I felt there were more pressing matters to which we should attend. "But the case, Grandfather. A man is dead!" I sounded just like my mother.

"And he'll still be dead after we've availed ourselves of some much-needed sustenance. Now we must decide which of the fine establishments here at Kilston Down we should charge with providing our victuals."

I looked about the square for the tenth time that morning. "Do you mean Dotty's Teahouse or the pub?"

"Precisely, my boy." Without stopping to hash out the matter between us, he walked in the direction of The Holly Tree Inn. Like many buildings in the village, the public house was Tudor in design, with a black timber frame and white walls. It had once been a coaching inn and still offered weary travellers a poke room for the night and old men a place to sit all day drinking.

As it happened, I had never set foot inside the place before as, for most of my life, I'd been too young to enter. Furthermore, the last time I'd been at home for more than a day, I'd still viewed pubs as dens of iniquity that could only lead men to ruin. My thoughts on this fine British institution had changed somewhat in the intervening months and years, and I was eager to discover the delights on offer within.

"A pint of Shires, please, barkeep." Grandfather didn't sound quite so toffee nosed for once. He rubbed his hands together like a labourer about to enjoy his first beer of the day.

"And an apple juice, too." I, on the other hand, still couldn't stand ale of any kind.

I had expected the place to be quiet at eleven thirty in the morning, but most of the nooks and alcoves of the irregularly laid out room were occupied by people I recognised. As we reached the bar, a chorus of voices went up to greet me.

"Hello there, Master Christopher," Reverend Deacon called, and the refrain was immediately echoed by half a dozen others.

"Hello, everyone," I sang back in harmony, and I received a few bemused looks for my trouble.

It was a perfectly cosy place for lunch. There was a well-tended fire in the huge, blackened hearth opposite the bar. One wall was covered in horse brasses depicting scenes of rural life, and another was cut in two by a line of diamond-leaded windows that gave onto the square. I spied a table in the corner and left Grandfather to obtain a pair of menus. Delilah was more concerned with getting dry and went to stand beside the fireplace.

From my vantage point at our table, I could see my fellow drinkers quite clearly and noticed a few significant figures. In addition to the reverend, our very own Mayor Perkins was leaning against one wall with his elbow on a shelf for support. He was all alone and stared into his glass as though it were a crystal ball.

Gareth Heywood was tucking into some pork chops with a striking blonde woman at the table closest to the fireplace, and Dastardly Dean Henderson was there, too. He had apparently stowed his wheelbarrow somewhere cold, and was tucking into a plate of sausages, gravy and mashed potato. I had no love for the boy he'd been, nor the man he'd become, but I did approve of his choice of meal. This raised an important point as, at what time does breakfast finish and lunch begin?

Grandfather had suggested a late breakfast, but by the time it was served, it would surely be an early lunch.

With a dead man on his way to the local coroner's office, and the possibility of a string of killings in Kilston Down, this should not have been my primary concern, but my musing soon led me to wonder whether I could link my childhood bully to the crimes.

Dean Henderson was an uncouth villain by most standards. He certainly didn't appear to have grown up since I'd last met him – and any man who spends his morning planning to irritate some cats is a rotter in my book. Sadly, though, there was nothing to connect him to the grocer or Miss Evans as far as I knew. Nevertheless, I would keep him at the top of my list. I wouldn't tell Grandfather that, of course, but I'd keep him there all the same.

"Here we are," my dining companion muttered as he reached our table carrying a pair of slates. "Two menus, though the steak and ale pie has already taken my fancy."

He placed them down in front of me and had a long sip of his coppery bitter. The head of the beer left a creamy line on his moustache – a sort of over-moustache, if you will – but I decided it was polite not to mention it.

"What will you have then?" he asked as my hungry eyes darted back and forth across the chalked list of dishes. As I'm not insane, I immediately dismissed the five options in which offal featured. Grandfather's pie and the bully's sausages were both appealing, but was that really what I wanted to eat on the twenty-third of December?

"I'll have roast chicken with roast potatoes, roast parsnips and roast carrots."

"Would you like some roast gravy to accompany that?" he asked in a teasing tone, and I replied just as smugly.

"I would if such a thing existed. In fact, if I could choose, I would roast all my food. Just imagine roast jam on roast toast. Delicious!"

He laughed and went to do something that was quite rare for him; he performed a simple task without the help of his servants. He ordered for the both of us, and we settled at our table, with Delilah now sitting on our feet to keep herself and us warm.

"I have some questions for you, Christopher." With his hands linked together like a miserly banker, he sat up straighter to loom over me.

"Shouldn't it be the other way around?"

"I beg your pardon?"

I tried to extend my neck and stretch my back to rise to his level but failed. "Shouldn't I be the one asking questions? I tend to know far less than you."

His prickly eyebrows wavered. "Not today, and you must stop thinking in such terms. You are almost twenty-one and have been of vital assistance to me for several years now."

I did not acknowledge this point. It was not just modesty that prevented me from agreeing with him; I genuinely struggled to think of myself as anything but a lucky amateur when compared to my mentor.

"Very well. What is your first question?"

He took a moment to size me up again – not like a tailor, I hasten to add, but a rival across a chessboard. "I brought you here to discuss the case as it appears at this early stage. It is more than possible that the killer has completed his task, and we have already found all the evidence that exists. On the other hand, this could well be the calm before the storm of a great massacre."

His voice had risen up and become infused with fervour, like a Puritan preacher in the time of Oliver Cromwell. It certainly drew some sideways glances from the neighbouring tables, the occupants of which were already discussing the grocer's death. In fact, the only person who didn't look over at this strange and violent proclamation was Mayor Perkins, whose only interest was the bottom of his glass.

"Perhaps you could speak a little less excitedly," I warned my companion in a whisper, but our fellow drinkers had already returned to their conversations.

"Very well, but I haven't asked my first question yet." He cleared his throat affectedly and continued with what he was saying. "Assuming that there will be no further killings, what do you think might link the crimes?"

This surprised me, as I felt quite sure that he would set aside Old Miss Evans's death until we could prove that she had been murdered. I stared blankly for a few moments as I tried to summon an answer.

"I'm in no hurry." He sat back casually in his chair. Well, as casually as possible for a man in a black silk cravat and dove-grey morning suit with a rabbit-skin top hat on the chair next to him.

"To answer your question," I began, to buy myself some more time, "I don't think I can answer your question."

He released an infuriated, "Pfwah! Come along, Christopher. At least try to use your imagination."

"I thought one of your many maxims was that my imagination makes a proficient magnifying glass, but a terrible compass. Should I not base all my conclusions on facts and hard evidence?"

"When that hard evidence is lacking, imagination may be the very thing we require. I would say that you, even more than I, could be most adept in that department." He was clearly excited by the possibilities before us. "So what do you imagine connects Maude Evans and Nigel Tibbs?"

I puffed out my lips in frustration. "I would love to answer you, Grandfather, but my imagination is not what it once was. You have trained me out of using it and, much like a muscle that goes unused, it has become flabby and weak."

He tutted, sighed, shook his head and bit his lip to show his discontent. "Really, Christopher. You're like a full glass of water."

"Thank you very much," I said, trying my best to take this as a compliment.

"It wasn't a compliment," the blasted mind reader replied. "I was implying that, for every new thing that settles in your brain, another spills from the top. It is a failing which you are yet to address."

"Or a reason to be happy with the knowledge I already possess, and a reminder not to try too hard to learn anything else."

This time, he restricted himself to a mere tut. "I'll pretend I didn't hear that, but I will take this opportunity to exercise your imaginary muscle. Look at that man." He turned to motion to a scruffily dressed individual standing at the bar. "He came in while I was ordering, and I found him rather puzzling. He speaks with the voice of a gentleman but is dressed like the lowliest of peasants. As a fun little exercise, I would like you to imagine the circumstances that have led him to this humble state."

I stuck my tongue out a short way between my lips and studied the old man. "He is an interesting case. I'll grant you that." I shifted in my seat to get a better look at him. It was rather exciting how quickly my words came to me. "Let's say that his name is Joe... No, Joseph. In my opinion, he is the son of a long-deceased lord of this parish. His father, Baron Kilston, was a spendthrift and a gambler. The family was reduced to selling their manor house out towards Wotton... No, I take that back; he has the look of a man from Gomshall. The family had lived in the area for centuries but were left near penniless by his father's profligacy, which led him to move into an alms cottage with his mother, who recently died at the age of ninety-six."

Grandfather looked ever so pleased with me. "That's wonderful. I must retract any criticisms that I made and even more that I was thinking."

"You are most kind." I closed my eyes modestly, but my trick was soon undone when another of the old regulars wandered into the bar and said in a loud, deep voice, "Joseph Bickle, you still owes me a cider from last Friday, and I 'ave come 'ere to claim it."

"You know that man, don't you?" Grandfather looked at me with a scowl. "Cheats only cheat themselves, Christopher. I thought better of you."

"Of course I know him. Sir Joseph, as I've always called him, has been practically living at the Holly Tree Inn since I was old enough to totter about the village as a child. I didn't have to use my imagination because I already know far too much about the eccentric old fellow. When he's not here, he sits on the bench beneath the clocktower and, if you give him a bullseye or a mint imperial, he will tell you tales of his childhood growing up in the splendour of Gomshall Abbey."

Grandfather looked glumly down at the hound at his feet. Delilah peered sympathetically back at him, like the caring mother dog that she was to the pair of us. I was quite sure that she would receive a juicy chunk of steak from his pie as a reward.

"Oh, fine," I said when the guilt overwhelmed me. "I'll try again with someone here that I don't know." I looked about the place and realised that the one person on the premises who was not familiar to me was Gareth Heywood's companion.

The pair of them were sitting sideways-on to the rest of the pub, and so the young lady with long peroxided hair didn't notice me staring. I imagine that a great beauty like her would be used to such attention in a backwater like Kilston Down, but I still did my best to be subtle.

"Heywood over there is with a woman of around twenty-five. She is quite exquisite, and from the way she is looking at him, I would say that she is deeply in love. For his part, I do not believe that he is quite so enamoured. He doesn't always meet her gaze and—"

"I'm not interested in what you can see," Grandfather interrupted. "I want to hear the story that the scene tells. What do her clothes suggest about her? Do the lines around her eyes reveal that she has a troubled existence."

"She doesn't appear to have any lines around the eyes." This made me wonder whether young people can age so rapidly, and I might have got a little distracted by the idea. "Do I have lines around my eyes? Is my whole face as wrinkled as a scrunched-up piece of paper?"

"Concentrate, Christopher. Tell me her story."

I turned back and did what I could. "Very well, I think her name is Melodie, and she was born to a family of…" I was going to say something silly like travelling acrobats, but even as the thought formed, it felt wrong. "No, she is the daughter of a school teacher and a craftsman of some sort. Let's say he was an *ébéniste*." To tell the truth, I'd read this word in a book and wasn't quite clear what it meant.

"A French cabinet maker?" he asked a little dryly.

"Yes, why not. That's why she's called Melodie with an I and an E at the end instead of a Y." I paused to study her a little longer and noticed the way her sharp fringe cut diagonally across her face so that she could presumably only see clearly out of one eye. It would have bothered me no end, and I decided that she was either terribly patient, or partially blind. "She has known Heywood for several years and is waiting for him to confess his love. In the meantime, she has written whole books of poetry to capture the torment of her troubled heart. She has enjoyed some success in certain lofty publications, including the Criterion, and is holding out hope that the Hogarth Press will agree to print a collection of her work."

Grandfather didn't say anything, but he smiled almost paternally. This was a rare thing for him but was even rarer for my real pater.

"Of course, none of her friends knows of her literary endeavours. She publishes under a pseudonym for fear that her amour will discover the truth about her. She is caught in the Tantalean hinterland between love and rejection, fame and anonymity, but her overriding optimism keeps her going from one day to the next. She is, in short, a romantic.

And we all know what happens to her sort at the end of sad stories."

I believe I'd left him the tiniest bit speechless. "Christopher... I..." Well, he'd managed to get two words out, but it would take him a while longer to produce anything of note. "Yes, I must say that was splendid. I take back every criticism I've ever laid at your door."

"So I don't eat too many cakes, and speaking in full sentences isn't as important as you have often claimed?"

"I meant intellectual criticism. You are clearly far more imaginative, perceptive and creative than I previously realised. On the basis of this experiment, I believe that you would make a fine writer. Perhaps you should talk to our friend Marius Quin the next time we are in London. He may be able to give you some useful tips."

I was about to ask him whether he'd prefer this to my continued presence at his side, but a more important question came to me. "That's all well and good, but will you please now tell me why you wanted me to indulge in such daydreaming in the first place?"

He leaned a little closer over the table and his voice dropped to a whisper. "I asked you to use your imagination as I have been doing the very same thing, and I did not wish to shock you."

I showed no shock. In fact, I stared back expressionless. I might even have had a brief yawn.

He took the hint and continued with what he was saying. "Certain factors today have indicated at a possible link between the two dead bodies. And yet the narrative I have concocted is not based on reliable evidence, as I would usually insist. As a result, it may still come to nothing."

I was eager to hear this, not least because I love a good yarn, but first he had more questions for me. "Is there anything that you have noticed that could explain why both Maude Evans and her local grocer were murdered in remarkably similar ways? Have you discovered a thread that could connect them?"

I smiled then, as I would finally have the chance to show off about the tea that I predicted would exist. "As a matter of fact, I have. You see, the doctor noticed—"

"Except for the tea, Christopher." He huffed out a breath, and it was clear that the brief moment of his amazement at my abilities had sputtered out like a malfunctioning firework.

"Then, no. I have tried my very best, but the truth is that I haven't a clue what could link them. I was hoping that we could ignore Maude Evans's death entirely."

He closed his eyes, then slowly opened them again. "Think back to what the woman's sister told us when we went to her house yesterday. Think of the scant facts that we know about Nigel Tibbs, and then fit them together like two hands intertwining."

"Lillibet thought you were the rotter who loved and left her big sister." I turned to look back at the bar as a thought hit me.

"Yes, and so what connection could there be between Old Miss Evans and a fifty-year-old man who never knew his parents?"

"You don't mean?" I began, and before I could say what he didn't mean, the door to the pub flew open and Ethel Perkins let out a piercing scream.

CHAPTER FOURTEEN

"How could you just leave me like that?" she yelled at her husband.

For his part, the mayor didn't appear to know how to react. He was still rather stiff and distant, perhaps trying to comprehend why it should be his job to comfort his wife when her lover had been murdered.

"Ethel, I know you're upset, but please keep your voice down." The innate desire for decorum that most politicians have around their voters was evident in him. He continued in a whisper that was still loud enough for everyone to hear. "You may be feeling sad now, but all wounds heal."

This was not what Mrs Perkins wanted to hear, and she let him know at the very top of her voice. "How can you be so callous? My close friend has had the life stolen from him, and you're suggesting I calm down."

He moved across the room to reason with her as all the old boys there sipped their beers and enjoyed the show.

"It's for your own good, Ethel. I don't want you to be overcome with emotion. We will all miss poor—"

"Oh, yes, you were bosom pals, isn't that right? You and Nigel were the best of friends and I'm sure you're in here crying into your drink at the thought of his demise."

"I wouldn't put it like that exactly," he replied in an even tone, and I noticed that it wasn't just the regulars in the pub who were listening. Heywood and his friend were just as keen to hear what the mayor and his wife had to say. "But I didn't want anything bad to happen to the man."

Mrs Perkins restrained herself as she fashioned her response. "I don't believe you, John. I don't believe a word of it." She had to swallow, as though the very thing she was about to utter was hard for her to imagine. "I came here to ask you the truth. Did you kill Nigel Tibbs?"

The whole pub was silent at that moment. I'm sure that I use that expression too often, but in this case, it was true; there was not a sound as we awaited the mayor's answer. Before he said anything, he turned to us as the jury tasked with condemning him to death or granting salvation.

He held the lapels on his long black coat and, straightening his back a little to appear both taller and more respectable, he denied the claim. "Of course I didn't kill him, Ethel. I would hope that, if there is one thing you know about me, it's that I'm not a violent man."

His wife stared at him without showing a hint of what she was feeling, but this couldn't last long, and her emotions soon burst like the clouds on a stormy day. "I'm sorry, my love…" A tear rolled down either cheek in perfect synchronism. "I know you would never hurt anyone. I just can't see how to make sense of what has happened. Why would anyone kill poor, silly Nigel? He was the daffiest man I've ever met."

It was at this point that the mayor rushed forward to embrace her. I thought perhaps he was afraid that she might fall. She pushed her heavily made-up face into the crook of his broad shoulder, and she stood there sobbing for some time.

The spectators' initial interest, as we hungrily awaited new grist for the Kilston Down rumour mill, now turned to embarrassment. This was no longer a sensational entertainment for us to enjoy. We were eavesdropping on a married couple as they suffered through a difficult time. A sense of discretion returned to the Holly Tree Inn, and we went back to our drinks, meals and discussions as if nothing had happened.

The barman brought our lunches, and Grandfather and I spoke at great length of the deliciousness of well-cooked country food. My roast everything was delicious, and the unroast gravy was just as good. Delilah enjoyed the chunk of steak that Grandfather kindly gave her and, as soon as the mayor and Mrs Perkins had left, the place exploded in chatter and conjecture.

"Well, what did you think about that?" I found myself asking with just as much joy as any one of the gossiping regulars at Dotty's Teahouse. "They put on quite a show for us, don't you think?"

Grandfather was less effusive. "What exactly do you mean, Christopher?"

I looked at the neighbouring tables, but their inhabitants were too engrossed by their own speculation to worry about ours. "It's all a bit convenient, wouldn't you say?"

"Let us be clear." He put his hands together over his near-spotless plate. "Are you suggesting that the mayor of this village murdered the grocer with his wife as an accomplice, and they chose to argue in a public place in order to suggest to all those present that they had nothing to do with the crime?"

An immense smile curled its way up to the centre of my cheeks, and I nodded gleefully. "That is exactly what I hand in mind."

My heart jumped in my chest for a moment as his stern expression remained right where it was… for approximately five seconds or so. "Bravo, Christopher. We have no evidence to show that anything you said was true, but I approve of the way you have taken a perfectly innocent interaction between husband and wife and turned it into something sinister."

For some reason, I lost my excitement then.

Grandfather continued in the same vein. "Though you must tell me, why would they do any such thing?"

This was always the question I feared when I put forward a theory. It was all very well using our imagination from time to time, but there is generally an underlying factor that I haven't considered which my grandfather immediately identifies.

"Well… Perhaps…" I should probably have taken my time to think before speaking, but an idea finally came to me. "Perhaps the glamorous Mrs Perkins was never really interested in dull Mr Tibbs, but she feigned affection in order to…"

"Gain a place in his will?" Grandfather mumbled just as speculatively.

"That's it! She made him change his will so that she would inherit everything. That would explain why our beloved mayor has shown no compunction over his wife's dalliance with another man."

"Yet it also provided a point of division between them, thus offering the chance for a very public argument, which could be used to imply that the two of them were not working together!" He nodded approvingly a few times as he considered what more he might add. "All they need now is a reliable alibi to rule themselves out of the poisoning, and they'll be home and dry."

Grandfather still had the dregs of his drink at the bottom of his glass, and he now proceeded to tip them down his throat. He was clearly satisfied with our conclusions.

"Is that it then?" I asked, quite amazed. "If we discover that Tibbs's will favours Ethel Perkins, is that the case solved?"

"No, of course not, Christopher." He rose from his seat and

Delilah shot out from under the table. "This is merely pub-talk. We have enjoyed a brief voyage through the valleys of our imaginations, and we must now return to the cold, hard world beyond these doors. We must return to facts, evidence and proof."

I sighed and pulled back my chair. "I knew you were going to say that."

"Lord Edgington," the young musician, Gareth Heywood, called as we walked past his table towards the exit. "Don't forget the party this afternoon."

"I wouldn't miss it," Grandfather responded as he smiled at the young lady to whom we would not be introduced. For her part, she looked sad not to be included in the conversation, but Gareth was in fine form.

"Half the village will be there, and it should be a jolly good whoopee."

Grandfather's mouth turned a little mischievous behind his moustaches. "There is nothing I like better than a jolly good whoopee."

"That's wonderful." Gareth laughed in his usual warm, giving manner. "You're welcome any time from six o'clock."

We said farewell, and I braced myself for the snow and cold air that hit us like fifty mallets to the face as soon as the door was flung wide. If anything, the weather had got worse since we'd entered that happy bubble of an establishment. The flakes were coming down by the cupful, and so I pulled my scarf higher to cover my nose and mouth.

"One thing is certain. Gareth Heywood is not the killer."

Grandfather's eyebrows rose disapprovingly. "I beg your pardon, Christopher, I didn't understand a word you just said."

I pulled the scarf back down and repeated myself. In reply, he laughed disbelievingly, and so I offered some evidence to support my claim. "What foolish person would invite Britain's finest detective to his house for a party if he'd been busy killing his neighbours? Furthermore, Gareth is new to the village and probably hasn't had time to build up the rage and rivalry that long-standing members of the community have spent decades cultivating."

The wind whipped around us, but I held my ground. I felt, for once, that I was on a firm footing in eliminating a possible suspect, but Grandfather would not accept so obvious an argument.

104

"Then you don't find it curious that a working musician, who must surely spend several nights a week in London for concerts, should wish to move to a close-minded and poorly connected village in the heart of Surrey?"

"Perhaps he likes the country air." Even as I said this, I knew it would only lead to more derision.

Grandfather walked off along the pavement but continued the discussion as if I were right next to him. "As for a suspect keeping a detective close, that is no evidence of his innocence. Pre-meditated murderers are, almost by definition, the most arrogant people ever to walk the earth."

Delilah and I ran to catch up with him, as what he was saying was actually rather intriguing.

"They believe that they will be better than all who came before them: all those men who have killed and been found out – those who swung from the hangman's noose and those who rotted in prison for the remainder of their sorry lives."

He once more sounded like a priest delivering his message from the pulpit, and he cast his arms about with great energy and expression. "How many times have we met killers who believed they were our match? A cocky young chap like Gareth Heywood is just the type to think that he could plan the perfect crime. Befriending the investigating detective would be an excellent smokescreen for one's intentions."

There had been so many theories and so many potential killers put forward over the last few hours that I was quite lost by this point. "So you *do* think that Gareth is to blame?" I must admit, my head was reeling.

"No, of course I don't, but that doesn't mean we can dismiss him as a suspect."

"And Ethel and Mayor Perkins?"

He stopped on the corner of the road as a lorry carrying freshly cut Christmas trees rolled past on its way from the Gimbel family farm. "I am open to the possibility of their involvement."

"Then what about your untamed imaginings? Would you like to investigate the idea that the first victim was the second victim's mother?"

It was his turn to look rapturously contented. "That is precisely what I wish to do. Come along, Christopher. We have a wild theory to explore."

CHAPTER FIFTEEN

I don't know whether it was the Christmas season that had imbued the old detective with an impish air, but he was full of spirit as we rushed through the village to the residential streets away from the square. I would even say there was something childlike in his manner, and I half expected him to stop to build a snowman.

Though, during my life at least, he had spent comparatively little time in Kilston Down he appeared to know the village well.

"I have a good memory for places," he explained, having delved into my thoughts to discover what I'd been pondering. "Mine is not quite photographic, but it is a useful tool to sharpen." He stopped at the turning to the first road we reached. "So tell me. Where does she live?"

I was used to being confused by everything he did, so I didn't even point out what a ridiculous question this was. "Where does who live?"

"Young Miss Evans, of course. I assume that she has a cottage in this part of town."

I would have liked to say, *Ha! That's where you're wrong, Mr Know-it-all.* But his guess was spot on; Lillibet Evans resided on that very street.

I tried to imagine how his mind worked and decided that he had brought us here on the basis that Miss Evans did not have a great deal of money and would therefore live in one of the smallest houses around – of which Sunday Drive held several. He wasn't quite the magician he pretended to be, but I still found his mental agility impressive.

With the wind pushing us half a step backwards for every three we took, we straggled along the quiet road. There were no cars visible, though there was a large mound of white blocking the pavement where I imagine an Austin or perhaps a Vauxhall had been parked before the snow fell. I caught sight of a pair of eyes and a woollen orange cap peeking over it, but they did not belong to Miss Evans; Dean Henderson was there with his wheelbarrow, still waiting for the unfortunate felines to make their appearance. We hurried past him, and I was grateful that he didn't launch any projectiles in our direction.

The younger of the Evans sisters lived in the house where their parents had once resided. It was little more than a wattle and daub hut and made poor Maude's cottage look like a mansion. I once more questioned whether Lillibet Evans could have murdered her sister for the inheritance, as meagre as it was, but before I could suggest any such thing, the door to the house opened and there she was.

"Afternoon, gentlemen," she said in her usual cold, slightly suspicious tone. She sounded as though she were forever dealing with people who wanted to sell her something. "Have you had any luck finding Tibbs's killer?"

She was wrapped up for the cold and gripped an empty string bag in one hand, which reminded me of a lobster pot. It didn't take a master detective to conclude that she was off to the shops.

Grandfather answered for the both of us. "I'm afraid that we are still at an early stage of our investigation, madam. Has anything of interest occurred to you?"

"You have talked to that Ethel Perkins, haven't you?" I believe this was a rhetorical question, as she didn't wait for an answer. "I grant you that she's an odd choice for the killer, considering that the two of them were carrying on together, but perhaps they'd quarrelled. Perhaps the husband finally had enough and, when Ethel tried to call things off with Nigel, he was having none of it. An argument ensued, and she killed him."

I couldn't fault the woman; this really wasn't any more farfetched than the ideas that had come to us in the pub… except for one thing.

"An argument ensued, and she poisoned him?" I clarified. "It's hardly an instinctive reaction. For one thing, she would have had to be carrying the stuff with her, and arsenic isn't as easy to obtain as it once was."

"Fly papers!" She was an odd lady, but this was a strange reaction even for her.

"I beg your pardon?"

"Just before the war, there was a woman who was sent to prison for killing her husband with arsenic she got from fly papers."

"How curious." Grandfather was once more charmed by her quick mind. "I believe that was the Mortimer case. I remember it well."

She shrugged and tied her headscarf more tightly against the cold. "Anyway, I'm no detective. I was just expressing an idea. Now, what are you doing in this out of the way spot?"

Grandfather took a hesitant step onto her property. The path up to her door was the only clear ground for yards around. "I don't wish to pry, but I have some more questions about your sister."

She looked along the road and then back at her house before pulling her Welsh shawl around her shoulder and opening the door. "You had better come inside then."

We didn't argue, as we were happy to get out of the cold. Of course, when the door shut behind us, Delilah looked up at me as though she believed it was warmer outside. The floor was made of unburnished stone, and there were no carpets or soft furnishings to take the cold edge off the barely decorated living room that opened directly onto the outside world.

There had long been a rumour that Old *Mrs* Evans (the Evans sisters' mother) had been something of a hoarder, but this did not appear to be true, as her daughter lived in practical squalor. The one bright spot was an unlit altar candle sitting prettily on the windowsill. Its vibrant red hue and green tissue-paper surround stood out in the otherwise dull room. Young Miss Evans must have noticed my interest, as she came over to stand next to me.

"It's lovely, isn't it? That kind Mr Heywood sent one to me and one to my sister before she died." Knowing the sort of person she was, I could tell how difficult it was for her to say something nice about one of her neighbours. I was also aware that her opinion of him had changed immeasurably since the last time she'd spoken of him. "It was on my doorstep this morning, but I've decided to save it for Christmas Eve."

She stood admiring it for a few moments longer, and then Grandfather brought us to the matter we'd come to discuss. "Perhaps you can tell us about Maude. We won't take up too much of your time."

Back to her usual sour-faced best, Miss Evans turned to address the detective. "I can't think what else you might want to know about her. She was a simple woman, just like me. She lived alone. Never had any family, and she died with little in the bank. You'll know by now that her cottage belongs to the parish? I inherited this place from our parents because Maude already had somewhere to live."

Sadly, this seemed to rule out my sororicide theory. Or at least the obvious motive for one sister killing the other.

"I have a specific question in mind." Grandfather was ever so good at steering our witnesses back to the point without sounding too forceful. "You see, after Mr Tibbs was found dead this morning, I remembered what you'd said about your sister's relationship with a rich or aristocratic man in her youth."

Lillibet Evans's expression turned even harder, and she rolled her fingers into fists as though the swine-hound in question had just stepped through the door. "I remember. She was only twenty-two at the time and a pretty young thing."

"You mentioned 'the state' in which this man left her. Would you mind elaborating?"

Miss Evans's brow creased, and I wondered if it were her sorrow over her sister's tragic life which caused such consternation or her usual abhorrence of sin and sinners. "I don't know the details, mind. Our parents kept me in the dark about all that nasty business as I was two years younger. What I do know is that Maude had her heart broken by a heartless mongrel who came from high stock."

"You don't know his name then?" I asked when she seemed to have run out of things to say.

"No, she never told me, but she was very much in love for a month or two before Christmas and quite heartbroken afterwards."

Delilah was still doing laps of the room, presumably in search of somewhere to sit that would provide the comfort a lordly dog comes to expect. Or perhaps she was trying to keep warm.

"I have to ask something a little indelicate." Grandfather stepped closer to our witness to urge her to answer the key question which had weighed on his mind for at least the last hour. "Can you tell me whether your sister fell pregnant?"

"Pregnant!?" the word came out of her accompanied by a good number of laughs. "My sister, pregnant? Don't talk nonsense. She never had a child. I already told you that."

"Ah, I see." Grandfather's breathing was so expressive that I could tell just how disappointed he was. "Then we have apparently wasted your time."

Miss Evans looked back and forth between us to suggest we really were a pair of prize idiots. "Maude was never pregnant, but her name was certainly dirt in this house. That's why my parents sent her away to stay with our maiden aunt in Camberwell for a year. I didn't see her that whole time and, when she came back, she were a changed person. She'd been a carefree type before, but Auntie Margaret drilled some sense into her. She became ever so pious and upright. Never looked twice at a man for the rest of her life."

Grandfather's soft breathing suddenly took on a more optimistic tone. "How very interesting."

"That's why it makes me so angry to think of that Ethel Perkins running around with anyone she pleases, and her husband looking the other way. He's not a real man, our mayor. He can't be if he lets his wife behave in such a manner. When I think of how our parents punished my sister for kissing a—" She was unable to finish this point and, when she spoke again, she had returned to her usual harsh and unwavering tone of voice. "Still, it did her good in the end. Set her back on the straight and narrow and all that. My poor sister..."

"Indeed, madam," Grandfather muttered, and I was sure he hadn't heard a word she'd just said. "I must request one last favour. Could we borrow the key to Maude's cottage for another look around? There is an increasingly strong possibility that her death may be linked to that of Nigel Tibbs."

"I can't imagine..." she began, having already moved off towards the bare dresser in the corner of the room to open a small drawer. "I mean to say, I'm grateful that you'd think of looking into the matter, but I can't imagine why anyone would kill her."

Grandfather allowed a few seconds' pause before replying in a dramatic, stagey voice. "That is for us to determine, Miss Evans. And determine it we will."

.

CHAPTER SIXTEEN

Lillibet was – for her at least – comparatively obliging and gave us the key on the understanding that we were to drop it through her letterbox posthaste when we had finished our task. We said our goodbyes, and then the three of us (plus one dog) set off in the exact same direction back towards the centre of the village. This was rather awkward as we had to thank her and say our farewells all over again at the turn for Maude Evans's snow-logged street.

We soon reached the tiny cottage and, within a quarter of an hour, Grandfather had rifled through the sum total of the deceased Evans sister's meagre property, overturned then set right chairs and mattresses, and come to the conclusion that there was nothing at number two Bitterly Close for us to find.

"I was certain that she'd been sent away for a year to have her baby without anyone in the village knowing of it." Once we'd returned Lillibet's keys, Grandfather motored along the frozen pavement like a… like a… motorcycle? "But if she'd had to give up a child, I believe there would have been some trace of a memento of what happened. Not necessarily a photograph of the baby, but a letter from the adoptive parents or her diary from the time explaining how she had felt. Of course, this doesn't rule out my hypothesis, but it does make it difficult to prove."

I didn't like to tell him that we'd been barking up the wrong proverb, but I very much felt that must be the case. "Don't be so downhearted, Grandfather. We can contact the dead man's brother and put the possibility to him. I believe that Mrs Tibbs said he was older, so that might mean he—"

"The brother!" Grandfather came to a sudden halt and banged his forehead with the ball of his hand in frustration. It almost sent his top hat flying. "I completely forgot about the brother. How could Maude Evans have been Nigel Tibbs's secret mother when he had an older brother?"

He really did look desolate at that moment, but I was determined to pick him back up again. "Or perhaps the same thing happened to Maude twice, and she had to take two trips to her maiden aunt to hide her pregnancies. Wait, no! The older brother was probably born to an entirely different woman, but the two were adopted together."

Delilah pawed at his trouser cuffs. I'd like to believe that this was a sign of her innate awareness of her master's mood, though I think she was more likely telling us that she was finally tired of the snow and wished to go home.

"I appreciate your efforts to make me feel better, Christopher, but I've taken the wrong path entirely. Tibbs wasn't Maude Evans's son; that was wishful thinking on my part."

I didn't dare ask the obvious question out loud, though I must have thought it terribly clearly as he fixed his eyes upon me and said, "Next, my boy? Next, we must go home to spend time with our family and make the most of Christmas. You can help your brother decorate the house, and I will sit in a comfortable chair where a man of my age belongs and doze off as our relatives busy themselves with preparations for the coming days."

I bit my lip for a moment or two, but it wouldn't work. Laughter burst out of me, even as his moustache drooped, and he peered down desolately at the ground.

"Christopher, why are you laughing?"

I really tried to hold it in again, but I couldn't. "I'm sorry, Grandfather, it's just…" Great booming guffaws broke from me, and I had to start again. "It's just that you look so hard done by. I believe we must have more in common than I ever knew."

He tipped his chin back dismissively. "I do not consider myself hard done by, you impudent urchin. I am merely dismayed that we are several hours into the investigation of a crime, and we have failed to settle on the motive for the murders."

This did nothing to stem my enjoyment. My face was wet with tears, which stung my cheeks as the cold wind continued to rage around us. "You're ready to give up. I would say that is really very hard done by."

His dejected air was blown away, and he now looked quite perplexed. "I'm sorry, but have you not considered that this is an essential part of the process of any good detective? We must stare into the abyss of failure before seizing victory."

I was still tittering. "That's beautifully put, Grandfather, but surely it would be better to focus on victory from the beginning instead of

114

heading back to the manor to sit in a chair and fall asleep?"

"That's all well and good, young man, but…"

He couldn't think of a way to finish his thought, which made me very happy indeed. "Yes, old man? What were you going to say?"

He looked back at Maude Evans's cottage, which was just about visible through the near blizzard. "I was going to point out that it's all well and good saying that we should focus on victory, when the most likely scenario at this moment is that Old Miss Evans died because of one of the many illnesses from which her sister told me she suffered. And if that fool Nigel Tibbs died from poisoning, it's probably because he picked up the wrong bottle in the kitchen and drank bleach or rat poison or something unpleasant."

"You don't believe that," I told him with certainty in my voice. Gone were the days when a word from my august grandfather could convince me of any half-truth he felt like tossing in my direction.

"Yes, I do." The very fact that the eminent Lord Edgington was standing in a snowstorm with his grey overcoat turning white, arguing with a boy who possessed one tenth of his intelligence, proved that this was nothing but stubbornness on his part.

"You can disagree all you like, but that doesn't make it true. You say that we have run out of theories to investigate or evidence to inspect, but we are yet to talk to two of our main suspects. We have uncovered a pair of suspicious deaths in a village in which the mayor's wife was openly carrying on with one of the victims, and we haven't even put the case to Mayor Perkins."

"'*Two* suspicious deaths'?" he repeated back to me, and I realised that the tables had turned once more. "We have found nothing – not one thing – to connect Evans and Tibbs, and you know that."

"It doesn't matter." I set off along the road at this moment, and Delilah gave a bark of approval.

"I beg your pardon?"

"You heard me," I called over my shoulder and this time he had to hurry to catch up. "It doesn't matter whether there's a connection between them. If we were to give up now, we would never discover the truth, and I know you couldn't stand such an outcome. It's as you said this morning; we're on the hunt for a killer; let it be damned whether or not he exists."

We stopped once more and did something quite bizarre. No, he didn't burst out singing 'As a Porcupine Pines for Its Pork' or belch the national anthem. He put one arm around me and said something terribly kind. "You really are a wonder, Christopher. You've snapped me out of a blue funk in record time. Let's go and find this mayor of yours."

For a moment, I didn't notice just how cold I was or what the wind – which was not blowing in gusts anymore but had become a constant, unceasing force at our backs – was doing to the tails of our coats. For a moment, I almost felt warm. It was a feeling that only comes to me once or twice each year. It was both rare and unmistakable. With these fond words, he'd made it feel like Christmas.

I rubbed my gloved hands together to fend off the cold. "Yes! Let's go and put the no doubt wicked and murderous mayor to the sword. Only then will we pop home to see how everyone is doing."

"That, my dear Christopher, is a very good plan indeed."

CHAPTER SEVENTEEN

We looked for the mayor in his office in the town hall, which had been a school before I was born, but it was locked and silent. There was no sign of him in Dotty's Teahouse, either, though his wife was in there getting all the sympathy she could need. And that wasn't all she was getting.

The place was packed to bursting, not least because two-thirds of my father's side of the family had invaded and were making merry with tea and mince pies. I say they were making merry but, for them, the sole entertainment was looking glum and listening to my great-uncles hold court.

Terry was at the table next to Edith Perkins and Reverend Deacon, and to say he was lavishing her with attention would be an understatement.

"You poor, dear woman. I cannot imagine how you must be feeling at this moment. Life is but a spark which sputters out far too quickly."

"I know, I know!" the grieving lover complained, whilst batting her eyelids and admiring her reflection in a spoon. "It is my lot in life to suffer."

I suppose we should have taken the time to interview her, but it was an unappealing prospect and could wait until no other options remained.

Terry's brother Thomas was complaining about the worrying spread of wireless telegraphy and the possible risks to children's brains. My cousin Gerald had approximately nine empty cake cases in front of him and still had a plateful of fondant fancies to devour. Philippa was voicing her approval of everything that her father said. Aldrich was issuing orders to his family in his usual naval fashion, and Grandfather took two steps into the café before turning back round to leave. Luckily, no one spotted us, or we might well have been trapped there all day.

I considered returning to the pub to look for the mayor when I spotted him sitting on a bench beneath an overhanging yew tree in front of St Eustace's church at the opposite end of the square. It was a strange sight, as the spot where he was perched was the only bare ground as far as the eye could see. It was sheltered from the snow by the branches overhead and the wind by the wall that runs around the churchyard. We crossed the road to reach him, and he didn't even look at us through the metal railings that topped the rough stone.

"Mayor Perkins," I began, as I knew the man somewhat better than my grandfather did. "Would you mind if we spoke to you?"

His eyes shifted about the scene as though he couldn't be sure from where my voice had emanated. "Ah, Christopher… Lord Edgington…" He sounded like a teacher taking a register. Now that the check was complete, he could answer my question. "Yes, of course— Or rather, no, I don't mind the company."

"I'm sure that you've had a difficult morning, not just personally but professionally too. At times like this, we look to our leaders for guidance." For a moment, I sounded far older than my twenty years. Don't worry though, I would soon say something silly or insist that we have a snack.

"I can't say it has been a red-letter day for me," he replied. "It is hard to know exactly what to do at a time like this."

"Yes," Grandfather said, though I believe he meant the exact opposite. He knew just what to do at a time like this, and he was in the process of doing it. "What was Mr Tibbs actually like?"

There was something cautious and not quite natural about the mayor's manner. He was never a relaxed sort of person and, with his ever so small head on his immense body, he had the look of a child dressed as an adult.

He was particularly apprehensive as he answered this simple question. "Nigel was… Well, he was the grocer. Everyone knew him, though I can't say we spent a great deal of time together. It was one of those strange cases in which you see someone all the time but rarely stop to speak to him."

"Quite." With this one word, Grandfather was saying, *I know all about the unusual arrangement between the dead man and your wife, and it is evident you aren't telling the whole story.* He didn't utter any such thing aloud, of course. No, he made a few sympathetic noises and asked, "Was he popular with the locals?"

The mayor had one of those faces that are hard to age with any precision. His wife looked very good for her fifty years on earth, whereas if you'd told me he was sixty-five, I would not have been surprised. The lines on his forehead seemed to deepen with worry

118

each time he had to speak.

"We all love the man who sells us sweets and dry goods, don't we?" He really wasn't keen to admit what we all knew, and so it would fall to me to make him.

"I imagine what you are avoiding saying is that you did not like him." Once I'd started, it was hard to stop, and the glaring fact that no one had been willing to pronounce jumped from my mouth. "He stole the woman you love away from you, and you despised him for it."

"Tibbs didn't—" He was more nervous by the moment, but some new reality seemed to find a place in his brain then, and he changed his mind. "Or rather, yes. You are quite right." The truth appeared to liberate him somewhat, and he nodded ever so slowly. "I hated him. He wasn't worthy of my dear Ethel, and yet I was too weak to stand in their way."

"Were you so weak that you chose to poison him last night? Did you perhaps give your wife something to offer him as a gift? A bottle of alcohol, perhaps?"

We hadn't found any bottle of alcohol other than the whisky that Tibbs's brother had sent, but that didn't stop me asking, and it didn't stop Mayor Perkins's face from turning even more grim and grey.

"I didn't kill the man. I wouldn't do that." He put his hands down on either side of him. The green wooden slats of the bench must have been ice cold, as he immediately brought his arms back up as if he'd burnt himself. His skin looked almost translucent. It had turned such a shade of blue that I had to wonder what he was doing out there without any gloves.

I took my cue from Grandfather and didn't say anything more. Leaving a suspect to talk himself out of a corner is an important skill he'd taught me, and it was worth it just to give the mayor a few moments to squirm.

"I'm really not a violent person," he said for at least the second time that day. "Do you think that I would have let them go around together for so long if I were?"

"Claiming that you don't have it in you to murder is not evidence that you didn't do it," the senior detective told him, looming intimidatingly over the bench. "If it were, even the most savage killers could make that simple statement in court and walk free."

"But it's true." The mayor looked from side to side in frustration.

I wondered if he was searching for a way out or an explanation. "I've never been the sort to pick a fight. I'm too scared of prison to risk my neck in such a foolish enterprise." He shuddered and I couldn't imagine it was from the cold. "I would take the long drop over a life spent rotting away in a cell. I've had nightmares of that very thing since I was a boy."

Nothing he'd just said was especially convincing, and my grandfather looked back over his shoulder to wink at me without winking. I know that sounds impossible, but not only was he the most skilful human being I'd ever met, we'd been working together for so long by this point that, just occasionally, I knew what he was thinking. With this wink that wasn't a wink, he told me that we had the feeble character where we wanted him, and it was time to increase the pressure.

"Is that all you have to tell us?" His voice was thickly lathered with incredulity. "You've had all this time to think up a reason for why we shouldn't suspect you, and all you can say is that you're not violent and you're scared of going to prison? Christopher here is no great lover of heights, but he'd still climb a mountain if there were a remarkably good bakery at the top of it."

I would have liked to disagree with this statement for two reasons, but neither would have been true. He'd captured my nature to a T. I really am a nervous person. I will do almost anything for pudding and, from time to time, I can surprise myself by being braver than I generally imagine.

"You've got this all wrong," the mayor moaned, and his tiny black eyes seemed to shrink back into his skull as he looked up at his accuser. "What good would killing him do me?"

"Stop lying, man. You're the only obvious suspect. We know that—"

"Am I?" he shuffled back in his seat, but did not seem so apprehensive as he previously had. "Do you really think that I'm the likely killer?"

His sudden change had set my grandfather off guard, and so I continued to apply the pressure.

"Of course you are. Everything we've seen today suggests that you murdered your rival."

The problem now was that I couldn't think of any evidence to support my claim. Normally I would have said something like, *Your fingerprints were all over the weapon!* or *The maid saw you leaving the scene of the crime.* But the only thing we knew about the relationship between the grocer and Mayor John Perkins was that the former had been involved in an affair with the latter's wife. Which wasn't to say that I couldn't exaggerate a little.

"After all that we've discovered and what we've heard from various sources, I can't see how anyone else could be to blame."

Whatever relief the previous explanation had provided, it was now forgotten. Dejection suddenly coursed through him. He looked like a man with only weeks to live. I almost felt sorry for him.

"I…" He began, but the emotion was too much. It affected him like a physical pain. He had to close his eyes for several seconds before he tried again. "I don't know what I was thinking. I really wish that I hadn't been so rash."

"What are you saying, man?" Grandfather demanded, but Perkins just stared down at his hands.

"Do you mean that you poisoned Tibbs?" I put to him.

The mayor shook his head a few times, more in bemusement than denial, and when he finally answered, I think that I was more taken aback than my grandfather. "Yes, but Ethel had nothing to do with it. I would never have involved her, and she wouldn't have gone along with it anyway."

"If you're the killer," I said, apparently now happy to argue against my previous position, "When did you poison him?"

"It was yesterday afternoon. I simply went into Tibbs's house when I knew that both he and Nora were in the shop."

Grandfather was the next to prompt him. "How did you get inside?"

Our suspect looked back and forth between us. "They don't lock their front door. Few people in the village do." He needed no further prompting but offered the information we required. "I'd heard him boasting about the fancy bottle of whisky his brother had sent him for Christmas. I knew that Nora would never drink anything so strong, so all I had to do was tip something nasty into it and creep back outside. It was already dark, and the snow was so heavy that no one paid me any attention."

"What did you use?" I asked, though the moment I said the words, I knew that his answer would prove nothing. The details of Mr Tibbs's death were common knowledge in the village, and the mayor, more than anyone, would have been able to find out the finer points of the case.

"Arsenic."

"Where did you get it?"

The wind really screeched around the square just then, and he waited for it to die down before answering. "I looked through the shed in my back garden and found a very old packet of something nasty looking. I don't remember how it got there, but it did the trick." His lip was trembling; I couldn't say whether this was due to his anger at the man who had stolen his wife, or his fear of what came next. "I rid the town of vermin, and I'd do it again if I had to."

I could probably have reeled off another five questions, but Grandfather put his hand out to stop me. "Mayor Perkins, you do know that we will have to hand you over to the police now?"

Even though this was undoubtedly true, it would take the soon-to-be prisoner a minute or so to move. He remained sitting perfectly upright on that cold wooden bench, and I realised that I had no feeling left in my hands. I was wearing leather gloves, but each finger felt as though it had frozen, like a string of sausages in an ice house.

"I'm ready," he finally muttered, then rose to standing in order to drift off ahead of us and out of the graveyard.

There were still a few lights on in the grocer's, but I had the definite impression that most shopkeepers had given up for the night or were on the point of closing. One institution that would stay open for some time was the police station beside the Holly Tree Inn. It was a squat, unremarkable building, and I was sure that the most exciting crime that Sergeant Keel had investigated in all his years there was when Mr Gimbel's sheep were stolen – though he eventually discovered that the farmer had left the gate to his field open, and the herd had wandered off into the woods.

I was sure that Grandfather would have some wise words to impart, but Perkins did all the talking. We saw him into what one might have expected to be an office but was more like a small, cosy salon. It was certainly more comfortable than the room we'd visited in Lillibet Evans's house. There was a steaming radiator, a kettle already on the boil and even a fire lit in the grate.

Warmer still was the look that we received from the sergeant.

"Hello, one and all. It's nice to have a bit of company. I hadn't expected anyone to come calling in this weather."

The Mayor, as he still was for the time being, couldn't look at the man. He kept his eyes on the whistling kettle and confessed to his crime.

"I'm sorry to tell you, Eddie, but I'm the man you're after."

Keel was such a jolly fellow that I half expected him to make a joke about Mr Gimbel's sheep, but he could see that this was no laughing matter.

"You don't mean…" He said, and his perfectly round cheeks inflated in surprise. "Not Nigel Tibbs?"

The mayor's head only fell further. "You're a good policeman. That's exactly what I mean."

Grandfather stood in the doorway, and I couldn't interpret the expression on his face nor imagine what he was thinking. His thoughts were a secret and would stay that way for some time.

"I suppose I should lock you up then, at least until someone more superior than me gets here." The sergeant pointed towards the back room. "Would you like some tea in your cell, or should I look for something stronger?"

Mayor Perkins was escorted to an adjoining room into which I had never before stepped. The sergeant took no notice of me, but I trailed behind them to see that our culprit was handled correctly. As the white metal door closed on the cupboard-like cell, a question occurred to me that I should have already asked.

"Mayor," I called, and he looked back through the bars to see what I wanted. "What about Old Miss Evans?" I didn't say anything more. I knew it was best not to give anything away.

"What about her?" There was no energy left in the man. He spoke these words much as if he'd been told that the bank closed an hour early on Wednesdays or there would be no kippers at the fishmonger's this week.

"Don't worry," I replied, unsure whether this was the most important thing I'd heard that day or another piece of evidence that would lead us nowhere. "I hope you don't have to stay here too long."

CHAPTER EIGHTEEN

"But he didn't react in the slightest when I mentioned her name," I told my grandfather as we were blown back home with Delilah stalking through the snow ahead of us. The tranquil beauty of the white world that I had so admired that morning had been replaced by the rage and intensity of our very own blizzard. I was beginning to worry that Kilston Down's usual Christmas Eve festivities would have to be cancelled.

"Perhaps he's trying to save his own neck," Grandfather blustered. "There's no guarantee he'll be hanged for killing the adulterous grocer. However, if he's found guilty of two murders, he doesn't stand a chance."

"You didn't see what I saw. He was a man without hope. He looked totally defeated, and I don't believe for one second that he had the composure to conceive of any such subterfuge."

"So then we were wrong," he answered from behind the turned-up collar of his coat. "Maude Evans wasn't poisoned. She was an old lady who died of natural causes, and we read too much into the circumstances for the simple reason that neither of us wished to remain at home with your unbearable relatives."

"Do you really believe that?" My voice was so soft and uncertain that I doubted whether these words would reach him in the swirling air.

"It's not a question of what I believe, Christopher. All that matters is what the evidence we have gathered proves." He apparently realised that this would not satisfy me as he continued speaking. "I must remind you that, try as we might, we haven't found a single connection between the grocer and Old Miss Evans except for their preference for tea." He gave me a good-natured wink. "Have I overlooked something?"

"No, but—"

"Then what about a motive for the first death? Is there anything that anyone in the village has told us that could explain why she was murdered?"

"Well…" I really looked for one, but he was right. The day had been something of a wash-out. "No, we've no reason to believe that anyone had a specific grudge against her, and there's nothing to say that even her sister gained from her death."

"Whereas, Mr Tibbs was having an affair with a woman and rubbing it in her husband's face. I feel sad for all involved, but the mayor has admitted to his part in the crime. He appears to know how the poison was administered, and we've no reason to doubt his confession."

I looked up at him as the snow settled on the brim of his hat. I don't think I'd ever known anyone to wear a top hat in the snow but him. Normally, I would have laughed, but all I could summon was a sad and empty sigh.

He took pity on me and sought a consolation. "I know you were hoping for a complex conspiracy which takes in various intriguing motives, any amount of backstabbing and plenty of jealousy. I wanted the very same thing. Indeed, the readers at home (in newspapers that cover our cases) would like nothing more than to read such a story in time for Christmas. But it simply isn't the reality."

"Tell me the truth: have you ever come across such a simple solution to one of your investigations before?" I asked in a truly innocent tone, and he had to reflect on the matter.

"Though relatively rare, it does happen. Every single one of my cases has required a great feat of mental agility to solve, but I have, on rare occasions, heard of officers who arrived at the scene of the crime to find that the killer was willing to confess."

"How bizarre." This concept was quite foreign to me, and I wasn't sure I believed it possible.

"I will admit," he said as we turned off the now silent road towards the manor, "that it does feel strange to solve a case even before Christmas Eve. Normally we'd be rushing to finish when there are still presents to be wrapped."

We puzzled over this unprecedented scenario as we crunched our way back to the house. The snow was thick on the trees and, to punctuate the sound of our crunching boots, there was a regular flutter and thud whenever large clumps of the stuff went falling from laden branches.

I was still considering the chances of stumbling across such a very straightforward case when we arrived at our front door. "Really," I muttered to myself as much as to my grandfather, "one murder, unconnected to any other, and the killer turns out to be a wronged husband. I never thought I'd see the day."

Before Grandfather could answer, the door swung open, and our loyal butler Jessop was there to welcome us.

"Good afternoon, gentlemen," he intoned in that special, calming voice that only butlers have. I had to wonder whether they learnt it somewhere, much in the way that rabbis practice for years to chant the Torah. "And may I say how wonderful it is to have you here with us?"

"It's good to see you, too, old friend," I replied and took the opportunity to shake him by the hand. He had worked at the house since before I was born and had always been a dear companion to me. "And as I haven't had the chance to say it yet, Happy Christmas, Jessop."

Grandfather followed my lead, and the three of us exchanged festive greetings. I noticed as soon as the door closed behind us that something felt quite different about the place. It wasn't just the change from the cold outside to that toasty warm house. There was a totally new atmosphere. For one thing, I couldn't hear the cooks shouting at one another down in the kitchen. My first thought was that Maggie had murdered poor Henrietta, but something told me that this was unlikely.

No, there was a feeling of harmony there that I hadn't experienced for years. Once we'd discarded our boots and outside clothes, we walked towards the salon at the back of the house. Several of the Cranley Hall staff waited to greet us with huge smiles on their faces. Alice, our maid, was holding a plate of mince pies ready for our arrival. Halfpenny was pouring snifters of hot parsnip wine, the smell of which hit me from halfway down the hall. Meanwhile, Todd stood beside the entrance to the rear salon with a few words on his lips just for us.

"I can't tell you how nice it is to have all the family together, M'lord." He bowed and opened the door to let us pass.

Inside, my parents were standing beside the Christmas tree as though waiting to have their photograph taken. Mother looked a picture in a red dress, which was brave in ribbons and had a neat green velvet collar. Father wore his best suit. I was even more surprised to see Granny at the piano, playing most pleasantly as my brother sang. It must have been the first break he'd taken from his decorating since I'd arrived the previous day.

> **"Angels we have heard on high**
> **Sweetly singing o'er the plains,**
> **And the mountains in reply**
> **Echoing their joyous strains."**

It really was the most heartening scene I could have imagined. Our staff crowded in the doorway to listen as Albert's beautiful voice swelled around us. And in that moment, I was at peace with the world. Our case had been resolved. The killer was behind bars, and I could now spend a few days celebrating my favourite holiday with the people I loved most.

My brother was just about to ring out the glorias when the front door opened, and we heard people entering the house.

"All I'm saying is that it's fine to be a tourist and gawp at the hoi polloi for a few hours, but I wouldn't want to do it on a regular basis. You don't know what sort of diseases these people carry."

The sound of Uncle Terry's voice cut through the beautiful music, and everyone became tense once more. Granny darted from the piano to hide behind the Christmas tree. Albert muttered something about needing to decorate the pantry, and I watched as the strain came over my parents' faces.

The whole rabble of my father's extended family ploughed through the entrance hall and into the rear salon. My cousins (and Gerald in particular) instantly cleared the plate of mince pies, and then moved on to Cook's lovely parsnip wine before I could have any. They were like a swarm of locusts but with less warmth and humanity.

"What a disappointment," my mother said as the uncles claimed their place in the two armchairs closest to the fire, and their broods filled in the gaps around them. "You've arrived just as we're going out."

Thomas and Terry were plumping up their cushions and didn't respond. I knew the signs; they had found the best spot and were all set for a nap. On a good day, those two could doze right through from lunch to dinner, but they were famously light sleepers. In past years, this had meant that no one could do anything even slightly jovial in their vicinity, and our Christmas afternoons were unthinkably sombre.

"Where are you going?" Terry demanded with a yawn and a suspicious look.

Granny was still behind the tree, but I could practically feel her willing my mother to think of something that would help us escape her brothers, nieces and nephews as soon as humanly possible.

"We're going to…" Mother tried, looking at her father for inspiration.

He was without inspiration for once, and so it fell to me to answer. "We're going to a party in a very small house. There will only be room for my parents, assorted grandparents and brother if he isn't too busy."

Thomas had already closed his eyes by this point, and I noticed that our staff were mysteriously absent, as my cousin Gerald enquired, "I don't suppose there's a chance of a nip of something potent before you leave? Personally, I would enjoy a hot toddy, not that anyone has offered me one." He finished what he was saying and downed the last of the parsnip wine.

"Best of luck with that, Gerald," Grandfather replied and, seizing his daughter and son-in-law by the arms, he sallied out to the hall.

I stayed behind to watch my grandmother creep out from her hiding place. She hadn't waited long enough, and her brother Terry opened his eyes. "Loelia? What on earth were you doing behind that Christmas tree?"

She pretended not to be alarmed by this question and answered with her usual confidence. "There was a bauble on the other side that wasn't quite shiny enough. I thought I should take it to the ironmonger in the village. He'll fix it up there and I'll bring it back here."

She didn't even need this extra reason to leave the house, but I suppose that she now had one in reserve for later. Whenever we were next at home, she could say that the ironmonger had been too busy, and she would have to make a second trip.

The one thing she was missing was the aforementioned bauble, so I dashed around the tree to grab the first I saw. "We wouldn't want to forget that now, would we!"

My family and I got changed and ready in record time. Todd fished out a few bottles of good French wine from the cellar, and I rang ahead to Gareth Heywood to make certain that he really had meant it when he said that the more people we brought with us, the merrier he would be. He was his usual good-natured self and laughed down the line as he confirmed the extended invitation.

Best of all, I finally had a chance to wear my black woollen opera cloak that Grandfather had bought me two years prior. I realised that we weren't going anywhere so formal as an opera house, but it was cold enough to wear a cloak, and I thought I looked rather suave. My parents seemed to approve, and we all piled into Father's

Bentley, which wouldn't start.

Luckily, Todd had already prepared Grandfather's Daimler on the off-chance it would be needed. He had even fitted chains to the tyres. I'm sure we hadn't possessed any such device before that day, so he'd evidently had a busy afternoon. I invited him along, but he said he had plans with the other members of staff, and I felt he'd probably enjoy himself more without his employer around.

So then we were off... very slowly. Even with the chains on the wheels, the car struggled in the deep snow that coated every road on the normally two-, now six-minute journey. I had a feeling that we would be inundated like this until the New Year, and I can't say I honestly minded. In a few months' time, Grandfather and I would be heading to the sunny climes of Italy and who knows where else on the Continent. I intended to savour the winter and enjoy my time with my family.

I'd never seen him drive so carefully, even in snowy conditions, and I had a feeling that he was trying to avoid any criticism from my always sharp-tongued grandmother. She still found a few things to observe as we reached the square.

"English villages were far prettier in my youth. I don't know why they have to knock down old buildings just to put up new ones when the first ones were perfectly lovely."

Mother smiled at her husband in the back seat and, as they were both too polite to say anything, I answered her. "By that logic, we should all still be living in primitive huts with straw roofs."

There was a rather wistful look in her eyes. "I may be traditional, Christopher, but I have my limits. Sixteenth to nineteenth century architecture is fine by me. We don't have to go all the way back to the stone age."

Perhaps she realised just how similar she sounded to her dreadful brothers, as she perked up after that and was actually rather good company. Don't worry. It wouldn't last. She'd be back to her acerbic best in time for Christmas. And besides, she didn't have too long to complain about anything, as our destination was already in sight.

CHAPTER NINETEEN

We pulled into Bitterly Close, and I could hear the sound of loud music blasting along the street before Grandfather stopped the car. There was a willow tree outside Gareth's house that had been re-painted for the season. On top of the snow, someone had placed long, sparkling garlands of silver and gold, and there was a large star dangling from the highest branch, which spun in the now softer wind. I had to wonder how anyone had got it up there in the bad weather.

I was surprised how excited my grandmother and (no relation) grandfather were, even when they saw the crowd of young people gathered in the freezing front garden. It was a welcoming scene, and as we reached the front door, I heard calls of "Lord Edgington!" and "He's really here!"

I could see a Christmas tree through the downstairs windows and spotted a few familiar faces. Reverend Deacon was chatting away in the hall as I scampered after my family. He was talking to the beautiful young lady whom we'd seen eating lunch at the Holly Tree Inn. I was tempted to ask her whether her father was a French cabinet maker, but she was too bored by her talk with the reverend to notice us. Her petrol blue eyes flashed in the light of a pendant lamp as I passed.

Every room we saw was packed with people. It was no mansion, but there must have been fifty guests enjoying a drink, a chat and the jazzy music, the source of which we eventually located in a large sitting room on the right-hand side of the house.

We managed to push through the clogged doorway to a well of space inside, where we finally caught a glimpse of Gareth Heywood and his band of musicians. I counted six in all, including a drummer, double-bassist, plus two trombonists and a clarinet player. For his part, Gareth had a saxophone on a strap around his neck and, when he wasn't accompanying his friends, he would sing at the top of his voice.

> **"Hark! the herald angels sing**
> **'Glory to the newborn King**
> **Peace on earth and mercy mild,**
> **God and sinners reconciled!'"**

It was not the usual slow, ponderous rhythm which I was used to from school assemblies and carol concerts. There was a certain vibrancy that is hard for me to describe because I know nothing of modern music. What I can say is that it made me want to dance, as several couples were already doing on the opposite side of the room. I hadn't seen such freedom of movement since our first trip to the Gargoyle Club in Soho. It was remarkable.

There was a fellow a few years older than I, who, judging by the colour of his skin and his exquisite foreign clothes, looked as though he must be from India or some far-flung country I don't know. He was dancing with a very large woman who, for some reason, was wearing a Red Riding Hood costume, though no one else had come in fancy dress. I couldn't take my eyes off the gyrating pairs, and I had certainly never expected to see people dancing like that to a song written hundreds of years earlier. Even Granny was tapping her foot – though she made up for this by looking disapproving.

The song wasn't sung straight through. Instead, between long musical interludes, different members of the band would take a verse whenever they felt like it. I had the definite sense that they were prolonging the inevitable conclusion because they knew just how much everyone was enjoying themselves. Occasionally, the dancers would swap partners or even fish people out of the crowd when someone got tired of all the swinging and shimmying and what have you.

I can't honestly tell you the name of their dance. It was far faster than any I'd seen before, though I suppose there were elements of Charleston and foxtrot. What amazed me was the way that some of the men could pick up their partners and swing them around as though they were as light as kittens. All thoughts of murder and my horrible relatives were cast from my mind.

My father was so bowled over by what we were seeing that I thought he probably needed a nice sit down. Love him as I do, Daddy can be a rather staid individual, but I believe he was quite taken by the scene before him. I rather wished my brother had been there to marvel at our old man's reaction. Over the course of my grandfather's tutelage, I've come to realise just what an impact experiences outside of our everyday life can have on an individual, and I think it would have done the manic decorator good to remember that there were more important things than ensuring each upstairs bathroom had paper snowflakes attached to the windows.

The song built towards its conclusion, and our host took over vocal duties once more.

"Born to raise the sons of earth,
Born to give them second birth.
Hark! the herald angels sing,
'Glory to the newborn King!'"

Every last person in the band called out the final line in triumphal fashion before the room was plunged into the briefest moment of silence. The place was immediately overtaken by whooping and applause.

This was life. This was living. I could forget all about the petty jealousies and gossip of Kilston Down as, from this moment on, I would remember my village for the sensational music I discovered there one December. I clapped so loudly that my hands hurt and, standing next to me, Grandfather offered his usual polite, near-silent applause (but with a touch more gusto than usual).

Gareth noticed us there and waved. He said something to a returning trumpeter, who went to take his place at the centre of the band, and my new friend came to talk to my family.

"Welcome, all!" he went between us, shaking hands and offering us a smile each.

"It was so kind of you to let us come," Mother told him with great sincerity. "And at such late notice, too."

"Young man," Granny said to interrupt her daughter-in-law, "that music was…" She looked around the simply decorated room as if she hoped to find the word she needed on the mantelpiece or a shelf somewhere. "It was loud… but I can't say I entirely disliked it."

"It's called jazz." His response was in no way patronising. It was as if he really wanted to share his passion for the music with us, regardless of whether we knew what it was.

"It was phenomenal," Father assured him, and I'd rarely seen him so interested in anything that wouldn't get a mention in The Financial Times. "I wonder if I could have a word with your drummer before the evening is over. I'd like to know how he does what he does."

It was quite odd seeing my parents in such a youthful milieu. I was more used to my grandfather associating with people my age than my stay-at-homeative folks.

"Come along, dear," Granny said to guide him away. "Let's find you a drink before you offer to join the band."

"We heard that you caught the killer, Lord Edgington," Gareth told us as my parents reluctantly trailed after her. "That's fast work even for you, isn't it?"

Grandfather looked away as though he was too modest to accept such a compliment. He contradicted this idea with his less than humble reply. "There is no such thing as fast work. There are only astute detectives." I was about to laugh at him, but he must have realised how this sounded and added a caveat. "I'm talking of my grandson, of course. His skills of deduction are second to few." He still sounded a touch arrogant, but I was willing to let it pass.

Gareth did not seem concerned about any of this and kept asking questions. "I've spoken to Mayor Perkins a few times, and he seemed like a stand-up chap. It's hard to believe that he could be a murderer, but then men do strange things when it comes to love."

I noticed that he glanced out of the room towards the corridor then, and I wondered what sad, romantic tale was his to tell. I couldn't exactly switch from light conversation to asking what had happened between him and the charming young lady that he already hadn't introduced us to once that day.

Grandfather didn't do a bad job, though. "Christopher and I were wondering how you came to live in Kilston Down. It's not known for modern music. You must spend half your time shuttling back and forth to the city to play in clubs and concerts."

Whenever he was amused by something, a thick line appeared in his forehead just over his left eye. "Admittedly it isn't the most central location, but I came for a drive here one Sunday and fell in love with the place. People talk of the charms of the Cotswolds and the south coast, but they often overlook Surrey. It's a gem right on London's doorstep."

If Grandfather hadn't liked him before, he certainly did now. "You are a wise man, Mr Heywood."

"You must still call me Gareth," he reminded us, and we both nodded in accession.

"I don't know anywhere I'd rather live than right here." Grandfather sounded a trifle wistful. "Were you born in the south of England?"

That wrinkle I'd noticed disappeared. "No, I'm from further north. My people live in Kidderminster, and I moved to London as soon as I was old enough to leave. I've nothing against the place, but its small-town attitude wasn't suited to me… at the time, at least. Our ideas change as we age."

As we were speaking, the band played a slower number to give the dancers a chance to catch their breath, though there were already calls for Gareth to return to his post.

"I'm terribly sorry. I'd love to talk more, but a host must do as his guests demand." He gestured with his saxophone that was still around his neck.

"I hope we get to see more of you later," I told him. Of course, he had so many friends there, I couldn't imagine why he would bother talking to me.

"Help yourselves to drinks," he continued as he backed away. "Talk to some interesting people and have a marvellous time."

CHAPTER TWENTY

Grandfather slunk off through the crowd, but I stayed for a few minutes to marvel at the musicians. Another fast, cheery melody soon started, though I didn't recognise it as a Christmas song. My mentor insisted that, with years of practice, I could one day be as good a detective as he was, but I felt there were certain instinctive abilities that made some people natural musicians and others natural sleuths. I had a sneaking suspicion that I was a natural wantwit, but I wouldn't give up hope entirely.

One thing that was certain was that I'd grown in confidence in the last few years. Back when I'd first started investigating crimes with my grandfather, the thought of being left alone at a loud party full of unusual people would have terrified me. I walked quite calmly through the house, greeting those who greeted me and even meeting their eyes. It was almost as if I thought myself the equal of real grown-ups who didn't need their grandfathers to point them in the right direction in life.

There were all sorts of entertainment laid on for the evening. In one small room, a queue of people were waiting to see a rather thin-bellied stripling dressed as Old Father Christmas. In exchange for a gift from his sack, each person had to sit on his lap and tell him a story. I noticed that he was mainly interested in hearing from the prettiest girls, and his shifting, slightly devious gaze reminded me of that terrible boy Dean Henderson who, happily, made no appearance that night.

Dotty from the teahouse was there, though, and she had set up a table with cakes, tarts, sandwiches and various refreshments. She did not even charge a story for the service, but then she was already quite drunk.

"Happy Christmas, Chrissy, m' boy," she bellowed as I peeked into the kitchen from the hall. She apparently found this rather hilarious as she burst out laughing and had to seize her sizable stomach to stop it from shaking. "Oh my gracious! Chrissy: Christmas. What are the chances of that?" She would have made a far better (and less self-interested) Father Christmas than the hobbledehoy.

"It's nice to see you, Dotty," I replied just as cheerfully, and she took a gulp of whatever pungent brown liquid was in her glass. "I don't suppose you have any—"

Before I could finish, she produced one of her taste-bud-tingling chocolate eclairs from a shelf under the table. "I heard you were coming and saved this for you. Don't tell the reverend; he's been scoffing my cakes all evening."

She motioned to a spot behind the door where our upstanding and much-admired priest was now snoring in a dining chair.

"I don't think there's much chance he'll find out," I told her, though I was speaking through chocolate, cream and choux pastry and may not have communicated this message particularly clearly.

"You've earned it," she assured me, and raised her glass of elderberry wine before pouring one for me. "Would you believe that our very own mayor went mad and murdered Nigel Tibbs? I never would have put it past him." She made a clicking sound in her mouth and peered off through the kitchen window. "You should have seen Ethel in the teahouse today. She was… well, devastated isn't the word for it, but she certainly wasn't herself."

"It must have been a difficult day for her." I'd drained my glass, so I raised my gooey pastry to return the toast and continued my exploration of the house. "Have a wonderful evening." The sound of Dotty belting a filthy song about a young lady from Bude followed me down the hallway.

As we were having all this fun, the thought of Mayor Perkins locked up in the police station came back to me. Something still seemed wrong about the case. It felt unfinished: that was it. The whole experience had been abbreviated, and I was missing out on the familiar scramble for answers as we looked to eliminate suspects and disprove alibis. The idea that the culprit could simply have told us he was to blame was still quite incomprehensible to me.

Before I could examine the matter any further, I found myself in a small room at the back of the house. It was rather hidden away from the main party and, having squeezed through a few merry fellows drinking and laughing together in the corridor outside, I finally had some space to stand and walk.

I must admit that I was distracted by the decoration of the room and didn't pay attention to a faint sound I heard. There was a wall covered in instruments. None of them looked to be in good condition. A tuba hanging high above eye level was so battered that I imagined it had been driven over by a lorry of some description, but it was a wonderful overall effect and suited my initial impressions of our lively and gregarious host.

When my ears finally made sense of the small, high-pitched squeak coming from the far side of the sofa, I still didn't know what to think. If anything, it sounded like a pet complaining of its lot, and I went searching for a wounded beast. Why the seemingly gentle owner of the house would have fitted the place with snares to catch local cats and dogs, I cannot say, but then I didn't think too carefully about this very foolish notion until I saw who was making the noise.

"I'm so sorry," I said, and Gareth's luncheon companion looked up at me from beyond her sodden hair. "I didn't mean to— Are you quite all right?"

She was sitting with her back against the side of the sofa, with her legs pulled up to her chest as though she wished to be as small as possible. Her mouth opened a fraction, but she didn't say anything. She just stared at me, and I thought perhaps she was trying to comprehend what I was doing there.

"I should leave. I really am sorry to have—"

"Please don't go." She reached her hand out and, without really meaning to, I took it to pull her up to standing. I could tell she wasn't expecting this and, to be perfectly honest, neither was I. What I noticed most in that moment was that she was incredibly light. It barely took any effort whatsoever to return her to her feet, but what I was supposed to do next I couldn't have told you.

We looked at one another, both of us shy in our own ways and obviously nervous to have found ourselves in such a situation.

"Thank you for caring." She looked down at her pale green dress in a self-conscious manner, as though afraid her attire was too casual. Her voice came as something of a surprise. It was clear and crisp as a bell... to begin with, at least. "I apologise for acting like a child, but I appreciate your..."

I don't know what she said after this, as she was in tears once more. She fell backwards onto the sofa without checking what was there, and it seemed I would have to follow her.

"Now there's really no reason to be upset," I told her without an ounce of evidence. "I'm certain that whatever is wrong can be put right." I sounded rather stupid. This was the kind of thing that people say without taking the time to think, and so I tried to do better. "Perhaps if you told me what the matter is, I can help solve the problem."

She turned away then and peered up at the ceiling. I wondered what she was thinking at that moment and whether she was suspicious of my intentions. Why would anyone trust a boy who talks such nonsense, especially one with chocolate all over his fingers?

"You're that detective, aren't you?"

I was about to tell her that she'd confused me with my grandfather but decided this was accurate enough. "That's right. You might even say it's my job to solve problems."

She shook her head and fixed her eyes on the door. "I am beyond fixing."

Whoever this young lady was, she was not making it easy for me to help her. When I'd been in such situations in the past, I'd found that putting the distressed person at ease by telling an embarrassing story about myself often did the trick. There were so many options to choose from, though, that one single example didn't spring to mind.

"Have you ever let someone down so abysmally that you were surprised he could still bear to look at you?" she asked when I failed to respond. "Well, that's what I've done."

I wanted to ask her name or talk about something a little more friendly first, but this was apparently what she needed from a total stranger, and so I answered truthfully. "I can't say that I have, but everyone makes mistakes. We all disappoint ourselves and our loved ones from time to time." My mind ran with anecdotes of falling over, misunderstanding simple situations and eating too much, but none of them seemed relevant to what she was feeling. "I am confident that nothing you have done can compare to the crimes that grandfather and I have investigated."

She put her hands together and squeezed them ever so tightly. I thought perhaps she was trying to punish herself, but I couldn't say for certain. When her words finally came, they were so quiet that they struggled to escape her throat. "I hurt somebody."

I gave her a few moments to recover from the trauma of admitting this, then continued in a quiet voice to match hers. "There you go. You hurt somebody, presumably only emotionally. I take it you didn't give

140

him poisoned champagne or shoot him in front of Westminster Abbey. You didn't pretend to be someone you weren't for months in order to find some stolen diamonds that never belonged to you in the first place."

Out of context, I admit that these scenarios may have been hard to fathom. However, they didn't appear to have upset my new friend any more than she already was, so that was good.

"I loved someone, and I betrayed him because I am an impatient child who's never known how to be happy with what I have."

I had to assume that it was Gareth Heywood she was describing, and the usual way that people betray their beloveds was also rather obvious, but I couldn't put that to her. Still, it was all so abstract that I had to do something.

"My name is Christopher Prentiss," I told her quite out of the blue. This announcement sat between us for a few seconds, but she finally responded in kind.

"Katherine with a K."

This time, I wasn't ready for her to take my hand, but that's what she did.

"Pleased to meet you, Katherine." I considered telling her that she had the same name as my deceased grandmother, but I doubt it would have made her feel any better. As I shook her hand, it gave me the confidence to do something that I'd just decided against. "Would it be terribly rude of me to suggest that it is Gareth whom you feel you have hurt?"

"Yes…" she was quick to reply. "Or rather, no. It wouldn't be rude, and you'd be quite right." Something about this seemed to remind her of our surroundings as she tucked her long, sharp fringe behind her ear and sat up straighter on the sagging sofa. "I don't know why I'm pouring my heart out. It's just as I said. I'm a child and I need everyone to feel bad for me."

"Whatever you've done, you're still here together. I'm sure that he will forgive you and, by this time next year, everything will be back to normal."

"If only life were so simple."

Katherine with a K shook her head and the look she gave me was so bitter and so frustrated that I finally felt a little of her pain. She rose to standing, and I hated the thought that I would hear nothing more of her story.

"Wait," I begged. "Just wait one more minute before you leave."

She lingered in the doorway and toed the threshold with her foot.

"Tell me, Katherine with a K, when was the last time you told Gareth that you loved him?" This might sound like a strange point to put to her, but I'd been wondering recently whether, by the age of twenty, I should have uttered those words to a young lady. It seemed to me that they were as powerful as any spell, and perhaps that was the magic she needed.

For the first time since I'd entered that room, she seemed a little shocked by something I'd said. "I've tried and tried to show him how sorry I am."

I stood up myself then. "That isn't what I asked. When was the last time you said that, no matter what has passed between you, you still love him with all your might?"

It was evidently more difficult to respond to this point than I had imagined. So when she couldn't answer, I kept talking.

"Try it the next time you are together." To be perfectly honest, I was out of ideas by this point and had begun quoting some advice I'd read in a column in a newspaper. "Tell him just what he means to you – and how dreadfully lonely you would both be without one another – and you'll know whether he has it in his heart to forgive you for whatever went wrong."

She wiped her eyes with the back of her hand and, still looking like a startled animal, whispered across the room to me. "Thank you, Christopher Prentiss. I appreciate your kindness." She caught her reflection in the shine of one of the brass instruments and shook her head once more as she left.

I felt rather foolish that, as the unremarkable assistant to a remarkable detective, I had so failed to get the rest of the story from her. And then I thought, *Gosh! I hope that was good advice and they aren't fighting because she ran over his pet ferret.*

CHAPTER TWENTY-ONE

That false-start of a conversation summed up my day. In fact, it summed up my holiday in its entirety. My return home had not been the harmonious affair of which I had been dreaming. Our festive preparations, not to mention the investigation into Nigel Tibbs's death, had only offered brief flashes of their usual pleasures, and I wanted for nourishment – not just intellectually (and digestively, of course) but of my very soul.

It felt terrible to be so tristful when surrounded by such joy, and I tried my best to enjoy the party once more. I found Grandfather holding court on the landing halfway up the stairs. There were people surrounding him on two levels to listen to whatever story he was telling.

"It really was a race against time to find the killer before he struck again, but I'm glad to say that the man is now behind bars. Of course, I couldn't have worked so quickly if it weren't for my bright and dedicated grandson, Christopher." I don't believe he'd noticed me there, and I was pleased to discover that he doesn't only give me credit when he knows I'm within earshot. "Together we eliminated various suspects, worked through a number of possible motives and finally secured the culprit's confession."

He made this all sound very exciting and, for a moment, I didn't realise that he was discussing the killing in Kilston Down. I knew that story well enough, so I moved on around the house. The rest of my family were back listening to the band. Gareth had finished his shift for the evening and was busy elsewhere, and Mother had convinced my father to sway along to a slower piece. I assumed he would favour a waltz – or perhaps an even older dance like a quadrille – and I had never thought to see him there shuffling his feet and turning his elegant partner under his arm in a spin. He almost looked young again.

I went to the lounge that I was yet to enter at the front of the house. This was definitely the most Christmassy of the lot. The tree was a small version of the one my brother had bought at Gimbel's, but the other rooms in the house could have used his now expert touch to add some colour and sparkle. I should have stayed with my family as, on entering the room, I was captured by Sir Joseph, the old man who props up the bar at the Holly Tree Inn. He was a dear fellow, and I loved the stories he could tell, but he was very difficult to understand when drunk.

"Chrissy, m'boy. I would like to tell you that oars are pilchard stew."

"Pilchard stew?"

He shook his head, his eyes never quite settling on me for a moment. "No, no, boy. I wanted to tell you that I saw a picture of you... in the newspaper. You looked most apple light and runcible." He had a metal tankard in his hand – his own personal one which he took to the pub each day – and he waved it about in the air so that drops of beer splashed about the place.

"Apple light and runcible?" I asked to check that it wasn't my hearing that was the problem.

"What do you mean, boy?" He examined me as if I were quite mad. "I said you looked upright and respectable. I haven't used the word runcible in my life. I don't even know what it means." He stopped then and gazed about the room as though unsure what he was doing there. "Anyway, as I was saying, there was a phonograph..." I understood this slurred word without asking for clarification. "... of you with your grasshopper."

It went on like this for quite some time. I particularly enjoyed a story he told from when he was a child on his family's grand estate. He was playing with his two best friends – a unicorn and a hacksaw – and they discovered a purple blancmange. By this point, I had given up asking what he really meant and tried to enjoy the bizarre story for what it was.

When I could finally get away, I left him to tell the same stories to a rather jovial man in a beret. They were soon firm friends, and I didn't feel so bad about abandoning the drunken local.

I drifted out to the porch at the front of the property. There was a long wooden terrace that covered part of the lawn, and it was quieter there now than when we'd arrived. I stood staring out at the beautiful snowy scene with Maude Evans's cottage on the other side of the road. It looked just like a house from a Christmas card, and I felt a touch maudlin to think of her apparently irrelevant demise. Now, I'm not saying she would have wanted to be murdered, but at least her death would have been more than a footnote which was subsequently crossed out altogether.

There was a pale blue glow to the scene, which you only ever see on really snowy nights. The sound of the band was dampened by a closing door, and I realised that there were two people talking just out of view at the side of the house.

"I wish I could make you happy," a woman said, and I instantly knew who it was. "I wish I could be the person you need, but it's impossible."

"I really don't think I'm asking too much." Gareth sounded quite emotional, and I pushed myself further into the shadows against the wall, even though there was no way that either of them could see me from where they stood.

"I can't tell Rodrick about us," my old teacher replied, and I could feel her anguish even without seeing her face. "I love spending time with you, Gareth. These last few months have been like nothing else I've ever experienced, but it would break my husband's heart if he knew."

There was silence then, and I tried not to imagine what they were doing together. To be perfectly honest, I was having a hard time accepting what I was hearing. And, yes, part of me was thinking, if Alisha Steele was intending to fall in love with a man who wasn't her husband, then it should be me. But it also stung to know that she had gone ahead and done so. Even Gareth, whom – I don't mind telling you – I had prematurely elevated to the status of nicest man in the village, now fell in my estimations.

"We can still see one another," she whispered in a coarse, desperate voice that wasn't her own.

"I don't know whether that's possible, Alisha."

There was the sound of snow crunching underfoot, and I believe he moved away from her a short distance.

"Seeing you with him will be a painful reminder each time. I don't know whether I'll move back to London now or…" His words petered out as he considered this grim future.

Perhaps it was wrong of me to think the worst of him. Perhaps they were very much in love. It was possible that the not-so-good doctor had treated his wife cruelly, which had forced Alisha into the arms of another man. The more likely scenario, however, was that the not-so-saintly musician had seen a woman who took his fancy and seduced her without poor Dr Steele knowing anything about it. I still couldn't imagine where Katherine with a K fitted into that story, but it would surely come to light in time.

This was a further reminder of how far imagination can get us in real life. Even my grandfather hadn't been able to harness his, and our fanciful thinking had wasted most of the afternoon. We'd gone chasing ghosts and hunting for clues that didn't exist. Nigel Tibbs wasn't Old Miss Evans's son, and there was no sense in making up a story to explain who was responsible for the cracks in Alisha and Rodrick's marriage.

I can't tell you how much the dalliances of a man I'd only recently met and a woman I hadn't spoken to for years suddenly meant to me. And then, as I was about to tiptoe back to the party, I caught the sound of someone approaching the house.

"Come along, Alisha," the doctor called from several yards away, and I rather wished I could have seen her face at that moment – not to glory in her suffering but to confirm the truth of what had played out just before. "It's time to come home."

I struggled to identify his tone of voice. There was a touch of anger in it – that was certain. But that wasn't all. Disbelief, uncertainty, fear: they were all there, though I think the overriding emotion in him at that moment was sorrow. His wife had sneaked out in the night to see a man little more than half her age. It was a wonder he wasn't shouting down the neighbourhood.

"Rodrick, you mustn't think the worst of me," Alisha responded without conviction. She walked into view with her arms out to plead with her husband, but he wasn't interested in discussing the matter.

"Come home, Alisha. We needn't talk about this ever again."

Gareth said nothing. He was still hidden at the side of the clapboard cottage, and from the conversation I'd overhead, I believe he'd already given up on her.

"Come," Dr Steele was more forceful this time. He turned on the spot and began the short but endless walk back to their house, three doors down the road.

Alisha turned to look at Gareth. Illuminated by the light that flooded from the front room, her face was full of hurt and despair. I suspect she caught sight of me lingering there, as she would say nothing more. She hung in space for a moment or two, then sighed and rushed off through the snow after her husband.

146

CHAPTER TWENTY-TWO

At home in bed that night, I thought back over a most extraordinary twenty-four hours. Though things might not have played out as I wished, I couldn't deny that the day had led to some surprises. The very notion of a murder in my picturesque village was shocking enough, but to find out that my once faultless school mistress had an inamorato, the mayor was capable of killing his love rival and Granny could tolerate modern music was a real turn up for the books.

I considered the awkward conclusion to the evening, too. I couldn't exactly run to tell Grandfather what I'd heard when he was surrounded by admirers with a million questions to put to him about his career. Mother and Father looked to be enjoying themselves for once, so perhaps informal environments suited him better than I'd previously expected. And as for Granny... Well, she sat down for a game of cards with a few of the musicians after the concert concluded, and I think it's fair to say that she left a richer woman than when we arrived.

To top it all off, Todd turned up for the last hour, just to be sociable, and he and I were soon brewing up smoking bishops for all who wanted them. As previously mentioned, I had only come across this drink in Dickens's 'A Christmas Carol', and it turned out to be a form of mulled wine. To begin, we stuck cloves into a whole armful of Seville oranges which I then roasted over the fire in the Christmas room. Meanwhile, Todd busied himself in the kitchen, boiling up a host of spices with a little help from Dotty. The house was immediately filled with the smell of nutmeg, mace, ginger, cinnamon and allspice. When the water he'd placed them in boiled down, bottles of port from our wine cellar at home were produced, and the now roast oranges were added. With some more heating and mixing, we ended up with the most pungent and delicious spiced concoction I could have imagined.

Todd's hour away from his colleagues' festive endeavours soon turned into three, as everyone at the party was thirsty and we couldn't satisfy demand. The reverend woke from his slumber and consumed at least three glasses himself. We ran out of receptacles to serve out the quickly depleting rations, and I ended up having to drink my portion from a small bowl, which was at least traditional for that time of year. It was even suggested that we should parade around the village singing carols, but Gareth argued that it would be better to reconvene on Christmas Eve, when the weather might be more hospitable to tramping through the streets.

And so, despite every sad moment I'd witnessed, I still managed to have a nice time. I went home with a mix of joy, woe and fortified wine bubbling inside me. As my family chatted away to one another, full of laughter and, yes, also fortified wine, I sat quietly looking out of the window at the white world that was captured in the Daimler's headlights.

When we got home, we tiptoed inside so as not to alert our relatives to our presence. Then, rather than nip down to the kitchen for a late-night feast with the others, I walked quietly upstairs, attended to my ablutions, and climbed into bed with a million things still to consider.

The grandfather clock between the two sash windows had rung for midnight by the time I fell asleep, and Christmas had officially begun, but I didn't feel the way I normally did. I knew that, whatever else might happen, there would be precious moments to savour, but poor Katherine and apparently treacherous Alisha were still in my head. Even Mayor Perkins, alone in his uncomfortable cell, perturbed me somewhat, yet none of that compared to the thought of having to spend Christmas listening to Terry and Thomas passing off their dry and uncharitable anecdotes as some form of amusement. I was quite certain that they had grown more reprehensible over the past year, and it seemed truly perverse that we should have to spend Christmas with them. Childermas would have been a more suitable day to have to put up with their clan... or perhaps All Hallows' Eve.

And yet, when I woke the next morning, some of my usual Yuletide excitement had risen to the surface. I looked out of the window to see that the snow hadn't disappointingly disappeared overnight, though the sun was shining. I listened to the sounds of the house before forcing myself out from under the toasty layers of blankets. The only thing I could hear was an occasional clank of pots clattering in the kitchen and the odd shout from one of the cooks. I was fairly certain that I would have the house to myself, and so I pulled on one of my many pairs of lambswool moccasins, wrapped myself up in a dressing gown and padded downstairs.

I thought I might sit a while in front of the Christmas tree to enjoy the atmosphere there, but before I reached the rear salon, I found my brother passed out in the hall. He was asleep on our dog.

"Albert?" I spoke in as quiet a voice as I could muster, but this meant that Delilah was the only one to wake up. She opened one eye (as far as I could see at least) to peer up at me and, finding nothing interesting there, she went straight back to sleep. "Albert, don't you think you might be overdoing the decorating just a touch?"

At the word 'decorating' he sat bolt upright. "My goodness, I fell asleep. We'll never be ready in time."

I looked about the hallway to comprehend how this could be true. A galaxy of paper stars hung from the ceiling. There were bright red garlands suspended between two candle sconces and fine metal tinsel had been threaded up and down the banisters. Assuming he didn't plan to decorate the carpet, it was hard to find a spot which wasn't already adorned.

He immediately pulled himself up to standing and brushed the dog hair from his clothes. I could tell that he was about to shoot off to continue with his presumably endless task, and so I grabbed him by both shoulders to fix him to the spot.

"Albert, I'm going to ask you a question, and I need you to give me an honest answer." I paused to make certain that my words had registered in his brain. "Is everything all right?"

In response, his voice hit a high C. "All right? Of course, I'm all right, Chrissy. Everything is tickety-boo. Why wouldn't it be?"

If I have one rule in life, it is never to trust a man who says "tickety-boo".

When I didn't respond, he continued lying. "It is Christmas Eve, which I'm sure you'll agree is the happiest day of the year. The anticipation of today is even more precious than the joy of tomorrow. I am excruciatingly close to finishing my preparations, and I just know that everyone will be so impressed with the results. Everything is going to be perfect."

He clapped his hands together to emphasise the point.

I still didn't believe him. "Yes, that's all very good, but I'm worried about you."

He held his hand to his chest. "About me?" He was a terrible actor. "Why on earth would you say such a thing?"

"Because you've never had the slightest interest in decorating the house for Christmas before, and you seem a little overwrought."

I had expected him to deny this at least once more, but instead he fell silent, and his face drooped.

"I'm not suggesting there's anything wrong with you," I said to cushion the blow. "I just wonder if perhaps you're pouring your energy into this petty endeavour to distract from something more…" I searched for a word that wouldn't offend him. "…more serious."

He turned and wandered into the front room like a man without a soul. There was something terribly ghoulish about him. His skin was sickly grey, his eyes had great bags under them, and he barely had the energy to lift his head as he crashed into an armchair beside the window.

"You're right, dear brother. Everything you've said is spot on. I'm a positive disaster, and I don't know what to do with myself."

I knelt down in front of him to look into his downcast eyes. "Things surely can't be all that bad." This was the second time in less than a day that I'd denied someone's suffering for the simple reason that it was the done thing in polite conversation. "What's made you feel so blue?"

"Not just blue, old stick. My mood has faded to black." He sat there, staring at nothing for a few moments before he remembered that I'd asked a question. "Everything in life has run to ruin. I tried being in love and devoting myself to a good woman (on a number of occasions) and that didn't go to plan. I threw myself headfirst into Daddy's business, but it turns out that it is mind-crumblingly dull. I thought I could at least create the perfect family Christmas before you and Grandfather swan off to the Continent, never to be seen again, and I can't even get that right."

I had to hold in a laugh, not because I am heartless, but because I struggled to comprehend how it fell to his little brother to know what to say.

"I'm truly sorry you are in a funk, Albert. If I'd known you weren't enjoying your work with Father, I would have done more to liberate you from it. You just seemed so dedicated that I assumed you'd found your calling in life."

"But that's it, isn't it?" I had to hope his question was rhetorical, as I certainly couldn't think of an answer. "I never do anything by halves.

150

When I used to fall in love with every girl I met, I was totally in love from the first moment. When I was at university, I believed that I would be the greatest scholar who ever lived, right up to the point that I scraped through my final exams with a just about adequate grade. And as for these silly decorations…"

He pointed to a shelf in the far corner where he had fashioned his own nativity scene complete with a farmyard's worth of friendly beasts, a platoon of shepherds, four kings followed by a menagerie of exotic animals and, of course, a smiling baby Jesus in the manger. It was pretty, though a little overdone.

Before I could reply, Delilah had wandered into the room to sympathise with him. Her low moan would do more to pick him back up than any speech I could give.

That didn't stop me trying. "They're not silly decorations. They're beautiful because, much like all those things that you just described, you put your heart into them and did your very best. You were a passionate student, a great banker or what have you…" (I still wasn't quite sure what he and Father actually did in the City.) "…and you would have made a wonderful husband if things had gone differently. It really isn't your fault that the bride's mother was murdered on the eve of the wedding and—"

He gritted his teeth. "Thank you, Christopher, but I'd rather you didn't remind me." My faux pas sapped the energy from him. His whole body seemed to flop, though he was already sitting down.

"I mean it, Albert. You put so much effort into your every enterprise, and your only problem is that you haven't yet found the path you're meant to take."

This wasn't enough to cheer him up, and so he murmured through those same gritted teeth. "Maybe I'll become a monk. Withdrawing from the world and devoting my life to silence might be just the ticket."

Delilah growled a little, either in disagreement or sympathy. It was hard to tell which.

"I think that may be too extreme a choice," this was me speaking, not the dog. "But a new plan would surely change your horizons. Just look at Grandfather. Five years ago, he barely spoke a word and appeared to be settling in for a nice long death. Now he's running about the country solving crimes, and he's about to set off on a grand tour across Europe with his loyal assistant at his side. All it really took was a change of perspective to get him on his feet again."

"Lucky Grandfather." He pronounced these two words in the middle of one long, hard-done-by huff.

"Why don't you come with us?" I asked before I could even consider whether this was a good idea.

He turned to look at the crackling log in the fire. "Don't be ridiculous."

"I'm not being ridiculous, Albert. You need a change in life, and I need to see my brother with a smile on his face on Christmas Day. So why don't you give up your job and come exploring with us?"

He turned back to me then, and the look on his face said *are you mad?* before he said, "Are you mad?"

"No."

He had to take a deep breath. "You really mean it, don't you?"

I shrugged, which I thought was a fairly accurate response.

"Christopher, you little star." He was still quite incredulous. "I don't know what to say."

"Well, you could just come."

He put his hands together in front of his face, as if he was about to lead us in a prayer. "No… I won't agree here and now. But I will think carefully about it."

A tentative smile had appeared on his face, which made me feel a lot better.

"That's a good start."

He looked thoughtful and pursed his lips before saying, "You are a curious character, Christopher Prentiss. I never know quite what to make of you."

I had nothing to say to that, so I changed the topic. "You do realise that, if you wish to make a perfect Christmas, you don't need to worry about decorating every room."

"Oh, no? Then what would you recommend?"

"Simply wrap Uncle Terry up in tinsel and bury Uncle Thomas in the snow somewhere. That would certainly do the trick."

"Hey! That's not a bad idea." His smile was back on his face, and he gave a cheeky titter before suggesting some solutions of his own. "Cousin Philippa would make a wonderful hat stand were we to have a party. Oh, and Aldrich is as dry as a pile of old newspapers, so we could use him to get a fire started."

"Yes, and—" I was about to add a no-doubt-hilarious manner of disposing with one of our relatives when I heard a noise coming from the front porch.

I immediately approached the window to see who was there, as it was difficult to imagine a milkman coming out in such bad weather, and it was too early for the postie to call. I couldn't make out a lot from the angle, but there was someone bent low to the ground on our front step. I thought about banging on the glass, but my grandfather had taught me too well to do anything so silly, and I raced from the room instead.

I was running so fast that I bashed into the front door and then had to unlock the deadbolt and remove the chain before I could go outside. By that time, whoever was lurking there had caught wind of me (hopefully only metaphorically speaking). When I made it through the door, he'd already shot off along the path. I tripped over a small box that had been left there and almost went head first into the snow but managed to steady myself on one of the columns that hold up the porch.

I wasn't giving up just yet, though, and despite the fact I was still in my slippers and nightwear, I bolted after him. I couldn't get much sense of the fellow from so far behind, but he was tall and skinny, and I thought I'd seen that dark coat before. He was way ahead of me by the time he got to the spot where the path bent round at an angle. I lost sight of him for perhaps ten seconds before I got there and, when I did, there was no trace of him.

He had presumably turned off into the woods, as there would have been less snow there. Before I could follow him, I noticed a car at the end of the drive and there was Sergeant Keel. I was already losing the foot race, so gave up entirely and waited for the officer to arrive.

"Did you see Dean Henderson?" I asked as he pulled level. When all that came in reply was a confused look, I explained myself. "I'm fairly sure I saw him lurking at the front of our house a moment ago, but he ran off when I gave chase."

"There's no time for that, Christopher," he told me through the window. "I've come to get your grandfather. Ethel Perkins was just found dead at home."

CHAPTER TWENTY-THREE

A rare thing happened that day; I had to wake up my grandfather because he was still asleep. It wasn't even particularly early by his standards, and I had the definite sense that the smoking bishops had left their impression on the celebrated sleuth.

"Grandfather? I'm sorry to wake you, but—"

He made up for his lentitude with a near clairvoyant prediction. "There's been another murder."

The sergeant returned to town to give his prisoner breakfast before the day got away from him. Delilah decided that she'd had enough of the snow and would not move from her spot before the fire. And then, just ten minutes after we'd received the bad news (and I'd put on some proper clothes) we reached Ethel and Mayor Perkins's house. One was dead, the other in a police cell, and as loose and incomplete as everything had felt the night before, the case had now burst wide open.

"Has the doctor arrived?" Grandfather asked the constable at the door. I didn't recognise him, as his predecessor had only recently retired.

"Not so far, sir." He was freckle-cheeked and nervous. I could tell that he was doing all he could not to stutter in the presence of the legendary detective. "I sent a boy to look for him, but he hasn't come back yet."

"Jolly good." Grandfather nodded appreciatively to the slight young man, who searched once more for his words.

"If I may say one thing before the pair of you go inside." The constable looked between the two of us for a moment, and then his eyes rested on me. "I just thought you should know that it has long been my dream to meet you."

"That's very kind of you to—" Grandfather stopped himself when he realised that this comment was not addressed to him.

"You're one of the reasons I joined the police, Mr Prentiss. To see a man even younger than myself have such success… Well, you're a real inspiration."

"How generous of you, Constable." I tried to sound humble. "I'm sure that, if I can do it, anyone can."

Grandfather released a quietly disgruntled note as we walked into the house, and I decided not to rub his nose in this rare moment of triumph.

We found poor Ethel in her room, tucked up in bed. The circumstances of her death weren't so different from the last two we'd investigated. Predictably, seeing as her lover had been murdered and her husband locked up for the crime, she was all alone. A book had fallen to the floor nearby, and I had to wonder whether she'd been reading by the candle on the bedside table when she died. I read the title which was "The Innocent Accomplice" by Mrs Baillie Reynolds, but I doubted it would make a great deal of difference to the case.

It was easy to assume that she had been poisoned like Nigel Tibbs, as there was a teacup on the nightstand and signs that she had suffered the same symptoms.

"It's a cowardly way to kill, don't you think?" I had to ask as we stood at the end of the bed, trying to make sense of the scene there.

Grandfather looked unusually short of ideas for once, but he replied with great resolve. "I believe that every man who kills is a coward. Murder is never the answer, and anyone who resorts to it clearly doesn't have the strength of character to face his problems."

"Oh, quite," I replied when I couldn't think how else to respond. "They do say that poison is a woman's weapon." Even before I'd finished this sentence, I could tell that it wouldn't please him.

"And what do you say, boy?"

The muscles in my neck became tense with embarrassment. "I say that's all stuff and nonsense. What do *they* know anyway?"

"Quite."

After this brief, tetchy exchange, he went back to staring perplexedly at the once glamorous woman in her bed. Without her make-up, she looked like an unpainted canvas. This effect was surely only enhanced by the sallow tone of her skin and the fact that she had died with her eyes closed.

"Do you think this means that the mayor found a way to kill his wife from within the police station?" I thought he might object to this too, but he remained calm.

"It's possible. I suppose that all depends on how the poison was administered." He increased his pace at this moment, perhaps to avoid mentioning the teacup. "If it were placed in her dinner after she'd prepared it, then evidently a second killer was involved. However, it's more than possible that whatever she ate or drank last night was already laced with arsenic – or whatever the substance was. It may be that she consumed it without any further intervention from the killer."

I stood there for a few moments longer to consider our next move. "Will Scotland Yard now be called? Will the men who know how to look for the slightest morsel of evidence be despatched around Kilston Down to reinspect the various houses of note?"

"Sergeant Keel will have called them, though I think it unlikely that they will arrive any time soon. Judging by the roads around the village, it will be difficult for any officers from London to reach us."

I punched my two fists together in frustration. It hurt. "I don't think we've ever come across such a subtle killer. Short of finding a fingerprint – which we are never lucky enough to do – I don't see how we can tie this crime to anyone but the mayor."

Grandfather raised one finger to contradict me. "You're forgetting the bottle of whisky that was sent off for testing. If it is proven that whatever killed Tibbs was put in that bottle, then Perkins is still the likely culprit."

He nodded.

I shook my head. "I know it might look that way, and he surely had every reason to want both his wife and her lover dead, but there's something wrong about all this. I've felt it ever since he gave his confession."

At almost the exact same moment as I spoke these words, I heard someone shouting in the street. "Lord Edgington!" the constable called up the stairs to us. "Mr Prentiss! The lad's back from the doctor's house."

We could tell from the tone of his voice that something had upset him, so we rushed outside to see what had happened.

The boy in question couldn't have been more than nine. He had a grubby face, a flat cap that was too big for him, and he appeared to be dressed for school in the summer term rather than a snowy day in December.

"Where are your trousers, boy?" I asked, pointing at the shorts he wore and his shiny red knees.

I don't blame either my grandfather for ignoring this question and getting to the heart of the matter. "What have you got to tell us?"

The constable helped conversation along. "Tell the gentlemen what you told me, Derek."

The young fellow showed no hesitation as he rattled off the answer. "I was at my teacher's house. Well, I was looking for the doctor actually, but he was out seeing a patient, and I found her."

Something about the way he said this upset me. "Mrs Steele? What do you mean you found her?"

"On the carpet in front of the hearth she was. Just lying there, coughing her lungs out."

"What happened?" Grandfather demanded. "Is she all right?"

"I think so," the lad replied, less certain now. "I helped her to her feet and opened the window to let in some air. She was looking a good bit fresher by the time I left."

"We must go. We must go to her right now." I looked over at the car, which Todd was already preparing for the short journey.

There was nothing we could do for Ethel Perkins up in her bedroom, and Grandfather did not object. In fact, he stood on the running board of the Daimler all the way to the large house at the end of Bitterly Close. I was too nervous to do any such thing and would surely have fallen off, but it served him well. When we pulled up there, he was off the car and through the large arched hedgerow before I'd got the door open.

"Mrs Steele?" He called as he entered the building ahead of me. "Alisha, is everything all right?"

When I stepped into the lounge, she looked quite dazed. There was the scent of something strong and unpleasant. It reminded me of what Mrs Tibbs had said when she'd gone to see her husband before he died.

"I'm fine, I think." There was none of her usual self-assuredness. She was clearly shaken by what had happened. Her silver-grey eyes glistened as she addressed my grandfather, who had sat down to inspect her. "I don't know what came over me. I was normal one moment and felt weak the next. My throat began to hurt, and I believe I fainted."

I wanted to comfort the dear lady as my grandfather had, but there was something I had to do. Something which had been lingering in my mind since we'd first visited Maude Evans's cottage finally made sense to me. I walked to a small table beside the window and blew out a red altar candle that was burning there.

CHAPTER TWENTY-FOUR

"The candle?" Grandfather was more surprised than the woman who had almost been killed. "You're saying that candles are responsible for the various deaths we've investigated?"

"It has a chemical smell that Mrs Tibbs noticed when she checked on her husband on the night he died. And thinking about it now, there was a similar scent in Ethel's bedroom."

Grandfather ran his hand through his long hair and then held it at the back of his head as he tried to make sense of it all. "But arsenic is odourless."

This really wasn't my area of expertise, though I felt that my theory might still hold weight. "Arsenic doesn't smell of anything, but then whoever made these candles and laced them with poison probably wasn't using the stuff in its purest form."

This brought my grandfather back to life. "You mean to say that the killer could have used an old medicine of some variety or... yes, more likely raticide. You've made a good point there, Christopher."

"Have you ever heard of such a method being used to kill someone before?" Alisha asked.

He was particularly slow and careful with his answers, as this whole idea was evidently only just sinking in. "Not outside of fiction, but it is rather ingenious. The candles would give off arsine gas." He looked about the spacious lounge for a moment. "Of course, yours wasn't potent enough here because this room is too large and airy. If you had been close to it for some length of time, it would have killed you, but I don't believe you inhaled enough to do lasting damage."

I tried to connect this information to what we already knew. "Whereas Tibbs, Ethel Perkins and Maude Evans were all in small rooms and had settled in for the night when they used theirs. They may have fallen asleep before the damage was done."

"That's right!" Grandfather shook his head in disbelief. "And there were definitely traces of candles in each of their houses."

"So it wasn't the tea after all," I mumbled to myself, but neither of them paid any attention. There was an obvious question we were yet to ask. "Alisha, where did you get it?"

Grandfather turned to look at her and we awaited her cautious response.

"It was on the doorstep when I came home from the party last night."

I moved to sit down beside her and take her hand in mine. "Was there a label attached? At least two of the others we've seen had a small label with Gareth Heywood's name on it. He supposedly sent candles to Old Miss Evans and her sister."

She raised her hand to her mouth in distress or perhaps fear. "Gareth? He wouldn't... I mean, I didn't notice any label, and I threw the paper away."

As she said this, she glanced at a wastepaper basket under an escritoire in the corner of the room. I went to inspect it, leaving Grandfather to ask another question. "What time did your husband leave here this morning?"

Alisha was all nerves. She bit her lip even as she replied. "He was out before I rose, but there was a note in the kitchen explaining that he'd gone to see the Gimbels. Their baby has been ill this week, so perhaps he's still there."

"As soon as we find him, we'll send him here to inspect you," he promised. "Do you think you'll be all right if we leave you to continue the investigation?"

"I'll be absolutely fine. I'm already feeling like myself again." Her smile was just as reassuring as her words were. "It was lucky that little Derek came when he did. He will certainly be a favourite pupil when we are back at school in the new year."

I'd found the label in the bin, but didn't tell the others what it said. It had been folded into the tissue paper, which explained why Alisha had failed to notice it. With this pocketed, I collected the candle from the window, and we bid farewell to the dear lady who had almost suffered a terrible fate.

Outside in the front garden, Sergeant Keel had arrived to receive his orders. "Is there anything I can do to help, Lord Edgington?"

"Good timing, Sergeant." Grandfather nodded to him as much in salute as confirmation. "First, you must drive to Lillibet Evans's house and remove the candle she was sent. There is a high chance that it is poisoned, and I believe she intended to use it today, so that is our most pressing concern. After that, you must ask around the village to see if anyone else has received one."

I was still holding the candle that Alisha had lit and now handed it over to him. "Perhaps you should keep all the offending items together so that the men from Scotland Yard can test them whenever they arrive."

Keel was a no-nonsense sort of person. He gave a brief, "Very good," and walked back to his nicely shiny, navy blue GWK. "I will do my very best."

"I know you will, Sergeant."

There was some more efficient nodding, as is common with men of their ilk, and he started the engine.

"Do you really think that the killer could have cast his net even wider?" I asked when the officer had driven away.

Grandfather turned to walk towards the Daimler, then stopped, as though he'd had second thoughts. "There is one scenario that I'm currently willing to entertain. You realise that our imagination has been of greater importance this time around because we have little real evidence upon which to build our case. However, it may be our best tool after all."

This was helpfully opaque, and so I pressed him for more. "Do you think that Gareth Heywood is to blame? His name was on the label sent to both of the Evans sisters. And I didn't like to say it in front of Mrs Steele, but hers had a similar one."

He seemed both unsurprised and unconvinced by this revelation. "The more important question you must ask yourself is why would he want to kill them?"

"I suppose…" A thought came back to me, and it throbbed like a headache. I hate it when nice people turn out to be heartless murderers. If Gareth really was the killer, it would ruin my Christmas. "Well, something happened last night that I didn't tell you."

"Oh, really?" He rested his elbow on the roof of his car.

"I overheard Gareth and Alisha having a tête-à-tête outside the party. They were in close confabulation, but then Dr Steele arrived and demanded that his wife return home with him."

"I see." The way he delivered this short response puzzled me.

"You're not surprised, are you?"

"Not in the slightest."

I waited for a few seconds in the hope he might explain further. To my amazement, that's exactly what happened.

"Think back to two days past when we first met Mr Heywood, and you introduced me to your teacher. What did they say about the last time they'd seen Maude Evans?"

With everything that had happened that week, it was difficult to remember where I'd eaten lunch the day before – though I did seem to recall that all I'd had for dinner were several of Dotty's delicious pastries.

The information I needed eventually came back to me. "Gareth had seen her coming home whilst he was throwing his Advent party. And Alisha said something similar, but she was in her living room at the time."

This all sounded very innocent, and I waited to have my understanding corrected.

"That's right, Christopher. But perhaps it's significant that Alisha Steele's living room is hidden behind that rather large hedge." He pointed to the foliage through which we'd just passed.

I swallowed to prepare myself for what I was about to say. "So she lied. She couldn't have seen Miss Evans arriving home."

"Well, she couldn't have seen her from within her house, but she might have from just across the road."

I once more felt that my head was about to split open as thoughts of a conspiracy between my beloved Alisha and that nice young saxophonist developed into a motive for murder. "Are you suggesting that they killed Old Miss Evans because she saw them…" I tried very hard to say this next word, even though I had no desire to do so. "… canoodling together?"

"It is one possible explanation. What I can say for certain is that Mrs Steele was quite alarmed when we mentioned her apparent paramour."

"Yes, but why would they have sent another candle to Young Miss Evans? What good would that do them?"

"Maude may have told her sister what she'd seen. They couldn't take that risk, and so they tried to kill Lillibet, too." He motioned to Todd, then walked past the car and along the pavement towards Gareth's house.

This was the kind of thinking which came naturally to Grandfather. He already had all the answers while I was still scrabbling in the snow (thankfully only metaphorically) to try to understand what was happening.

"Then what about Nigel Tibbs and Ethel Perkins? Are you saying that they also knew of the affair and had to die too? It all sounds a touch excessive, wouldn't you say?"

He had rarely looked more cheerful. Evidently, a killing at Christmas is the gift which keeps on giving. "As you well know, Christopher, murderers are not known for their self-restraint."

Several people had died. A woman for whom I greatly cared had just received and rejected her own invitation up the celestial staircase to those ornate gates, but I must admit that his enthusiasm had made me smile.

"Does all this mean that Mayor Perkins should now be released from his cell? Why on earth would he have confessed if he wasn't to blame?"

There was no doubt that it was the more advanced stages of the investigation my mentor enjoyed most. Though the end was now in sight, there were still so many threads to the case at which to pull.

"We'll worry about the mayor after we've spoken to the current favourite. A more urgent question though, is why, if Gareth is the killer, did he send Alisha one of the candles?"

I thought he was going to ask why, if Gareth was the mastermind behind all this madness, he'd signed his name on three of the murder weapons, but I concentrated on his point first.

"I suppose that, having murdered several people to keep the details of their liaison a secret, Heywood would have had little compunction about poisoning his lover when she wouldn't leave her husband." The clapboard house was in sight now, and I wanted to make sure I knew the whole story before we arrived. "Is that right?"

He stopped at the end of the path. There had been so many people at the party that it was one of the few well-trodden spots on the road. "It certainly fits with the conversation you overheard last night."

From this, it was impossible to say whether he would have put all his money on the hypothesis I had just outlined, or I was a thousand miles from the truth.

We walked up to the house, and I noticed that a few of the interesting characters from the night before were still passed out in the front lounge. Little Red Riding Hood was sharing a sofa with Reverend Deacon, and Dotty was lying face-down in the middle of the floor like a tiger-skin rug.

The door was open, so we didn't bother knocking, and we soon found Gareth in the room where I'd met his perhaps former girlfriend the previous night.

"Gentlemen," he said in a whisper, and I realised that Katherine was curled up asleep on the sofa. "To what do I owe the pleasure?"

He got up from the small desk where he'd been writing and came to greet us. His eyes were as bright and friendly as ever, and I reminded myself just how duplicitous some people can be.

"Alisha Steele was nearly poisoned this morning," I told him in as cold a voice as I could manage.

Panic immediately reshaped his features as he pulled us into the hall and closed the door behind him. "My goodness. Is she all right?"

If he was acting, then he'd gone into the wrong career as he was a natural.

I believe that even Grandfather was taken aback. "The method by which she was poisoned was unorthodox to say the least. We believe she inhaled the fumes from a candle laced with arsenic. She is lucky to be alive, but the same cannot be said for Mr Tibbs and Mrs Perkins."

Gareth looked down at the floor in something approaching shock. "You're saying that someone tried to kill her? But why?" He really did deliver a performance of the first water. "Why would anyone want to hurt the dear woman?"

"We were hoping you could tell us that." I tried to hide the emotion I felt and failed.

"How could—" He cut short his question and led us along the hallway to the front terrace. He was still in the loose, knitted jumper and slacks that he'd worn to the party, and he wrapped his arms around himself to keep warm. Now that we were away from the sleeping guests, he raised his voice a little. "Why would you imagine that I could tell you what happened to her?"

"Come along, Mr Heywood, we know all about you and Mrs Steele." Grandfather weighed the man down with the force of his words. "You would have had every reason to kill Miss Evans across the road if she'd seen the two of you together."

"So now I'm Jack the Ripper, am I? I bumped off countless neighbours for my own dastardly pleasure?"

"Then you don't deny that you and Alisha were having an affair?" I was ready to punch him in the nose, for Dr Steele's sake if no one else's.

"An affair?" Sounding quite overwhelmed, his voice shot higher. "I'm not having an affair with Alisha Steele. She's my mother!"

CHAPTER TWENTY-FIVE

"I overheard you," I told him as I struggled to comprehend how he could invent such a story. "I stood on this very spot last night and heard the two of you talking. She said that she wouldn't tell her husband about you because—"

"Because I am her son, and I moved here to be close to her. She was only young when she fell pregnant, and she gave me up for adoption."

Grandfather raised his eyebrows then. I believe he was saying, *Well, there you have it! The old imagination did a better job than we'd realised. There* **was** *a secret baby delivered to someone in this community; we merely picked the wrong mother and child.*

I was still making sense of things. "But the doctor found you together. He must have thought the worst."

"You are quite right, Christopher!" In exasperation, Gareth collapsed onto the white wooden bench that was positioned to the right of the door. "She would rather he thinks that she is in love with a younger man than admit she has lied ever since they first met."

"What an interesting case." Grandfather's impressions of the situation apparently shifted from one moment to the next. "You do realise that we'll have to confirm all this. If you're making it up, we will uncover the truth."

"I can show you my bally birth certificate if you like." Gareth's hands crashed down at his sides in anger. "I was adopted at just a few weeks old. When I was an adult, my parents told me the truth, and I went looking for the woman who gave birth to me. I showed up here a year ago and tried to talk to her but didn't have the courage. The only solution I saw was to rent this house and live here until I got to know her well enough to reveal who I am."

It was a compelling tale, and Grandfather and I waited to hear more.

"That happened in the summer, and she was both happy to see me and heartbroken over what my appearance might mean for her life here."

This raised another question, and I wasn't afraid to ask it. "So the doctor knew nothing of you until last night?"

"We've said hello to one another in passing but little more. If you ask me, he's a stubborn, aloof sort of person. That's why I can't totally blame Alisha for not telling him about me."

I leaned against one of the wooden posts that held up the porch. "Your name was attached to the candles which were sent to kill first Miss Evans, then her sister, and now your mother."

"And you thought that made me the likely culprit?" He looked at me as if I had just suggested we have *worms a l'orange* for Christmas dinner. "Why would I have signed the murder weapon?"

As I didn't know what to think of our guaranteed killer turned unlikely suspect, I watched my grandfather's reaction. Based on very little evidence except for the way in which he was chewing the inside of his right cheek, I decided that he was most likely considering whether any of this affected our hypothesis. Wasn't it possible that Gareth had signed the labels in order to say this very thing? Perhaps he had killed those people because they'd discovered the truth about him, then poisoned Alisha when she wouldn't acknowledge that he was—

Wait a moment, I appear to have already contradicted myself. So the answer to my unanswered question is, no. No, it wasn't possible in the slightest.

Before we could ask anything more, a face peeped around the front door and, a second later, there was Katherine, wrapped in a man's immense overcoat, looking far sunnier than she had the night before.

Gareth noticed and put his hand out to her. "Lord Edgington, this is my fiancée, Katherine Brookes. She can confirm my story while I find the proof."

He indicated for the young lady to sit down on the bench next to him and then rose to leave. It was a slightly unfeeling manoeuvre – rather like abandoning her to a small though highly focused pack of wolves. He must have realised this, as he gave her an affectionate stroke of the hair before slipping back into the house.

"I'll happily answer your questions, but first I have to say something to you, Christopher," she began before my grandfather could. "I must tell you how grateful I am."

"I see you've already met," the great detective commented, but she wouldn't pay him any attention until she'd finished.

"I listened to what you told me last night, and you were right. It had been so long since I'd told Gareth that I loved him, and the words unlocked something in both of us. We spent half of the night talking, and he says he really has forgiven me."

I must admit that I am the sort of person who hates not having the full story. I longed to discover what had gone on between them, but there was no way I could ask that now.

"That's wonderful. I'm glad I could be of assistance." I sounded like someone working in a department store. Along with hating unfinished stories, I'm also the sort of person who is very bad at taking compliments.

"Now," Grandfather said to move the conversation on, "we'd like to hear the story of why your fiancé really came to Kilston Down."

We left a quarter of an hour later, once Katherine had confirmed all the details we needed, and Gareth had produced his birth certificate, which bore Alisha Steele's (née Harris's) name. I don't mind telling you that all this left me feeling decidedly... undecided.

Todd had correctly interpreted my grandfather's earlier hand gesture as a sign that he should take the car home. Even in the snow, getting from A to Y in Kilston Down (it wasn't quite big enough to have a Z) never took long, and we wouldn't need the Daimler unless another emergency arose.

I couldn't rightly say how we were expected to feel about that morning's developments. As we walked back to the square, I was relieved that both my favourite teacher and my favourite saxophonist had not been outed as poisoners. And yet I still had that hollow feeling that always comes when there is a killer on the loose and his identity seems to be slipping further and further away from us.

For his part, Grandfather walked in silence, and I believe he was experiencing similarly contrasting emotions. We had come across two excellent solutions to the puzzle, and unless the mayor had something more to tell us that could prove he was guilty after all, we would have to start again from zero.

Before we reached the police station, we discovered that a crowd had formed around the clocktower. I noticed several of the old people from Dotty's Teahouse talking to a very animated Lillibet Evans. The postman had paused his round to see what the fuss was about, too.

"I've been warning for years that something like this would happen," Young Miss Evans said in her usual pessimistic tone, and there was some cooing of agreement from those around her.

Still in his long black coat, and with a glare in his eyes that made me shudder, Mr Marley was there with his bucket of salt. He stabbed his shovel into the snow at his feet to show his anger at the situation but said not a word. He really was a creepy sort, and I wondered if anyone had questioned him on his whereabouts.

"I want to know what's being done about it," Sir Joseph called amongst a chorus of other voices, and all eyes turned to the Kilston Down policeman.

"Now, ladies and gentlemen," Sergeant Keel replied before someone shouted another demand for answers. "Now, now. Simmer down, please. I understand that you're anxious after all that has happened this week, but if you listen to what I have to say, I will try to set your mind at ease."

He spoke calmly and clearly and had evidently reached his audience as the noise now died. "Thank you. The first thing I have to tell you is that we know how the three victims were killed." The level of chatter instantly shot up once more, but he would not slow down. "That's right. My colleague Lord Edgington believes that Maude Evans was the first person killed back at the beginning of the month. The good news, though, is that the killer is unlikely to remain a threat, so long as you don't accept gifts from anyone you don't know."

I believe he'd started far more strongly than he'd finished. If anything, the people were more frightened now than they had been before.

"Oh, and don't light any candles," the sergeant added and then went tearing through the crowd to reach us. "Lord Edgington, I must share a few details with you. We had a telephone call from the coroner. The manner of Nigel Tibbs's death fits with arsenic poisoning, but there was no trace of the stuff in the whisky bottle or teacup at his house."

I must admit that I was a touch disappointed that I couldn't tick off death by tea on my list of things that regularly happen around my grandfather. Well, not this Christmas at least.

"That's as I suspected," Grandfather replied in a solemn tone. "What about the candles? Have more been discovered?"

He nodded with the crisp efficiency that was common in his line of work. "We took possession of the one we found at Lillibet Evans's cottage, and there was another on the doorstep of the vicarage."

My first thought was that it was lucky the vicar was still passed out in Gareth's house, but I asked, "Was there anything to suggest when it had been left there?"

170

The sergeant moved closer as though afraid that the mob of, if not furious, at the very least peeved villagers would hear him. "The paper around the candle was dry, and there was no snow on it, which suggests that it had been left there since the weather changed early this morning."

Grandfather put his thumb to his lips to think for a moment. "Did you notice any footprints that led up to the vicarage? They could be important."

Keel stood up straighter, and it was clear that he was proud of his and his constable's efforts. "We did, sir. And they were noticeably smaller than the average person's. Most likely made by a woman or a child."

Or a man walking upside down with small shoes on his hands, I thought but didn't say, as I was distracted by a face in the crowd.

"Doctor Steele," I called before running over to talk to him.

He was surrounded by villagers reporting minor symptoms which very much didn't imply that any of them had been poisoned. Young Miss Evans was particularly worried about a sore throat that had been bothering her, whereas Sir Joseph suggested that a pint in the pub ought to ease her suffering.

I had to raise my voice to be heard over them. "Doctor Steele, I'm afraid you're needed at home." This did the trick, and the hypochondriacals reluctantly drifted away.

"Thank you, Christopher. I appreciate your saving me like that. Now, what can I do for you?"

"It's your wife, sir. One of the candles found its way to your house, and she lit it this morning."

"My goodness, is she—"

"She was fine when we left her. She wasn't in an enclosed space like the three people who died, and I don't believe she was exposed to the fumes for too long."

"I must go immediately." The panic clear on his face, he was already hurrying off. "Best of luck finding the brute who's responsible."

Grandfather and Sergeant Keel appeared to have finished their conversation and were walking towards the station.

"Come along, Christopher." The more demanding of the two waited for me to catch up with him. "It's time to find out why the mayor lied."

CHAPTER TWENTY-SIX

The three of us marched into the station, and Keel presented the keys to my grandfather for the ceremonial act which he was about to perform.

"Mayor Perkins," Lord Edgington said in a formal tone as he unlocked the cell, "you are a free man."

The prisoner looked understandably confused and perhaps a touch irritated. "But I'm guilty. I thought I'd made myself clear on the matter. I murdered Tibbs because of what he did to my marriage. He deserved to die."

Grandfather barely reacted to these claims. "Yes, I remember you saying that." He simply turned and walked back to the entrance-hall-cum-living-room of the station. "Meanwhile, I'm dying for a cup of tea."

The sergeant duly boiled the kettle as Mayor Perkins lingered in the doorway, uncertain what to make of my grandfather's little show. Nothing would be explained until we were all sitting down with a cup and saucer in our hands and milk had been poured into our boiling hot drinks.

"Won't you join us, Mayor?" Grandfather asked quite innocently.

Why we had to go through this piece of jolly theatre, I cannot tell you, but Lord Edgington always has his reasons. I imagine that the whole thing was designed to set the duplicitous civil servant off guard, and it undoubtedly achieved that aim. He walked to the one free armchair beside the hearth and, just as cautiously, sat down there before Keel obligingly provided a fourth cup.

"Now, where shall we begin?" Grandfather sounded so earnest in this entreaty that I believe the mayor must have searched for an answer to the rhetorical question. "You are not the first man to confess to a crime which he did not commit. During my time at Scotland Yard, it was quite common for those seeking attention to pop by and admit to some terrible offence. The number of Jack the Rippers I met was quite astounding. Of course, they were always tripped up by the details. One man claimed that he was responsible not only for the killings in Whitechapel, but the crimes of Charles Peace, too. And yet, when we asked him how he went about the murders, he knew little more than what had been printed in the newspapers."

"But it was me; I killed Nigel Tibbs. I promise I did!"

I must admit that this was when the penny dropped. It should have been obvious earlier, but I'd been so busy questioning who the real killer was that the reason for the mayor's subterfuge hadn't settled in my mind.

"You're protecting someone," I whispered, but everyone heard, so I might just as well have said it with more conviction. I soon made up for this. "You told us that you'd killed him because you know who really did it."

He closed his eyes and would say nothing more. He did have a sip of tea, but then who could blame him?

"Come along, John," the sergeant said in a confidential manner, as though talking to an old friend. "There's no need for you to suffer for someone else's ill deeds."

Perkins brought his fist down on the table next to him. The fact that he first had to transfer his cup to the other hand robbed this action of any drama. "I'm telling you, all of you: I poisoned him, and he deserved what he got."

Grandfather fixed his eyes on the man with great intensity. I'd seen this happen many times and still found it a little frightening. "There was no trace of poison in the whisky which you claimed to have dosed with arsenic."

Our suspect (of some crime other than murder, but still a criminal no doubt) immediately froze. "That's possible. I mean... I was evidently so flustered by the thought of what I was about to do that I changed my mind and put it somewhere else. Have you examined any beer bottles, for example, or perhaps—"

"Enough of this." Grandfather roared these words and brought his fist down on the arm of his chair to show the mayor how it was done. "I'm tired of your lies. We know how Nigel Tibbs was poisoned. More people have died since you were locked up here. So stop wasting our time and tell us whom you were protecting."

The man was surely terrified. He hid his mouth behind his teacup, but there was no doubt that my grandfather's show of fury had put the fear of God into him.

"Really, Mayor Perkins," I said in a suitably guileless tone. "More people could die if you hide the truth."

He looked into the cup as if hoping to read his tea leaves. I thought he might hold out a little longer, but then he sighed, and it was clear that he could see no other option.

"Very well, it wasn't me." I could tell just how much pressure was bearing down on his broad shoulders. "Not that I didn't have a good reason, mind you, but I'm no killer."

Grandfather said nothing to gee him along, and Sergeant Keel sat back in his chair, happy to observe the scene that his (retired) superior was directing.

"I told you that I killed Nigel Tibbs because I didn't want the real killer to suffer. You see, if I hadn't been such a weak man, none of this would have happened. If I'd fought for my wife when her head was turned, we would all be a great deal happier now."

I cannot tell a lie; it was a slow tale, and he was no great raconteur. His small audience sat in patient anticipation, waiting for him to get to the good bit.

"Two nights ago, after Tibbs had closed his shop, I overheard them. He and Ethel were shouting at one another, and they nearly came to blows. He said that she had been making eyes at Farmer Gimbel, and she said he was a jealous fool."

"Where was this?" Grandfather's eyes narrowed as he considered what he'd heard.

"In the street in front of the grocer's. There was no one else about, but I'd been for a walk to clear my head."

"Was that all you saw?" I asked when he added no more. "Was that the only thing that suggested Ethel was the killer?"

"Not quite." He apparently had no fear that his suspicion was wildly overblown. "Nigel stormed off and Ethel ran after him. I've seen that change in attitude in her before. She does that whenever she wants something. In this case, she was suddenly all sweetness and convinced Nigel to share a drink with her at the pub to put things right."

"I was in the Holly Tree for some time that night," the sergeant revealed. "I didn't see either of them."

The mayor put his cup down and looked despondent once more. "They never made it to the pub. Nigel said that Nora was out playing cards with friends, and they could drink at home."

The room fell quiet as his story came to an end. There was the faint hiss and crackle of a log slowly turning to ash in the fireplace, but nobody spoke for a whole minute as we considered the facts.

"I'm afraid we have some bad news for you, Mayor Perkins." This was not the first time I'd heard my grandfather utter such words. His voice was a fine instrument, and the resonance and solemnity he could achieve were impressive. "Your wife was found dead in your home this morning."

The mayor gasped, and we allowed him a few moments of silence to absorb the sad revelation.

"We believe that she died in the same manner as Nigel Tibbs and even Maude Evans. Each of the victims, and several far luckier souls who survived, were sent candles that were infused with arsenic, presumably from some household substance that is still dangerously easy to obtain."

"We can't entirely rule out the possibility that Ethel killed her paramour," I added, "but that would suggest she was carrying the candle when they went into the house. If they'd just started arguing, it seems unlikely."

"I don't..." The mayor placed his hand on his forehead. It was a good thing he'd put down his teacup, as he'd surely have dropped it. "Do you really mean that I lied for nothing?" He had to close his eyes then, as the relief at his impending freedom was surely tempered by the knowledge of his wife's death. "Poor Ethel. I know we had an unusual marriage, but I really did care for her."

I found the control he showed at this moment quite startling, but as tears graced his cheeks, I had no reason to doubt his sincerity. It is hard to imagine how anyone can bear such bad news. I've always thought myself lucky that, though my grandmother was murdered when I was just a boy, I didn't realise how she had died until a decade later.

"You cannot be put on trial for falling out with your spouse," Grandfather reassured him. "I am truly sorry for your loss, but it is never a good idea to interfere with an investigation as you have."

Another batch of crushing emotions weighed on him as he came to terms with what he'd done. "My goodness, I never thought of that. I was so sure Ethel was the only person to care enough about him to want him dead that my admission seemed as if it would cause no further problems. I never imagined there would be..." He stopped himself once more. "What have I done? She might not have died if I'd stayed out of her business."

176

"Precisely." Grandfather could often be soft with those who make mistakes but don't cross the line into true devilry. At other times, however, he liked to teach such people a lesson. "My grandson and I went home after you were arrested. Although I had my reservations, I was willing to believe that either you were the killer, or you knew something that could implicate your wife. I therefore concluded that there would be no more violence. Had I known the truth, I would have torn the village apart looking for the culprit."

"I…" The mayor looked to his fellow Kilston Downians for sympathy, and it was the sergeant who would give in first.

"The reality is that we can't say what would have happened if things had been different. It's possible that Ethel would have been targeted in just the same way."

"Sergeant Keel is correct." Grandfather pushed his chair back to tower over Mayor Perkins. "We will never know what damage you have done. The only comfort you can take is that we came to see what was really happening before even more people died."

CHAPTER TWENTY-SEVEN

"My gosh, Grandfather, you certainly didn't take it easy on the man," I told him as we left the police station. "Don't you think he was acting with good intentions?"

"You know what they say about the road to hell, Christopher…"

I believe that I almost definitely had a vague idea, but before I could give him the wrong answer, I caught sight of the Daimler pulling up in front of the bandstand on the nearside of the square.

"Lord Edgington, sir." It being Christmas Eve, Todd had to wait for a few package-laden shoppers to pass before hurrying over to us. Our factotum was always immaculately dressed in his chauffeur's livery, though he'd long since been promoted from that position. It was funny to see him stomping about in large, clumsy boots to cope with the snow. "M'lord, I thought you'd want to know about this immediately."

He was holding a small box in his hand. A box that I'd tripped over earlier that day.

"Where did you find it, Todd?" Grandfather asked before I could say anything.

"It was on the front doorstep of the manor house. There was no address or label, so it must have been delivered by hand."

I waited until the three of us could see the candle inside before telling them of my suspicions. "I know who left it. An old classmate of mine from when I was eight years old was there this morning. When I went outside to speak to him, he legged it into the woods."

Grandfather's perturbed expression said, *Really, Christopher, must you use such slang?* But his mouth said, "Really, Christopher, why didn't you mention this before?"

"Because I didn't know what was in the box. Soon after I lost sight of him, the sergeant arrived with news of Ethel Perkins's death."

Todd was far more diplomatic in his response. "What's this boy's name, Master Christopher? And how can we find him?"

It was easy enough to trace our steps from yesterday (not that they were visible anymore) to Sunday Drive where both Young Miss Evans and Dean Henderson lived. I was glad that Todd had accompanied us in case Henderson tried to escape, and we would have to engage in a snowball fight in order to stop him. Though this was, admittedly, an unlikely scenario, I had no doubt that our servant had a far better throwing arm than mine.

"He's always been a troubled character," I told my companions. "When I was seven, he put pins on my chair in school, and let me tell you this, they really hurt." Even as I spoke, I knew this would do nothing to convince my grandfather that my former schoolmate would be the violent criminal for whom we searched.

When we got to the tumbledown cottage where he had lived since we were babies, we discovered that he was no longer using his neighbour's car as a blind for his assault on the local feline population. No, he had built an igloo for that purpose.

I must admit that it was an ambitious construction. It had three thick walls as tall as my grandfather, and a hole near the top through which the assassin could despatch his projectiles.

"Don't make so much noise!" he yelled as soon as he saw us, and we all walked a little more softly.

"Why not?" Grandfather loudly whispered once we were just a few feet away.

"They'll hear you!" the crackbrain murmured back.

"Do you mean you still haven't managed to throw a snowball at a silly cat?" I could probably have spoken more quietly, but his bizarre plans were the least of my concerns.

Dean poked his head out of the hole and his orange hat fell backwards off his head to reveal a mop of messy brown hair. "That's the problem; they're not silly at all."

"Have you been outwitted by a feline?" Grandfather asked, and if I'd had the time, I would have warned him not to fall into a conversation with Dean Henderson if he wished to avoid uttering ridiculous statements like this one.

"I haven't been outwitted!" He scrunched up his face. "They just keep evading me."

I can't say that I managed to resist replying, either. "Isn't it possible that they're staying inside because it's cold?"

His eyes never stopped moving, and he searched up and down the road as he talked. "There you go, then! They're clever."

It would take the smartest of the four of us to get the investigation

180

back on track. Todd moved closer to his master to remind us of our purpose. "That's all very well, M'lord, but I believe that there is a more pressing matter to address."

He bowed and stepped away again, then the great sleuth cleared his throat. "Yes, thank you, Todd. We are here," he said this in an incredibly grandiose manner, and I'm surprised he didn't waggle his hand about in a courtly fashion as he paused for suspense, "to discuss the matter of a certain candle."

Henderson wasn't scared of the lordly old gent, and I considered in which direction I might dive if he were to cast a snowball in our direction. "I don't know nothing about no candle, and if I did, I wouldn't talk to you about it."

"I saw you," I told him before he could utter more lies. "I saw you at my house this morning, and we found what you left there."

I have to say that it was odd conducting an interview through a wall of ice, and I was quite glad when he stepped out from behind it and came to talk to us. "What of it? That isn't a crime."

Grandfather emitted a sound that was a mixture of disbelief and derision. "No, but murder is. Are you saying that it was a coincidence that three people have been killed with arsenic-laced candles, and you just happened to sneak to the manor house on the other side of town to leave an example of the very same thing on our doorstep?"

"No." He crossed his arms and looked bored.

I was unsure what he had just denied. "I'm sorry. Are you saying that it's not a coincidence or that you didn't kill anyone?"

He rolled his eyes like I was the stupid one, which I suppose was fair enough. "Neither! I'm saying that it's Christmastime."

Grandfather turned his head to one side. I'd rarely seen him look so utterly baffled. "My apologies, but you'll have to elaborate."

"It's Chriiiiistmaaaas!" he practically shouted. "People give each other presents, and perhaps you didn't realise this, but candles are common at this time of year. If you don't believe me, just watch the procession in the square this evening. Or ask Mrs Perkins who found one on her step last night after Dotty's closed."

This was all fairly sensible, especially by his standards, but there was one thing he hadn't explained.

"Then why did you run away when I came to see you?" I gave him a good hard stare, and I think he knew why.

"Because you went shooting out like a madman. I thought you were a dog coming to chase me off the property."

I almost believed him. "That's not true. You'd already moved before I opened the door. You knew that you would be in trouble if you got caught. You left the candle there to get your own back on me because we never got on at school. I bet that everyone else in the village to whom you sent one has upset you in some way or another, too."

Nothing until this point had got through to him, but this certainly did. "What do you mean we didn't get on at school? You were the only friend I ever had there."

If I fashioned a reply, it was only in my head, and it was presumably quite nonsensical.

"What are you saying, boy?" Grandfather asked. "And don't tell any more lies. If you are the killer, we will find out the truth."

With a huff, Dean clomped over to Todd to seize the package.

"Don't touch that," our factotum told him, but it was too late.

Our suspect had pulled the candle free of its cardboard container and out into the light. It was actually nothing like the other candles we'd seen. For one thing, it was made of sheets of rolled beeswax as opposed to the smooth, solid altar candles that had been sent to the people the killer had targeted. But that wasn't the most significant thing he would remove from the box.

"I sent you a candle, Christopher, because I wanted to be nice." He reached his hand back inside and pulled out a small, square envelope. "I ran away when I heard you coming, because I felt I'd made a fool of myself."

He held it out to my grandfather. I could see that my name was neatly printed on the outside.

As was his wont, the experienced public speaker cleared his throat before reading the card he'd extracted. "'Dear Christopher, I am so glad that you are back for Christmas and hope you'll have the time to meet up again before you leave.'" The words faded out, and yet the words ricocheted around my brain for a good ten seconds longer. "Ah, it would appear we have made a mistake."

I couldn't help myself. I had to shout out something entirely irrelevant. "But you put pins on my chair when we were in Mrs

182

Steele's class!"

"No, I didn't." He pulled his hat back down over his ears, as though he didn't want to hear what I had to say.

"I saw you doing it!"

As he completed the movement, something seemed to come back to him from all those years earlier. "I remember that day. Ryan Endacott put those pins on your chair, and I was taking them off. If you'd given me a minute to explain, you wouldn't have sat down on them."

I am unable to tell you exactly what colour my face had turned, but evidently my grandfather felt so sorry for me that he tried to defend my undefendable assumption that a boy was a murderer for the simple reason that I'd thought him a pain twelve years earlier at primary school.

"To be fair to my grandson, you are rather fond of torturing cats."

This was the final straw for Dean. He took his hat off once more to throw it on the ground. "I'm not torturing any cats. I'm trying to stop them from constantly coming into my garden and leaving unwanted Christmas presents on my lawn."

"Oh, I see."

Todd was possibly the only person who enjoyed this moment, but he is a very discreet chap and wouldn't let it show.

"This is so typical," Dean continued. "Everyone always thinks the worst of me. Just this morning, the doctor wandered past first thing and felt the need to criticise me for being rude to his wife when, as it happens, I think she is one of the nicest people on earth, and I would never utter a nasty word to her."

I immediately forgot about cats and igloos and even woollen hats and focused once more on our stuttering investigation. "What time was that?"

Dean was bewildered by my sudden change of tack. "I told you; it was first thing! Around nine o'clock."

I was already retreating. "Thank you. That's extremely helpful."

"Christopher?" Grandfather called after me. "Where are you going?"

"Hurry up, or you'll miss out." I realised that I was the one being rude now, but not to my grandfather, to whom no degree of civility is ever enough, but my misjudged former classmate. "Thank you for the present, Dean. Perhaps I'll see you at the Christmas Eve celebration if we manage to solve the case in time."

I hadn't felt this positive in days, and apparently neither had he. "Oh, that would be wonderful. Thank you, Chrissy. I'll definitely be there."

Grandfather had an almost plough-like capacity for moving through deep snow and soon caught up with me. "What was it you heard, boy? Why did you run away like that?"

I stopped to look at him and there was a truly contented smile on my face. "Dr Steele told his wife that he was at Gimbel's farm this morning. That's on the other side of the village, a mile past our house." I paused for my words to settle. "He lied about where he was at the time Alisha almost died."

CHAPTER TWENTY-EIGHT

Yes, yes. I know. We'd bounced from one suspect to the next that day and I really shouldn't have got so excited before this new possible solution was swiftly eliminated, but... well, it was Christmas Eve! If I can't be excitable on the twenty-fourth of December, when can I?

To keep my feet fixed to the slippery ground, I tried to think of reasons for why Dr Steele might *not* be the killer as we once more returned to Bitterly Close. For one thing, he could have been called to another patient's house, having already attended the Gimbels' sick child. Or perhaps his wife had got the details confused, and it was another address altogether to which he'd been called that morning. It also wasn't out of the question that he'd simply popped out of the house to buy her a present and made up an excuse.

This kept me going for some time, but then another thought occurred to me that I didn't want to acknowledge. It seemed that, by constantly judging everyone we met, as Grandfather had taught me, I had become a less forgiving person in general. I didn't want to end up like the Evans sisters, who could see no good in anyone. It was common for hardened detectives like me to think the worst all the time, and yet, many of my favourite books – including the one I had recently got up to read in the middle of the night– are about people's ability to change and expose the goodness within themselves. So the real question that I didn't want to answer just then was: am I becoming a Scrooge?

Luckily, it was only a short walk, and I soon pushed this doubt to the remotest corner of my brain. We arrived at the Steeles' property and walked through the archway hedge moments before a pile of snow dumped down behind us.

"Perhaps we're luckier than we realised," Grandfather suggested. "Let's hope we're finally on the right track."

Todd didn't look so sure and decided to wait outside. I wondered whether he was afraid that the angry mob from the square would storm the house if they discovered what we now knew, or perhaps he was simply enjoying the fresh air.

"Lord Edgington," Alisha said when she opened the door to us. "How kind of you to come back."

Grandfather was only caught napping for a moment. "Yes, we wanted to make certain that you were well. Has your husband examined you?"

"Please, come in." She stood back to allow us to pass. Rather than leading us into the parlour we had visited that morning, she pointed us towards a sitting room on the other side of the house.

Dr Steele was standing at the window, looking out at the snowy back garden. "Lord Edgington, Christopher, I don't believe I expressed my gratitude earlier."

Grandfather walked over to shake his hand as Alisha rang a small bell for a maid to bring tea. Theirs was by no means the richest household in the village, but they had always kept a maid and cook, and after our manor house, it was one of the prettiest abodes in Kilston Down.

"We really didn't do anything." Grandfather humbly closed his eyes. "As sad as it is that Ethel Perkins died, it is lucky that her body was discovered so early this morning, as it meant that the little boy from Mrs Steele's class was sent here to look for you."

"I don't like to think what would have happened if he hadn't come." Alisha still sounded shaken by her experience.

"I've thoroughly checked my patient, and I don't believe that she could have inhaled the arsenic in any great quantity. It's more likely that she reacted to whatever else was included in the candle when the killer meddled with it. Alisha has always had certain respiratory difficulties. She is sensitive to smoke and fumes at the best of times. It was one of the reasons we moved to the countryside in the first place."

If he had been busy that month plotting a campaign of terror against his fellow villagers, he was certainly very calm in front of us. His broad smile stretched his face, and he tossed his head back to remove his grey fringe from his eyes. The man was the very definition of charm, and though I'd always found him an appealing sort, this suddenly caused warning bells to ring in my head.

"Please sit down and share some tea with us," Alisha said when Grandfather had stood staring at the possible killer for some time.

It was all very awkward, if the truth be told. Not only had we invited ourselves into their home without notice, we were secretly there to gather information on the doctor.

"Has there been any progress with the investigation?" he asked as we took our places.

Grandfather and I sat on the sofa, and the married couple were in armchairs on either side of us. I had to ponder whether this division was a good metaphor for their situation.

"We do have a name in mind for the possible killer," Grandfather said quite confidently, and I admired that dear old fox even more than usual. "Of course, we cannot give anything away at this juncture."

"Of course, of course."

It was at this moment that the maid arrived with a trolley and began to serve tea. This did beg the question of whether, in this house, any bell rung automatically signalled the need for hot beverages.

"It is a complex and taxing case." Grandfather rocked in his seat, and I thought perhaps he was expecting me to broach the topic we needed to discuss. It was suddenly clear why Todd had remained outside; this conversation was guaranteed to be uncomfortable at best and more likely quite unbearable.

"I was so sad to think that our little community could be harbouring a killer," Alisha added sincerely, but Grandfather was too busy studying her husband, and so I had to answer.

"I feel the very same thing," I replied. "Despite the gossip and minor scandals, I've always viewed Kilston Down as an innocent place. It's something of a haven, away from the harsh world about which my grandfather has taught me so much." I had meant this to sound like a positive thing, but it didn't come out that way. "It turns out that my home village is a hotbed of violence, backstabbing and adultery."

This final word made it feel as if someone had taken an axe and split the room in half. Alisha looked furtively up at her husband, and I believe that her hands must have been shaking as he kept his eyes on us. This was surely why Grandfather took me everywhere he went. You could always guarantee that I would say something indiscreet and spark a reaction from our suspects.

"Three murders," the doctor muttered with a shake of his head, and I accepted a cup of tea that I didn't particularly want.

"Yes, three…" I said when everyone else fell silent and the only sound was the clinking of teaspoons on porcelain. "We considered the possibility that Maude Evans had been murdered when we first arrived for Christmas, but until we realised how she was poisoned, it seemed improbable." Things were already tense enough; I didn't need to tell them that we'd previously dismissed the idea entirely.

"It's such a shame that it should happen at Christmas," Grandfather said, though, in truth, he was happy to tax his brain at any time of year. He gets very glum whenever he goes too long without something to investigate. If we're ever lucky enough to have a murder-free Yule, I'm sure he'll end up interrogating our staff to discover who dealt the blow that finished off that year's turkey.

"You think you know people," the doctor muttered, and he finally cast a glance at his wife, "then you find out they're not what you've always believed."

My goodness. The atmosphere was so frosty that accusing him of murder could only have warmed things up a little. Grandfather must have agreed, as he finally threw down the gauntlet... in a roundabout way at least.

"It's a shame that you weren't at home when Alisha lit the candle." He sighed in a regretful manner and Dr Steele soon took the bait.

"Indeed, it is, but I'm often called out to see patients at unsociable hours."

Grandfather silently concurred, then waited for a few moments before saying anything more. He had a sip of his tea, but I refrained as I already required the lavatory, and such necessities rarely grace the great detective's mind.

It would fall to me to reply. "I heard that one of Farmer Gimbel's children is sick."

"That's right, but she was already on the mend yesterday. I only went there this morning as a precaution."

Ah-ha! We'd already caught him in a lie, and assuming he wasn't just saying all this to cover a secret shopping trip, it wouldn't take much more to expose his crimes.

Much like a musician, Grandfather was using these moments of silence to his advantage. Each one was quite insufferable, but it was fascinating to see the doctor writhe.

"Oh... so you weren't called out this morning." The wily sleuth was the picture of innocence. "You chose to go down there."

The doctor swivelled in his chair to look at us. "Did I say that the Gimbels had called me? My apologies. That wasn't my intention. I merely went there to set their minds at ease that little Aimee would be all right. She had a nasty case of flu but has taken a turn for the better."

"Yes, you said that." Grandfather was quick off the mark when it counted, and I could tell that he was about to ramp up his attack. "And what time did you reach the farm?"

I watched as Steele realised that we were not there for a casual conversation. He put his tea down on the low table that stood between us, and then smoothed the creases in his brown suit trousers.

"I would say it was around nine o'clock that I reached the farm itself. May I ask why it is of interest?"

"Oh, it's nothing really." Grandfather was suddenly all charm and good manners once more, but this just made me more nervous. "I'm sure there was some confusion or what have you, but we were speaking to young Dean Henderson, whom I believe your wife taught. Isn't that right, Alisha?"

She looked at her husband before replying, perhaps to ensure that it was acceptable to him to make this minor admission. "Yes, that's right. He was in Christopher's class. Although he was a rather unusual child." She hesitated over whether to say anything more, but Grandfather was still staring quite fixedly at the doctor, and her words ran dry.

"Yes, that's the fellow. You see, Master Henderson told us that he'd spoken to you on the other side of the village from Gimbel's farm. He said you seemed quite unnerved about something, and I had to wonder why that was."

On delivering this last word, he stopped dead still and smiled as he awaited the doctor's reply.

"Well..." He looked first at his wife, then at me. Having shown his apprehension, he now tried to adopt the same carefree tone that Grandfather was already using to such brutal effect. "You see, the thing is..."

"You didn't go to the Gimbels' farm this morning, did you, Dr Steele? You lied." Grandfather's voice was immediately harder and flatter. He had expertly laid on the pressure and would now show his advantage. "You were mysteriously absent at the time your wife lit the candle that oh-so-suspiciously appeared here at your home last night while she was out."

"No." Steele dropped the short-lived act. "You're mistaken if you think that I would do anything to hurt Alisha. No matter what has happened between us, I love her more than life itself."

"Rodrick?" the woman in question responded. She moved to approach him, but he raised his hand before she was out of her chair.

"Yes, I heard about the trouble you've been having," Grandfather practically purred.

Steele's hand was shaking now, not with fear but fury. "Oh, so now you're going to condemn me based on village rumours! What kind of detective are you?"

"I never rely on gossip or hearsay, Dr Steele. I always check, verify and confirm every scrap of evidence we encounter. It is not just tittle-tattle which leads me to believe that you suspect your wife of committing adultery with your neighbour, Gareth Heywood."

A new fault line was visible in that pretty sitting room. It ran right up the plain cream chimney-breast. I had to think that, if Grandfather continued with such dramatic revelations, the building would fall to pieces in no time.

"It was clear enough that you didn't like him when I mentioned his name in your presence yesterday." He paused to see what effect this would have on our suspect, but it was Alisha who reacted. She buried her head in her hands so that, although she couldn't stop Lord Edgington from saying anything more, she wouldn't have to watch as he tore her world apart.

Steele shot to his feet. It was such a swift and seamless movement that it reminded me of a cog suddenly spinning within a complicated mechanism. "I barely know the man; why do I have to like him?"

"I notice you haven't denied anything I've said." This was the kind of declaration for which a person of my grandfather's age and stature could be forgiven. I, on the other hand, would have been clipped around the back of the head for insolence. "You suspect your wife of a romantic liaison with the young man at number three. A man who only moved to the village this year, and whose name was on the label of at least three poisoned candles that were sent over the last month."

The doctor's mood kept shifting, and it was difficult to say whether this was proof of just how deeply he suffered the sticks and stones that Grandfather launched at him. "Do you really think that I would kill all those people to get my own back on Heywood? Why wouldn't I start

190

with him if that was the case?"

"Perhaps it would give you more satisfaction to kill the woman who betrayed you and make it look as though her lover were to blame."

Steele opened his mouth to respond, but he must have realised that it would do him no good, as he turned away from us. This wasn't enough and, a moment later, he walked to the window to stare through it once more.

Grandfather decided not to push him any further but allowed that painful silence to come rushing back into the room. It was as if every snowflake in town had melted and was now flooding inside to stifle the faintest sound.

"It's a clever theory," the doctor eventually whispered. "But it's not true. I admit that I didn't go to the Gimbels' farm this morning. I went for a walk to clear my head before Alisha woke." He breathed in so loudly that I could hear him from the other side of the room. When he'd composed himself, he turned back to us, but it was not his accuser whom he now addressed.

"I love you, Alisha," he said crisply and clearly so that there could be no misunderstanding. "It's not important what you've done. You could be the killer for all I care, and I would adore you just as much as on the very first day we met."

Alisha looked stunned and didn't move from her chair, but I caught a faint, "You would?"

Grandfather faded from the scene at this moment. He fell quiet and ever so still, and I questioned whether his intention in all this was not to rule out the doctor as a suspect, but to meddle in the couple's affairs.

Doctor Steele could take it no longer and ran to fall at his wife's feet. "As long as you still love me, my angel, we can put everything else behind us."

She did not hesitate to put her hands on his cheek as she gave him the good news. "Of course I love you, Rodrick." I must say that her response would have sounded even more passionate if the doctor's parents had chosen a more romantic name than Rodrick. "How could I ever not?"

I had begun to feel like an intruder, which, of course, I was. I was sitting just a few feet from the couple at one of the most important points in their lives, and the only thing I could do to hide was pretend to drink the now cold tea I still didn't want.

Alisha fought off tears to continue. "There's something I must say before we go any further."

"You can tell me, darling, whatever it is."

This time, she was the one who had to take a deep breath. "I've never been unfaithful. At no point have I wanted to be with anyone but you."

I can't lie. This did disappoint me just a touch, but I was too transfixed by what she was saying to worry about the feelings of lovesick Chrissy aged eight.

"I should have told you long ago, and I am so sorry that I have been a coward all these years." To give herself time, she stopped for a moment and stroked his stubbled face. "The truth is that I had a life before I met you. I was young and foolish, and I made a terrible mistake."

Dear old Rodrick straightened his back so that his eyes were almost at the same level as hers. "I don't understand what you're trying to say."

She breathed out this time as she came to accept that she really was about to share her deepest secret. "Gareth Heywood is not my lover." Another pause and her lip trembled. "He is my—"

"Come along, Christopher," my grandfather sang as he got up from the sofa to make his move towards the door. "This really is none of our business, and we shouldn't be eavesdropping."

CHAPTER TWENTY-NINE

"You never expected him to be the killer, did you?" I asked once we'd passed back through the Steeles' hedge and were heading (for the last time that Christmas) along Bitterly Close to the centre of the village. Oh, and I also made use of the facilities, which is something that barely ever gets mentioned in the detective stories I read.

"I can't say I did," Grandfather responded, "though I thought it was awful that the two of them should have kept such secrets from one another. From what you told me about their confrontation last night, it was evident that Steele was deeply hurt by what was happening. He seems like a decent sort and helped us greatly when we were examining the scene of Nigel Tibbs's death. There was no reason to think he would have killed half the village to get revenge on a man he could just as easily have murdered directly. It is difficult to determine how a person will react in traumatic situations, but I felt it likely that he would be more accepting of his wife having a son who was born before the two of them even met than the idea she had been untrue."

The level of complexity in this sentence, let alone all the thinking that had gone into it, was quite difficult to follow, and I came to a simple conclusion. "You really are a terrible stirrer."

"I certainly am not." He scoffed loudly. "I merely facilitated the establishment of a more harmonious arrangement between a devoted husband and wife."

The third member of our party was walking a few steps behind us and couldn't stifle a laugh.

"I heard that, Todd." Grandfather sent a keen glare over his shoulder. "Don't forget what day it is. If you're not careful, you might find that your Christmas Eve envelope is a little lighter this year."

Don't worry; we all knew that he was joking, and Todd only laughed more loudly.

"It doesn't count if you blackmail people to be on your side in arguments, Grandfather," I chastised him. "What hope have I got of ever winning one?"

"Very well, I take it back. I give you permission to disagree with me when necessary, Todd. Just try to make sure it doesn't happen too often or Christopher will grow a big head." Grandfather waited for his second favourite employee – never forget Cook – to draw alongside us. "You know, there is another Christmas Eve tradition that I like to observe. How would you feel about taking lunch with your master and his upstart grandson?"

Todd is an expert at hiding his true feelings when required, but he blushed at this request and couldn't look Lord Edgington in the eye.

"Thank you, M'lord. I would like that very much."

We bustled on through the snow, and I caught sight of Katherine and Gareth wrapped up in a blanket on the terrace of his house. This made me reflect upon exactly what my grandfather's intentions had been in our earlier visit there. Had he moved on from investigating crimes to problem solving for local couples?

There was one thing that hadn't been resolved in our time at the Steeles' house and that was the question of whether Rodrick had actually murdered anyone. My grandfather was apparently satisfied that this was not the case, and he was normally right on such matters, so I decided not to raise the issue again.

Considering that we'd been thoroughly defeated by the poisoner's clever schemes, I was surprisingly light hearted and full of seasonal spirit as we trundled all the way to Dotty's Teahouse.

The square was abuzz with people, and I'm happy to say that, unlike that morning when everyone had gathered there to swap suspicions and express their fears, the atmosphere had changed for the better. There was a queue outside Mr Brown's butcher's shop – not to mention the carcasses of twenty of the fattest turkeys I can remember seeing, strung up beneath the awning. Children were pulling on their parents' hands to divert them towards the selection of toys that appeared every December at the back of Pendergast and Pendergast, the gentlemen's outfitter. And under the octagonal bandstand, musicians had gathered to practise for the annual celebration.

From the look of that cheery place, you really wouldn't have thought that there could be a killer on the loose. Although, old Marley, with his shabby black clothes, long face and bucket of salt, did his best to bring down the mood.

"What do you fancy?" Grandfather asked us as we peered through the teahouse window, and I knew the very answer.

194

We went inside to find a table, and Dotty shouted over a welcome.

"Afternoon, fellas." The gigantic woman was not quite so full of force or rich of voice as she usually was and had to lean on the counter to steady herself as she was clearly still feeling the effects of Gareth Heywood's party. "I'll be right with you."

Todd took approximately three seconds to pick what he wanted, whereas my grandfather studied the menu as though it were an ancient text that deserved great care and attention.

I have a sad confession to make, and it has nothing to do with the case. The truth is… well, I don't really know how to say this but, you see… I had eaten too many cakes!

That's right. Having been so busy that I had subsisted on little more than pastries, buns and fruit pies for two meals out of three that week, I opted for millet and mushroom soup with a salad of winter vegetables. My companions must have been wondering what had come over me, but I stand by my choice.

As we waited for our food to come, all three of us forgot about the conversation we should have been having and allowed our ears to explore the room. I doubt I need to explain that they didn't physically wander about the place, but I will anyway; it was a metaphor.

The teahouse was so busy that we were lucky to have a table of our own, but I still had to remark how much had changed since our last visit there. Gone were Ethel Perkins and Nigel Tibbs, who had made such an impact on my grandfather's introduction to the place. Mrs Tibbs must have put someone else in charge of the grocer's that day and was sitting just one table away from us, and even the vicar was missing. I had to assume that he was either sleeping off or living down his over-exertions of the previous evening.

"I couldn't take it anymore," I heard Nora Tibbs exclaim to Mary Gimbel, the farmer. "As soon as I'd finished with the police, I left Sam's girl Clarrie in charge of the shop and drove to see my sister in Godalming. I barely got a wink of sleep there, and it wasn't just because of the hard mattresses she has. I couldn't stop thinking about poor Nigel." She seized a napkin from her lap and raised it to her nose. "And then what should I discover when I arrived back here just now?"

Clearly transfixed, Mrs Gimbel leaned forward to hear the answer. "I don't know?"

"Ethel, Mary! Ethel Perkins is dead."

Mrs Gimbel leaned back again, looking a little shamefaced. "Oh, of course. I did know that."

I stopped listening and moved on to the next table. There was a group of regulars of the Lillibet Evans variety. Each of them spoke in a conspiratorial tone and each had a different opinion of who was to blame for the killings.

"I've always thought that Sir Joseph was a dubious fellow, and he certainly didn't get on with Maude Evans," said a man I recognised from my childhood, whose name, occupation and address I couldn't recall.

"No, no, no," his wife exclaimed. "Sir Joseph isn't the one. It's that reverend of ours. Who else could sneak about the village without anyone noticing? If he was confronted when delivering a deadly package, he could simply say that he was visiting a sick parishioner or giving out bibles."

Her prune-faced friend sitting opposite did not like this idea. "Priests don't swan about the place giving out bibles, you know," the former headmaster of my school responded with a downturned mouth. "I say that Dotty is the killer!"

There was silence as the heads of all four members of the group snapped towards the owner of the establishment. "Why would it be her?" Lillibet Evans asked – I told you they were of the Lillibet Evans variety; she was right there with them.

"Whoever tampered with those candles would have to be good with her hands," Mr Henry replied. "Dotty is a master craftsman as anyone who has eaten her cream puff surprises can attest."

"What rot!" the extant Miss Evans immediately contradicted him. "That is quite possibly the worst reasoning I have ever heard."

"Come along then," he responded, hunching his shoulders as though he were hatching a truly unpleasant scheme, "who do you think is to blame?"

She looked ever so pleased with herself. "Not just one person. I think there were a pair of them."

It was my turn to lean closer to listen, but just as I did, Dotty, the living wall, arrived with our dishes and blocked out the sound. I wasn't the only one who was disappointed. All three of us sighed. Our chagrin was soon forgotten when we saw the delights that Dotty had

196

brought. The food she sold was simple, but I already knew that each mouthful would be delicious.

"Call if you need anything else," she reminded us, and then thundered off back to her usual post to look dozy.

"And if you ask me," Lillibet was saying when we could hear her again, "they deserved what they got."

"You're wicked, you are!" her three acquaintances said as one. They almost seemed jealous that she'd had the best idea of the lot of them.

"There you go, then," Grandfather said once he'd finished listening. He had already buttered a cheese scone and added a thick wedge of single Gloucester on top. "We have successfully ruled out every last suspect."

I grimaced at this comment, as I didn't want it to be true but couldn't put my finger on any relevant exception. "Isn't it possible that…" I blew on my soup then, mainly to give me time to think of a way to finish that sentence. Todd and my grandfather both looked at me optimistically, but the best ending I could think of was "… that we've overlooked something important?"

"Possible?" my mentor replied in a tone of intentionally exaggerated irritation. "It's more than possible, Christopher. It's guaranteed. The question is what? And for that matter, where, when and why?"

"Not to mention, who? M'lord." Todd said with a slight tip of the head as he picked up his thick ham and pickle sandwich and prepared to disconnect his jaw to fit it into his mouth.

"Precisely, man, and very well put. I knew I could rely on you to shine some light on our failings."

He would presumably have told us how welcome we were, but he could no longer speak.

It occurred to me that, based on the relatively small population of the village and the close-knit community it contained, someone in that teahouse was almost guaranteed to know a key fact that we hadn't discovered. There was a young mother at a table beside the counter with her tiny baby, and a major revelation finally occurred to me.

"The paper we found in the grate at Old Miss Evans's house!" I said, my eyes wide with amazement as I turned to my grandfather. "It was an advert for Cow and Gate baby milk. Couldn't that explain why— Oh, no… actually, never mind."

Grandfather had held his breath for a moment but now released it in one short, glum huff. I slurped my soup. He ate his doubly cheesy scone with a knife and fork for some inexplicable reason, and Todd presumably regretted trying to put so much in his mouth at one time.

"Wait just one moment." Grandfather put his cutlery down to raise his empty hand. "Might it not be possible that— No, no. We've already ruled that out. Pretend I didn't say anything."

Todd had finally finished his mouthful and apparently took pity on us. "Have you considered financial motivations for the killings? Money is always a powerful persuader."

"I'm afraid so," his employer replied. "But who would benefit from the death of the school teacher, the grocer and his lover, not to mention two of the poorest women in Kilston Down?"

"Then what about long-standing grudges?" Todd looked at me for a response.

"It is possible that I've missed something in the time I've been away, but so many candles were sent out, and I think I would have heard about such an important argument that affected all those people. My mother keeps me well informed."

"I suppose you're right." This was a rare moment when Todd looked defeated.

"I still don't understand why Old Miss Evans was killed at the beginning of December, but the others were murdered in the last few days," I muttered, though I didn't expect either of them to reply.

I should have known better, as Grandfather cannot leave a point unanswered. "Think of it like this, Christopher. Just as we imagined that Mr Tibbs was Maude Evans's son, and it later turned out that Gareth Heywood—" I believe he realised that the people at the other tables were just as likely to be listening to him as we were to them, as he cut the point short. "Well, you both know what we discovered. My point is, what if we identified other elements of the case correctly, simply in the wrong order or applied to the wrong suspect?"

I didn't see how this would help us and continued blowing on the same spoon of soup on which I'd been working for some time. "So what you're saying is that we've essentially already solved the case. We just did it the wrong way round?"

He could see that this offered little comfort, and his confidence disappeared. "Perhaps not."

We concentrated on our lunch for a while before Todd cleared his throat and reminded us of something important.

"Lord Edgington, Master Christopher, I hope I'm not speaking out of turn when I say that it is Christmas Eve, and the time may have come for you to take a break. We've been so busy over the last few years that you've barely had the chance to celebrate what I know to be your favourite holiday."

I would have liked to disagree with him, but there was a lot of truth in what he said.

Emboldened by our silence, he soon continued. "We now know how the killer has been operating, and the police have been going from house to house to look for any dangerous packages. No one is going to light a suspicious candle from this point on, so perhaps it's safe for you to take a day or two off."

I thought about how Mr Scrooge wanted Bob Cratchit to work on Christmas Day, and I realised that Todd was right. While it was true that we were not greedy money lenders but kind-hearted detectives trying our best to save innocent people from untimely deaths, we had reached a brick wall, and I didn't see any way to climb over it.

"Well, Todd," Grandfather looked sharply at his retainer, and I couldn't imagine what he was about to say, "most employers would not appreciate their servants talking to them in such a fashion. However, I am nothing like most employers. I am truly grateful for your ideas, and if you have your eye on anything in the sweet counter, I may even invite you to dessert."

We had failed in our task. The case had come to a halt, and I didn't even have the stomach for cake. But as our conversation started to flow and the three of us enjoyed one another's company, I didn't feel nearly so downhearted as I had.

CHAPTER THIRTY

When lunch was over (and Dotty had convinced me to have a small slice of apple tart), I left my two treasured companions in order to go home before the Christmas Eve procession began. The procession marked the beginning of the festivities each year, and there would be all sorts of entertainment from mummery to carolling and, for those who partook of such activities, gooding from door to door in search of donations.

Of course, what my grandfather said and what he did were two very different things. I walked back to the manor wondering whether he really would take time off for Christmas or, the more likely outcome, he was already plotting to draw the killer out into the open.

There was more than just the resolution of the case weighing on my mind. I was plagued by thoughts of my brother's dark mood, my own treatment of Dean Henderson and a Christmas Day spent with some of the most ill-natured grumblers, groaners, grudgers and grousers on the face of the earth. The one silver lining I considered was that my head being filled not just with my own concerns but the fears and preoccupations of those I held dearest might, in some small way, be a sign of maturity.

This was soon forgotten when I arrived home to find the smellfungi of my extended family in every room. There was not a yard of space left unoccupied by a cousin or uncle, and they all had their gripes to air. Much like the toxic fumes of the candles that the killer had sent, their bad humour seeped through the house and down to the kitchen where our two cooks were arguing once more.

The atmosphere could not have been more different from my arrival the previous afternoon. My poor parents were doing their best to entertain their guests, but whatever positive note my mother struck, Terry or Thomas or one of their odious acolytes would overrule her warm sentiment.

"I don't approve of frippery!" Terry announced as I poked my head into the room to which I had been so eager to come home just days earlier.

I ignored him and spoke to my parents instead. "Mother, Father, I've come to get changed, but I'll be going straight back out again to see the procession."

Father was across the room like an arrow from Robin Hood's bow. "We'll be joining you, Christopher."

"As will I!" a voice from the cupboard under the stairs called, and I recognised my grandmother's dulcet, though muffled, tones.

I flew to my bedroom and made the necessary preparations. I was just about to leave when I caught sight of my copy of 'A Christmas Carol' beside my bed and decided to slip it into my pocket. It was not merely because I believe people should have a book about their persons at all times. In Kilston Down, it was common on Christmas Eve for villagers to recite poems or read out a favourite passage. As a child, I had always been too shy to participate, but Christopher Prentiss, aged twenty, was not the same person he had been at sixteen.

By the time I got back downstairs, it was not just my immediate family who were champing at the bit to escape from the house. Mother had given our servants the afternoon off to enjoy the festivities, and half of the gang from Cranley Hall, along with Jessop our butler and the two new maids my parents had employed since I left home, were all bundled up in hats, coats and scarves, ready to go.

As Halfpenny opened the door for us to troop outside, and Delilah went shooting out into the snow, I heard Uncle Thomas say, "In my day, Christmas was a time of solemn reflection. We had none of this exuberance." I could only conclude that his day was back in the seventeenth century, when Oliver Cromwell and his cronies banned the celebration of Christmas.

I must admit that I felt a trifle sorry for my younger cousins, who barely said anything in their elders' presence. Midshipman Peter looked particularly morose and leaned to one side in his chair to watch us go. It was almost enough to make me run back in there and tell our great-uncles that they were the most pessimistic so-and-sos I'd ever met, and that they should allow their families to live in the twentieth century. To be quite honest, though, I was too happy to secure my own freedom to worry about theirs and didn't dare look back.

Mother conjured a warming smile, and I put my arm through hers... then realised it felt funny and offered her my own instead. Father was immediately the carefree character that I'd met at the party the night before and jovially walked along with us in a line of three.

Such was the joy of leaving his uncles behind it had transformed him into a normal person.

"You will come to visit us at some point when Grandfather and I are travelling, won't you?" I asked them as, quite suddenly, the thought of spending months or perhaps even years away from them was too much to bear.

"No, we couldn't possibly," Father said, just as Mother said, "Yes, of course we will."

His face assumed its usual anxious and uneasy expression, but then to my and no doubt his surprise he relaxed once more. "I'm not one for travelling, and it will not be easy to take time away from my work, but I will do my very best to come."

Mother's eyes sparkled in the light that reflected off the snow all around. "I've always wanted to go to Italy," she said, "and France, Germany, Spain, Holland, and… well, everywhere really."

"There you go, Father." I turned to address him. "You'll just have to plan a trip of your own to help make Mother's dreams come true."

That flicker of nervousness ran through him, but it didn't last as long this time. "Perhaps I will, Christopher. Give me a few years to reach an appropriate age for retirement, and then I'll show that I am more adventurous than either of you have ever conceived."

Mother laughed at her stick-in-the-mud husband. "I believe you have already contradicted your theory by mentioning the appropriate age for retirement in the same breath as your secretly daring nature."

Father squeezed my arm affectionately, and I passed the message on to my mother.

Behind us, the staff had taken up a verse of 'God Bless the Master'.

"God bless the master of this house,
Likewise the mistress too,
And all the little children
That round the table go."

I say that they were all singing, but the only voice I could hear clearly was our maid Dorie, who had lungs like a church organ and piped out the words into the darkening sky overhead. It would be a clear night, and I could see the first stars emerging. The moon would soon peep over the trees, and by the time we reached the centre of the village, the streetlamps were lit, and impatient children were already waving about thin white candles in preparation for the evening's entertainment.

"There you all are," Grandfather said when we arrived. His smile was as bright as the electric lights in the window of Dotty's Teahouse.

"It's nice to have you back," Todd came to tell me, and I suddenly started worrying that none of my grandfather's (and evidently my) favourite employees would be coming abroad with us in the new year.

There was no time to be glum, though. The square was filling up nicely and, as friends greeted friends and families huddled together to stay warm, a double-decker omnibus from Dorking pulled to a stop at the far side to unload spectators from the neighbouring towns. Closer to us, I noticed all the usual faces. There were those who had lost loved ones to the killer's distant hand, and others who looked quite oblivious to all that had occurred.

The shops around the square had now closed for Christmas so that all the merchants could enjoy the celebration. Mr Brown, Mrs Lamb, the two Pendergast brothers, Mr Dryer the fishmonger, Dotty and the Gimbel clan were all waiting expectantly, and I noticed that Mrs Tibbs was right at the front of the crowd with a smile on her face. Evidently her trip to see her sister had done her good.

Delilah went running off to sniff some other dogs, and then the clock on the clocktower rang four. A relieved-looking mayor was already in place on the bandstand and, when he stepped into the light, a hush spread about the scene.

"Ladies and gentlemen, our community has suffered terribly this week. I myself have lost someone I love, and the natural temptation at such moments is to hide away from the world." His small head teetered on his broad shoulders like a rock on the edge of a cliff. "However, I discussed the matter with the families of those who were lost, and we came to the decision that cancelling this wonderful event would only have suited the savage who has been terrorising us."

This inspired a burst of mumbling as, apparently, not everyone agreed with this decision. I was coming to realise that some people in Kilston Down will simply never be happy.

"Let me first put your mind at ease that the candles we will use for the procession have all been checked. Furthermore, as we are outside in the fresh air, the police and Dr Steele feel that there is little risk to anyone."

This speech must have been extremely confusing to the visitors from outside the village. Talk of dangerous candles and an unknown tormentor weren't usual Christmas fare. Well, not until we got to the part of the evening when Sir Joseph read a ghost story, at least.

"Sergeant Keel and Constable Adams are on hand should anyone need their assistance, but I am sure that we will enjoy this congregation just as much as we do every year."

I turned to the back of the crowd to see the two police officers watching from the far pavement. There was more space there, and I noticed Alisha and Rodrick Steele standing with Gareth and his fiancée. The doctor wasn't saying anything, but nor did he look as if he wanted to murder his newly identified stepson. Gareth caught my eye and waved. I still felt guilty for saying that he was the killer, even if his name was all over the murder weapon.

Back on the raised step at the front of the bandstand, Mayor Perkins struck a match to light a candle like the ones I'd seen in the crowd. He moved forward, and Nora Tibbs lit her own from his and then turned to do the same to the one that a small child next to her was holding. Each new candle that flared into life would light three or four more, and the square was soon a sea of shimmering flames. It was at this point that our always prepared factotum produced six identical white candles from the inside of his long coat and passed them out among our friends and family.

The multiplying light reached our part of the square, and every face was aglow. It was not just the light that had changed; smiles bloomed to make the world a brighter place. And yet, as the mayor and Mrs Tibbs led the party towards the church, and we all fell in line behind them, I couldn't ignore a familiar sting of apprehension within me.

Even if it had been decided that the celebration should go ahead, it seemed foolish (or at least insensitive) to continue with the candle lighting, no matter how much I had been looking forward to this moment for months. The sheen of joy and positivity that the scene held felt superficial, and as we went on our usual route to the graveyard to bring light to the darkest part of the town, my thoughts were with the recent dead.

"How could I have missed it, Christopher?" Grandfather drew

alongside me to ask as Delilah threaded herself between us. "I fell for their trick. How could I have been so naïve?"

I was about to ask him what he meant when some children pushed between us with their candles raised skywards. When the crowd closed once more, we were divided by several people.

"It's lovely," our page boy Timothy said as we found ourselves walking together. "I've never seen anything like it."

Mother put her free hand on his shoulder and smiled down at him. Her heart was full of joy all year round, so I can only imagine it was overflowing at this moment.

Grandfather moved onto the raised bank of snow to the side of the path in order to move around the parade of people. There was no way I could get across to him; he was a row or two from the front of the group and seemed content to stay there.

I watched him from where I was, so it was a good thing he was one of the tallest people in attendance. He kept his eyes on the leading row and still looked nonplussed by whatever it was that had caught his interest.

The procession was, thankfully, a short one. It went from the square to the church, around the two residential roads, which the gate at the back of the graveyard gave on to, before returning to the bandstand where we had started. The candles were especially beautiful that year, and it was nice to think that people had held on to a tradition in the face of such sorrow, but that didn't make it any less scary. I kept thinking, *What if the killer is here and has brought his own candles from home?* It didn't help that the dark figure of Mr Marley, the phantom salter, trailed behind the group looking as ghoulish as ever.

Still, we made it back to the square without anyone inhaling poisonous chemicals, so that was a blessing. We came to a stop just as the band started up, and we all joined in with a local carol.

> **"Here comes poor Jack a-howling,**
> **And don't know what to say!**
> **Please give him a few ha'pence,**
> **And let him run away."**

The tuba took the lead and, somewhere out of sight, a large drum pounded on the offbeat.

"A pocket full of money
A cellar full of beer.
I wish you a merry Christmas
And a happy New Year."

There were cheers when the song finished, but I still couldn't get to my grandfather, who had ended up on the other side of the crowd entirely.

We all knew the running order for the night. A song would be followed by someone speaking, and the first of these diversions was the mummers' play that the tiptearers put on each year. There were six players in total, all in their bizarre costumes. One was dressed as a criminal, one as Old Father Christmas and then there were two knights and a judge. The knights fought a duel, and the judge sentenced the criminal to death before a man calling himself a doctor came in to heal the knights' wounds and give evidence on the condemned man's behalf. It finished with Old Father Christmas forgiving all those who had done wrong, including the judge himself.

That's right; it was a very strange piece of theatre, and I'd never quite understood what point it was supposed to make. Nonetheless, my fellow villagers cheered and booed as necessary, and we all enjoyed it for the nostalgic piece of entertainment from centuries past that it clearly was.

More concerning to me this year, however, was my grandfather. He barely moved the whole time that the actors were at work. He watched the play as though he wasn't seeing any of it, and when the end came, he cut through the audience to mount the stage just as the band was about to play a gypsy carol.

"I'm sorry to interrupt," he said in his most commanding voice as he turned back to address us. The same caution that I'd seen in him before we'd become separated was still evident, and he hesitated for a moment. "I really won't take up a great deal of your time, but I thought you should know that I've discovered who the killer is."

This brought the biggest reaction of the day so far. I'd never heard such loud gasps, which were amplified by the sheer number of people. This was only a taste of what was to come, though, as Grandfather had more to say.

"I will admit that you were terribly smart to go about things as you did, Mayor Perkins, but I finally saw through your game."

CHAPTER THIRTY-ONE

Once the initial reaction had died down, the crowd fell silent, and everyone strained to hear. There was even a little jostling at the back as certain interested parties pushed forward to listen. Miss Evans looked particularly curious to discover what had happened to her sister, and the front row was made up of various familiar faces from the town, with Mayor Perkins right in the middle and Nora Tibbs at his side.

As Grandfather spoke, I tried to put together the story that he had apparently already constructed.

"For those of you who don't know what's happened this week, Mayor Perkins's wife Ethel was found murdered this morning. At the time, he was in a cell in the police station, having admitted to killing Nigel Tibbs, his wife's lover who had died the previous day."

There was some loud discussion coming from the less local section of the crowd. They must have been quite appalled by all this, especially after a cloud of shushing wafted over in their direction. I didn't want to miss Grandfather's explanation, but I'd realised something significant and so I sidled over to Sergeant Keel to request a favour.

"I'm sorry to bother you, Sergeant. I need you to check someone's alibi before Lord Edgington finishes his speech."

He was an obliging fellow and, as Grandfather continued to accuse our former and now current main suspect of murder, the sergeant ran to the police station without the slightest complaint.

"The mayor was very convincing in his confession." Lord Edgington directed every word down at the killer. "It was clear to me that he really felt the guilt that he conveyed. And yet the information which he gave us to prove that he was responsible for the murder of Nigel Tibbs was later proven to be false. When I spoke to him before his arrest, he assured me that he had put the poison in a bottle of whisky that Mr Tibbs greatly prized. Though we didn't know it at the time, it is highly likely that each of the victims was killed with the fumes of a poisoned candle, a number of which have been sent to villagers this very day."

Grandfather was rooted to the spot at the front of the bandstand, and I must say that the band didn't look happy about the interruption.

The crowd, on the other hand, was rapt.

"While the possibility of Mayor Perkins confessing to a crime he had not committed entered my mind, I assumed he was protecting someone else. Indeed, when we discovered that Tibbs was killed by the candle – the remnants of which were visible in the room where he (and an unfortunate mouse) inhaled the venomous smoke – Perkins explained that it was his wife whom he wished to protect, as he believed that she was responsible for the crime. By that time, though, Ethel Perkins had met a similar fate to her lover, and so it seemed unlikely that she had been involved in the previous murder. This also meant that the mayor appeared to be off the hook for the two killings."

Another surge of noise rose and died back down again. His audience was clearly fascinated by the story, and just as eager to hear what came next.

"But what if he really had murdered Tibbs but lied about the details to get himself arrested and later freed? What if he was working with an accomplice to ensure that their two biggest problems were removed from this messy equation? If that were the case, he had provided himself with an alibi for the time when he knew that his wife would be slain."

Silence – true, unmistakable silence, the type you rarely get at large gatherings – took hold of the scene. Grandfather's cool grey eyes scanned the crowd before coming to rest on a woman in the front row. I had moved close enough to see her clearly, and I could just make out that her left hand was entwined in the mayor's.

"Nora Tibbs, you must have been tired of your husband making a fool of you. He ran around after Ethel Perkins like a puppy, and it's hardly surprising you should seek comfort in the arms of another man."

"Now steady on, Edgington," the mayor finally interrupted with far more indignation than he'd shown when it was his head on the chopping block. "Nora and I may be in love, but that doesn't mean we—"

Grandfather had heard enough and spoke over him. "I was right that you were protecting someone when you confessed to killing Nigel." He paused for a moment and timed the next line to perfection. "You were protecting yourself! You claimed to have seen Ethel and Nigel arguing, but that wasn't true, was it? You made that up to explain why you had given an apparently false confession. In fact, you were trying to rule out your own involvement."

The accused looked to his fellow villagers for support, but I doubted that it would do him much good. "I admit that I lied, but not to give myself an alibi. I lied to protect Nora. I knew that she and Nigel had been alone at home together before he died. I couldn't imagine anyone else having the opportunity to kill him, and I came to the wrong conclusion."

"There you have it, everyone. We must all believe the word of a self-confessed liar." My grandfather's often overblown delivery was, for once, free of melodrama. He was hard and serious in his speech, and I believe that he was a little appalled by the man. "I'm sorry, Mayor, but that isn't possible. You killed the two people who stood between you and your new lover. You killed her husband and Nora Tibbs did away with your wife."

His accomplice cried out in something approaching pain. She looked up at the sky, knowing that there really was no escape now. They must have believed that they'd planned the perfect murder. The mayor ruled himself out of the first killing, and it was widely accepted in the village that Nora didn't give a ha'penny about her vain, foolish husband in the first place.

The pieces all fitted together. Grandfather was just listing the final scraps of evidence that, come the court case in a few months' time, would secure the despicable killers' convictions when Sergeant Keel stepped from the police station and waved to get my attention.

I was so caught up in Grandfather's story that the interruption startled me. The sergeant stepped onto the low wall in front of the building to ensure that, when he gave the confirmation with a slow, solemn nod, I could see over the heads of my fellow Lord Edgington admirers.

I suppose I must have been stunned for a few seconds, as it took me that long to spur myself into action. I rudely pushed through the crowd and up the steps to the bandstand, breaking Grandfather's concentration so that his discussion of times and key discoveries was cut short. By the time I reached him, he had stopped talking altogether.

"Wasn't that wonderful, ladies and gentlemen?" I said in an artificially enthusiastic voice. "I know it's traditional to switch between music and speech tonight, but my grandfather simply couldn't wait to explain one potential solution to the recent rash of murders which our beautiful village has endured." This made it sound as if Kilston Down had suffered a nasty reaction to some stinging nettles, rather than a string of violent deaths.

"A round of applause for Lord Edgington and his most entertaining performance." I started clapping, even though everyone else was quiet. "Of course, my grandfather and I dismissed this fascinating theory when we discovered that our dear Mrs Tibbs was away at her sister's in Godalming at the time that the candle which killed Ethel was left at her house, not to mention the others that were sent this morning to Mrs Steele and Reverend Deacon."

There was a truly half-hearted patter of applause, and I pushed grandfather out of the way for the musicians to take our places. They seemed reluctant to move, and so I put my hand in my pocket to check that my book was there.

"I will be back shortly to read from Charles Dickens's 'A Christmas Carol'. So that will be nice," I said, because I had to do something. "And now, let's all enjoy 'The Cherry Tree Carol'."

I urged the band to play with a beseeching look, and they eventually started the song. The crowd slowly, somewhat uncertainly, began singing their part, and, by the end, it sounded like any other rendition. I could only imagine that people were still wondering what they'd just witnessed – none more so than Nora Tibbs who was crying into the mayor's shoulder.

Grandfather was just as confused. "What were you thinking, Christopher?"

I pulled him to the back of the stage before answering. "I was stopping you from making an enormous mistake. Didn't you hear that Nora Tibbs left the village yesterday afternoon and only came back around lunchtime?"

"How would I have heard that?"

"She was sitting at a table near ours in the teahouse."

He looked away, apparently dismissing the point. "Maybe it's another lie."

"I just asked the sergeant to call her sister in Godalming to confirm the time she was there. Unless her sister is also lying – and no one here saw Nora darting about the place delivering candles – which, I'm sure you'll admit, is beginning to sound improbable, I don't think that you picked the right killers. The mayor confessed to killing Nigel Tibbs to save his paramour, but he was in a gaol cell, and she was out of the village when several of the candles reached the victims."

There were obviously various ways around any of this – another accomplice, the candles delivered by an unwitting third party, the weapon being left in advance and only discovered later – but he could see just as I did that the case against his chosen culprits was no longer solid.

"I've been such a fool." He buried one hand in the palm of the other. I would have sympathised – if not contradicted him entirely – but he continued to lament the situation. "I was so eager to solve the case before everyone shut themselves away for Christmas that I failed to confirm every necessary detail." His expression would only turn graver. "You must believe me when I say that it was not out of vanity, Christopher. I wished only to prevent any further deaths."

I believed every word he said, of course, but there was no time to reassure him as the band had finished the carol, and I was called back to address the crowd.

Mayor Perkins did not look happy to see me. He stood with fists tightly formed, even as he patted Nora on the back. It was lucky that Grandfather was safely out of the way or punches might have been thrown. It was the first time he'd picked the wrong killer in the four years I'd been working with him. I could see now why he was normally so careful.

"So, ladies and gentlemen," I began, and then cleared my throat because the words came out hoarse. "Yes… My book is… As it happens, it's one of my favourite books. If you haven't read or attended a performance of this most redemptive of tales, then I really do recommend it… and strongly at that."

I looked at the faces peering up at me and wished that I had chosen a cheerier moment for a reading. Miss Evans looked particularly unimpressed that we had failed to pick the right culprit. My new-old friend Dean appeared confused by the whole thing and, at the back of the audience, Dr Steele was stern and silent, as though waiting to hear what I would say so that he could disagree with me.

I ignored them all and opened the book to the first page. I should probably have planned in advance which section to read. The Ghost of Christmas Present was my favourite and, had I been able to locate the scene easily, I would have skipped to the description of the Cratchit family's meagre, though much-appreciated, feast.

As the audience was already restless, I decided to start as soon as possible. "Everyone knows that Ebenezer Scrooge was 'a tight-fisted hand at the grindstone'. And if there is one quotation from the novel that any of you can recite, beyond a brief 'Bah, humbug!' or a 'God bless us, everyone', then it's surely that the miser was as 'solitary as an oyster.' He is a truly nasty figure at the centre of a tale that will never grow old, but the part that shocked me when I first read it as a child comes just after that famous passage."

I would have sounded a touch more confident had my brain not gone wandering off on a strange journey. As I'd started the address, a possibility had occurred to me, and I was only vaguely aware of what I was reading.

"Let me remind you that, 'External heat and cold had little influence on Scrooge. No warmth could warm, no wintry weather chill him. No wind that blew was bitterer than he, no falling snow was more intent upon its purpose.'

I paused to show that the quotation was complete. "The idea of this man not just being selfish, misanthropic and cruel hearted, but physically repellent to warmth of any kind was a frightening thought when I was eleven. The thought of never being able to shake off the cold of winter sounded like a curse from ancient mythology. But perhaps that was why I was so eager to witness his transformation. His greed is so great and his lack of charity so pernicious that only supernatural intervention can save him."

I waited to see whether people were still listening. To my surprise, they really were. They didn't look at me as some silly boy sputtering on about a book he liked. I believe they could tell just what the story meant to me, and they paid almost as much attention as they had to my grandfather.

"Of course, it is not really the four ghosts who help change Ebenezer Scrooge. He learns his mistakes through the people his visitors show him, but also through the season they represent. He sees what he has been missing, and it makes him want to be a better man. He realises just how precious a gift humanity can be because it has been absent from his life for so long."

214

I was rolling along nicely and didn't dare slow down. "As Dickens explains, 'Nobody ever stopped him in the street to say, with gladsome looks, 'My dear Scrooge, how are you? When will you come to see me?' No beggars implored him to bestow a trifle, no children asked him what it was o'clock, no man or woman ever once in all his life inquired the way to such and such a place, of Scrooge. Even the blind men's dogs appeared to know him; and when they saw him coming on, would tug their owners into doorways…"

I almost lost track of what I was reading then. A new and enticing possibility was ringing in my head, much as if someone had struck me with a huge beater from a dinner gong. I managed to reach the end of the paragraph, and I was fairly certain that, by this point, everyone understood what a rotter Scrooge was.

I took a deep breath before saying the hardest thing that I had to tell them. "We all make mistakes in life. I am no less guilty of that than anyone else. I sometimes have the tendency to judge people without knowing all the facts." I spotted Dean in the crowd at that moment, and he grinned up at me. "I can be immature, self-indulgent and I'm often impatient with my brother." Albert had earnt a smile of his own. "But what makes us good people is not a life free from all error and vice, but the ability to make up for the things we've done wrong."

I was aware that I had laid on the moralising a little too thickly, but I was ever so close to the point I was trying to make. "Of course not everyone accepts life's lessons with humility. Some people judge those around them because they genuinely believe that they are superior human beings. We don't all get a parade of ghosts to show us the error of our ways, and just imagine what Scrooge would have been like if he hadn't had the opportunity to change. Imagine what would have happened if his black soul was left to fester without correction. Would he have remained the same bitter, lonely person, or would he have become even worse?"

I allowed myself one last pause, one last look about that expectant crowd. I considered telling them what they all wanted to know but perhaps didn't expect to hear, but I'd learnt from Grandfather's mistake and changed my mind.

"So what I really wish to tell you is that, as we spend time with our families and loved ones tomorrow, we should spare a thought not just for the needy and downtrodden, but the cold of heart who will never know the joy we feel."

In the middle of the crowd, Mother hugged Father tightly, and Albert certainly looked moved by my soppy speech.

"Happy Christmas, everyone. I hope that every moment of it is filled with joy."

I closed the book and put it away in my pocket, then took my grandfather's arm to lead him from the stage. There was some polite applause, but I wasn't expecting anything more, and I was relieved when the band started playing "Away In a Manger".

"That was lovely, Christopher," Dotty told me, but it wasn't her that I needed. I threaded through the mass of huddled bodies and finally found the right person.

"Hello, Mr Scrooge," I said when I was just a foot away from her, and Lillibet Evans practically jumped out of her skin.

Turning to see who was whispering in her ear, she was immediately irate. "What are you babbling about now, you simpering fool?"

I was hoping to do this discreetly, but her loud voice had already caught the attention of those around us.

"You've looked down on your neighbours for decades, haven't you, Miss Evans?"

She stared back at me without saying anything.

"Even when I was a child, I remember how you and your sister acted as though you were the moral arbiters of the village. Did your superiority turn you to hate just as Scrooge's love of money drove him to solitude? Is that why you killed three people and tried to murder several more?"

216

CHAPTER THIRTY-TWO

Now, I know it's not a competition, but I'm fairly sure that the reaction this time was even louder than Grandfather's big moment. Of course, not everyone could hear me, so they didn't all groan or sigh, but those who were close enough certainly made their feelings known. There were not just gasps, but a few boos, and a definite hiss from Sir Joseph who threw down his tankard in disgust.

For his part, Grandfather stood perfectly still to hear me cut through the woman who had caused so much suffering.

"You, Miss Evans, are a miser who has never learnt her lesson. You condemn those around you and never question whether you are any better than they are. My grandfather, on the other hand, is a generous man. He gave me the opportunity to reveal who you really are and only described one of our theories that turned out to be wrong."

Surprisingly, it was the silence of the people listening that I believe caught the attention of the wider crowd. A space began to form around us, and I could tell that my audience was growing.

"Even if Nora Tibbs hadn't had an alibi and the mayor hadn't been in a cell when Ethel was killed, we discovered no reason for them to kill Mrs Steele, your sister, or any of the other people you targeted. You, meanwhile, as you so proudly told us, hate everyone."

Lillibet Evans was such a terribly proud woman that she wouldn't even deny my claims. If anything, she seemed to take them as a compliment, which made me dislike her all the more.

"Even this week, as we stood in the house where you'd murdered your sister for the sins you were so sure she had committed in her youth, you described the ways that various people in this village had done wrong. Mrs Perkins was an adulterer. Mr Tibbs: a foolish man led astray. You said the vicar was weak and indulgent of his parishioners, and I can only imagine that you saw Alisha Steele with young Mr Heywood and thought the worst of them – I suppose that is why you put his name on the candles that you sent out to kill your foes.

"You were frightened that someone might realise what you were doing, and so you even kept one at your house and spoke warmly of Gareth in order to deflect our suspicions onto him. I found it odd that you could be so forgiving of a young man who plays loud *modern* music. I'm sure the very idea is appalling to you."

No cries of anguish came back to me. Miss Evans didn't beg for mercy or explain her actions, and the longer this went on, the more convinced I became that my grandfather was about to do the very same thing that I had and point out a flaw in my argument.

But Miss Evans is allergic to wax, Christopher! She would never have killed with candles.

I became more nervous with every passing second, and this wasn't helped by the horrific gap-toothed smile on my chosen culprit's face.

"You are not the kind of person to whom anyone here would send a present," I told her. "You have a shard of glass in your eye and can only see the worst in people. Your hypocrisy is so great that you believe murder to be less of a sin than Ethel Perkins's unfaithfulness, or your sister's dalliance with a man fifty years ago."

This tipped her over the edge, and she barked out a response in her usual angry tone. "You blithering infant! You can say what you like about me, but that doesn't make me a killer. Has your grandfather never explained that you need evidence to convict a person of a crime?"

She was right, of course, and we didn't have a great deal, so I returned to the very first thought I'd had when we'd inspected her sister's cottage. "You had access to two of the houses where people died. You could have brought the candles into their homes to ensure that they would be used."

She bristled and stamped her feet one after the other. "Of course I brought them inside. I found the candles on their doorsteps. I was hardly going to leave them there with the weather we've been having."

It has to be her! I told myself to block out any other plaguesome thoughts. Everyone was watching me, and their previous wonder had turned to doubt. Even my family were muttering amongst themselves, but I concentrated on what I had to do.

It has to be her, I thought again. *No one else would have wanted all those people dead. She has to be the killer.* When we'd first considered her guilt, we hadn't known how the victims had been killed. I was sure that, somewhere in the largely empty and cavernous corridors of my mind, the evidence I needed was waiting to be found.

Grandfather looked at me, his expression grave, and I wondered how long it would be before he felt he had to interrupt.

"As a cleaner here in the village, you could go into people's houses and find out their secrets," I said to buy time until I could think of something more substantial. "You knew the worst of everyone, and it soured you against us."

"Facts, boy!" the despicable woman yelped, and it sounded just like something Grandfather would shout at me. "Where are your facts?"

I had imagined myself slowly moving closer to put my claims to her, but the opposite was true. Step by step, she made her approach, and the look on her face was one of pure spite.

"You..." I tried, but I suddenly felt rather hot despite the snow still decorating the trees around the square and on the pavements that hadn't been trampled on that day. "You..."

"Give up, boy." She was full of confidence as she jabbed me in the chest, and everyone I could see was pitying me. "You think that I must be a killer because I'm an old woman who speaks her mind? You think I'm wicked because I tell the truth?"

"No, it's not that," I wanted to contradict her, but it was all going wrong. "I'm... You see, I'm..."

Miss Evans turned to speak to the band. "Gentlemen, I think we've had enough talking. This was quite the diversion that the young lad put on for us, but perhaps you could play another song. I've always been partial to 'Mary Sat Weeping' if you happen to know it."

I looked across to my mother and father, who had both been so happy when we arrived there. Even my grandmother looked sympathetic, and she once told me, when I fell over as a child, that my scraped knee was a punishment from God for eating too many Scotch eggs.

I was breathing more heavily now, at a loss to know how to prove my case. I turned to my grandfather, but I'd made the same mistake he had and there was little he could do. He moved to put a comforting arm around my shoulders and was just about to address the crowd when a stream of triumphant words gushed from me.

"I'm so sorry, Lillibet, that you became not just the miser, but the misery of the village. You have had every chance to learn your lesson. You could have devoted your time to helping others, but instead you appointed yourself the judge, jury and now the executioner of Kilston Down."

Her face crumpled in that distinctive way of hers. She looked like she'd just mistaken a clove of garlic for a mint imperial. "Why are you blathering like that, boy? Are you too dim to realise that you've failed?"

"But I haven't," I said, stepping away from my mentor. "I know you're the killer. You knocked off your sister first, perhaps to see whether you could get away with it, or because you remembered what she did all those years ago and wanted to punish her. And when it was clear that no one – not even a great detective – had realised what you'd done, you decided to clean up the rest of the village."

She still wouldn't take me seriously but turned to my grandfather. "This boy hasn't a brain in his head! No doubt it's your fault for giving him ideas that he might one day make something of himself. People are forever trying to build up children's expectations when the world would be a much better place if we kept their feet nailed firmly to the ground."

"You missed my point, Miss Evans." A thrill passed through me as I knew that I'd finally got her. "I know you're the killer because you left a clue at the scene of the first murder."

Now she didn't answer me for another reason entirely; now she was scared.

"If Gareth Heywood really had sent candles to kill you and your sister, he wouldn't have put his name on them. But you needed something to confuse the evidence in case anyone worked out how the poison was administered."

"This is all tommyrot." Her mouth dropped open, but I doubt she'd worked out the significance of what I was saying. I imagine she hoped that I really was as stupid as she believed (and I sometimes claim to be).

"You kept going back to your sister's house in order to feed her cat and keep the place clean. The parlour where she died was spotless when we visited, but you left the remnants of a messy candle with the label on it in plain view because, if Maude's death was tied to that of Mr Tibbs and Mrs Perkins, you wanted the police to blame the upstart newcomer with his loud parties and modern habits instead of you."

"His type are ruining this village!" she yelled before she could control herself, and that's when I beat my grandfather (not that it was a competition). That's when the shock of the revelation was so great that every last person in earshot, whether they lived in Kilston Down or not, sucked in a noisy breath.

She turned to the crowd, not in search of sympathy or support, but to tell her neighbours that she was right, and the rest of the world was wrong. "The Ethel Perkins and Nigel Tibbs of this world are destroying our society. Good, old-fashioned English morals have gone out of the window, and all we are left with is—"

"Oh, do stop talking. You're a murderer, and nobody has any interest in what you think," I told her, because I was tired of her voice. "You've been telling us how terrible we all are for decades, but do you know the truth?"

She had turned into a particularly repulsive statue and waited for me to continue.

"The truth, Miss Evans, is that you are the worst person who has ever lived in Kilston Down."

CHAPTER THIRTY-THREE

There was drinking, dancing and a little delirium in the village that night, but not before Sergeant Keel locked up the killer in the police station. As terrible as it was that three people had died, I still found myself feeling sorry for the men who would have to put up with Lillibet Evans until she was transferred to the local prison. Just imagine the poor constable shut up with her on Christmas Day!

In no time at all, the right side of my body was sore from all the people who had come to shake my hand. Perhaps surprisingly, the mayor and Mrs Tibbs were most grateful of all, but I still thought it was good of my grandfather to offer a sincere apology.

"I really am very sorry." It is one of the few times that I can remember him looking so ashamed. "I honestly wouldn't have confronted the pair of you so publicly if I hadn't been confident that you were to blame."

"And...?" I said to prompt him.

His embarrassment had disappeared, to be replaced by mild annoyance at my impertinence. "And... I admit that I should have considered Christopher's point that, even if you had wished to kill your respective spouses, it would have done you little good to kill Miss Evans or any of the other people who received candles."

"And...?" I said, because I was enjoying the moment and hoped he might have something more to tell them.

"And that is all I have to say on the matter. Thank you, Christopher!"

Before the human-after-all detective could get any angrier, the mayor stepped forward to accept the apology. "Well, Lord Edgington, I appreciate you saying all that, and I admit that we were fools to carry on like children. Holding hands on the very same day that my wife was killed was a very silly thing to do, but I've been in love with Nora for over a decade. We weren't the type to get divorces, no matter what Ethel and Nigel did together, and I genuinely thought I was destined to live out my life in perpetual melancholy. When I realised that Nora really hadn't murdered anyone, and we could be together, I decided not to waste another second."

"I feel just the same way, my darling," the former Mrs Tibbs replied, and they put their foreheads together and looked one another deep in the eyes.

"I'm glad everything worked out for the best," Grandfather told them, though they were no longer paying attention. We moved to talk to the next group of people and, on the way, he said, "It's a good thing Lillibet Evans wasn't around to see that. She definitely wouldn't have approved."

I made the most of the opportunity and persuaded my grandfather to apologise to each of our other suspects in turn. We had a lovely conversation with the newly patched together Steele-Heywood family. Katherine and her future mother-in-law were already discussing the details of the wedding as Gareth and Dr Steele did their best to get to know one another in as short a time as possible.

When the festivities were winding down, and my family were ready to return to the manor, there was one person I still needed to see.

"You go ahead," I told them and, as our dog had been stuck to my side for much of the night, I decided that she wouldn't mind staying out a little longer. "I have Delilah to keep me company. I'll follow you shortly."

Ever the gentleman, Grandfather offered Granny his arm to navigate the icy route back to the house.

It didn't take me long to find Dean Henderson. He was sitting on the wall in front of the pub looking thoroughly frozen. "Sorry it took so long, old stick!" I told him in a voice that sounded quite different from my own. "Everyone wanted to talk to me, and I couldn't get away."

"That's all right." He was shier than usual and looked away. "What you did was truly impressive. Not only did you catch the killer, after all these years, someone finally stopped Young Miss Evans's nasty tongue."

"That was definitely one incentive." I tipped my head back to laugh and again didn't seem quite myself. Is this what growing up feels like? Do you eventually change so much that you no longer know how you're supposed to act or sound?

"I'm really glad she's where she belongs. If I had to pick a killer, I would have thought that creepy old fellow Mr Marley was to blame. It shows how good a detective I am."

There was an awkward moment then, and I didn't know how to change the subject to the thing I wanted to say. It was tempting to

224

forget all about it and go into the Holly Tree for a glass of mulled wine, but I persevered.

"Dean, you must let me tell you how sorry I am." It was definitely a night for apologies. "Practically every book I've ever truly loved talks about people's capacity to change, and yet I realise now that I've never applied those lessons in my own life. Especially since I've started working with my grandfather, I've come to view everyone as either good or evil, and I rarely consider people's capacity to flit between the two."

"I don't think I was ever quite that bad," he said with a half-smile. "Well, not to you, at least."

"That's just it. I based my whole opinion of you on two or three memories from when we were still just children. I should have kept an open mind, and that's why I want you to have this."

I reached into my pocket and pulled out my copy of 'A Christmas Carol'.

I'm not sure he knew what to make of it. "Oh... an old book. How kind."

"It's not just any old book. It's one of my favourites, and I know you'll enjoy it."

He studied the green leather cover with its embossed holly design and blew his fringe from his eye before replying. "That really is very kind, Christopher. I'm sorry I haven't got anything for you."

My half-smile became a whole. "You sent me a candle. That was plenty." I immediately had second thoughts. "Though you could buy me a drink, as I think I've left home without my wallet."

He laughed and punched me on the arm. "Come along then. Let's go."

He put his hand on my back to push me towards the inn, but there was still one thing that I needed to say.

"I am very happy that we get the chance to be friends, but I must admit that I don't understand why you went so far with your wheelbarrow to get snowballs when there is literally snow everywhere at the moment."

He looked a little mysterious, but then the door opened, and Sir Joseph shuffled past singing a rude song. As the light from inside the building hit Dean, he shrugged. "I'm a curious fellow, Christopher.

You should probably know that about me."

I ushered him ahead of me, uncertain at first how to respond. "Well… that will surely make for a far more interesting evening."

CHAPTER THIRTY-FOUR

Ever since we were tiny, my brother and I have had a Christmas Day tradition. We wake up early and pad downstairs as quietly as possible so that Mother and Father don't hear and tell us to go back to bed. If we make it through this first challenge, we are free to enter the Christmas room.

We like nothing better than to light the candles on the tree and sit in their glow. Sometimes, we'll pick up the presents and see if we can guess what they are just from their weight. Of course, Mother can always tell if anything has been moved so, more often than not, we just explore them with our eyes.

I wasn't sure that Albert would be in the mood to continue this practice after the last conversation we'd had, but, in the end, he was the one to wake me. We tiptoed out of my room, carefully avoiding the creaking floorboard on the landing. We took two stairs at a time to make less noise and, on seeing that Delilah was asleep at the bottom, I believe that we both held our breath to avoid waking her.

When we reached the doors to the rear salon, we both put our hands out to open them, and what we saw inside was truly... disappointing.

Uncle Thomas and Uncle Terry were in the armchairs on either side of the fire, snoring away loudly.

"What should we do now?" I silently mouthed to my brother.

"I don't know," he replied. "Dogfish cluster-cup sunbeam?" I've never been particularly good at lipreading.

Before we could make a decision, Terry gave a sudden start, which woke up his notoriously big-eared brother. So then we were stuck.

Terry blinked a few times to make sense of the intrusion before presumably recognising us. "Good morrow, young fellows, and a happy Christmas to you both."

"Yes, all that and more," Thomas added.

"You know, I can still remember being your age. I was already a one with the ladies. In fact, the first girl I ever loved lived right here in Kilston Down. We used to come here for holidays to visit a wonderful old uncle of ours, and I can still feel the young wench's lips on mine as if it were yesterday." He started rubbing his hands together enthusiastically at this point, and I tried not to listen to another word he said by singing 'Here We Come a-Mumping' over and over in my head.

Albert looked as though he wanted to dive through the window to escape, and then the whole extended family came traipsing downstairs, talking of what light sleepers they were and questioning why anyone would make such a lot of noise so early on Christmas Day. I felt like a prisoner in my own home. They didn't even wait until everyone was there to open their presents but simply passed them out and then moaned about whatever it was they'd been given. I noticed that the servants were keeping to the kitchen once more, and I didn't blame them one bit.

Finally, my parents, grandmother and grandfather could hide no longer and came downstairs in time for a light breakfast that Todd brought up on his own to save his colleagues from having to deal with the monstrosities who were ruining my Christmas.

"It's a perfectly nice cardigan, Loelia," Thomas said when he unwrapped the present that his sister had bought him, "except for the colour, the cut and the material."

"I'll tell you who looked good in a cardigan," Terry began, and I once more tried to block my ears without being seen to do so. Sadly, I had no beeswax to hand, or I would have popped behind the sofa and done the job.

As I was thinking this and singing "Jingle Bells" over and over in my head, Grandfather watched the two uncles very closely.

"That's not the first time you've mentioned a young lady you used to know in this village, Terry." His eyes became two paper-thin slits, and I wondered what he was about to do to the man. It was difficult to feel sorry for my unpleasant great-uncle, but my grandfather could be quite cruel when his ire was pricked. "I believe that you said you met her in 1878?"

Terry had completely misinterpreted Grandfather's tone and emitted a vulgar, *Wahhhaa.* "I'll say! I don't recall her name, but I remember exactly how she—"

"In 1878, Maude Evans was sent away from her home for a year after she'd been carrying on with a young man of aristocratic stock."

He still didn't recognise the look of fury on his interrogator's face. "Evans! That was it! Or was it Smith? It was certainly a common name. She was nothing special in terms of breeding, but get her behind the post office, and I'll tell you—"

Grandfather shouted this time so that there could be no doubt in his meaning. "Everything that has happened here this month is down to you."

Terry's face turned as white as the curtains. "Now, hold on, Edgington. I don't know why you would say such a thing."

"You took an innocent, underprivileged girl and robbed her of her dignity. Lillibet Evans grew up hearing of her sister's indecency after Maude was sent away from home to give birth to your child in secret."

"My child?" He gazed around the room in horror.

My grandmother, meanwhile, couldn't believe her luck and watched her brother being taken down a peg or ten with unchecked joy on her face.

Grandfather's criticism kept coming. "I don't think I'm going too far to say that, if it weren't for what you did to her sister, Lillibet might never have become the cruel, judgemental person that she is, and three people in this village wouldn't have been murdered."

"Sorry," Thomas said as though he were waking up from a short nap – which, now that I think of it, is more than possible. "Who's been murdered?"

Grandfather stood up from his chair. His every movement was controlled by the anger he felt, and I'm surprised he didn't end up belting the man. "My daughter and her husband are too polite to say anything, so I'll do it on their behalf. We would all like you to leave this house and never cast your shadow here again, unless you wish me to take out a notice in The Times to explain to anyone who sees it just what a rotten person you are."

Terry was up on his feet in a second. "Now, now. There's no need for any of that." His family couldn't quite believe what was happening and, to a man, appeared to have frozen where they were.

"And the rest of you can join him!" Grandfather threw both hands forward as if to shoo away a flock of persistent sheep.

Aldrich, Philippa and all the abhorrent cousins looked quite bamboozled but eventually drifted from the room.

"I haven't had any crumpets yet." Thomas complained. "I don't like travelling without a good breakfast."

"Out!" Grandfather practically yelled the word, and they began to move a little faster. "No, not upstairs. We'll send on your possessions after Christmas. Leave this house this instant before I do something I regret."

Even my parents were amazed at this, but no one would say another word until the front door had slammed shut and the house fell quiet. I listened as Grandfather stomped back down the corridor towards us. He came to a stop in the doorway and transformed in an instant.

"Loelia," he said, his eyebrows high on his forehead as he looked across the room at Granny, "Happy Christmas."

"You wonderful man," she replied, unable to believe what had just happened. "That is quite the nicest present anyone has ever given me."

"Well, they were rather irritating. I had to think of some way to get rid of them."

"You don't mean…" my father began, and when he couldn't find an end to that sentence, my brother tried instead.

"You don't mean that you made it all up? About the killer and her sister and everything else?"

Grandfather went to put his hand on Albert's shoulder. "My dear grandson, I can honestly tell you that, short of a few coinciding dates and the presence of the two of them in this village at around the same time, I have no evidence that Maude Evans and your great-uncle ever knew one another."

"And the abandoned child?" Mother asked. "How did you know that Maude was pregnant?"

"We don't," I replied on his behalf. "In fact, it's unlikely that she was."

Grandfather smiled. The smile became a grin, and the grin was soon erased as he'd started to laugh. "Oh, Terry's face was a picture!"

"It really was." Granny rose to offer her arm to one of her favourite adversaries. "This is the first Christmas I can remember when one of my brothers got what he deserved."

They looped around one another like drunken sailors, and I had a request of my own to make. "Can we start again now?"

Mother was a little startled by the sight of her mother-in-law and father getting on so well. "I beg your pardon, Chrissy?"

"Can we start this day again but do it better this time?"

CHAPTER THIRTY-FIVE

Ever since we were tiny, my brother and I have had a Christmas Day tradition. We wake up early and pad downstairs as quietly as possible so that Mother and Father don't hear us and tell us to go back to bed.

And this time, now that the rubbish had been cleared away, the unopened presents were back where they belonged and there were no longer two abhorrent prigs snoring in the armchairs, everything was perfect. Even before we opened the door, the smell of pine needles, cinnamon and a burning log curled up into our nostrils. And when we entered the salon, the only living being in there was our sleepy dog in front of the fireplace.

We sat, exactly as we had planned to, imagining what each present might contain. And after ten minutes chatting away like this, Albert suddenly changed the topic.

"I'm sorry, Christopher," he said as we sat on the floor next to one another with our backs against the sofa. "I really appreciate your invitation, but I won't come with you to France or Italy or wherever you end up going." He paused and I could tell it was hard for him to say any of this. "All that... well, it's your adventure, and I think it's time I found my own."

"That sounds like a wonderful idea, Albert." There was a slight itching sensation at the back of my throat, and I was having trouble expressing myself. "But if you change your mind, you'll always be welcome to join us."

Before he could say anything more, we heard footsteps on the stairs, and then our parents and grandparents came to share the thoroughly decorated room with us.

"I never imagined there could be such a thing as too many paper snowflakes," Granny said in a tone that was both impressed and bemused, "but you've certainly proved that it's possible, Albert. Well done."

"Come along, everyone," Mother said to get the day started in earnest. "It's time to open our presents."

She set to work passing out boxes and packets, packages and bags. Because she likes to spoil us, and she knows that part of me wishes to be twelve years old forever, I had a stocking full of small toys with everything from tin soldiers and whistles to a squeaking duck, a train driver's hat and decidedly – after what had happened when I was nine years old – decidedly no toy gun.

Granny gave me some brown slippers – people are forever giving me slippers – and Albert bought me some grey ones. Mother bought me some nice festive red slippers, but if the truth be told, it was hard enough to pretend I was happy the first time. All I could say was, "Slippers always come in handy!" and I didn't like to mention that I now had enough of the blasted things for each of my fingers and toes to have a pair.

There was a surprise to come, though, as I was about to find out why Father had been so concerned about the package he'd been expecting.

He handed me a box and looked unusually keen to see my reaction. Normally, he left presents and affection and that sort of thing to my mother, so I removed the red and white paper carefully, in case some spring-loaded snakes were to jump out at me. I'm relieved to say that is not what happened.

"They're Prism binoculars," he told me as I knelt in front of the tree, inspecting the gift he'd chosen. "I read up on which are the best ones, and from what I understand, these are rather good. I had to order them especially from Deraisme in Paris."

I didn't know what to say, and so I said nothing.

"I know how much you like birds but thought they might also be useful when you go abroad. You can look at all those wonderful landscapes and…" He searched for his words then. "I thought you might think of us back home when you use them."

I still didn't know what to say, so I threw my arms around him and squeezed him as tightly as I could. I certainly didn't feel like crying at the thought of being so far from home for an indefinite period.

In time, I patted him on the back in manly fashion and, clearing my throat because it had become dry, said, "Thank you, Father. It is a very thoughtful gift."

There were no cries from the kitchen that morning. I even heard Henrietta and Maggie chortling away together, so it seemed that the removal of our unwanted guests had helped to heal wounds. The staff came upstairs for a glass of sherry, and my mother and grandfather distributed their Christmas envelopes.

232

"Sadly, we've got too much food now that your relatives had to leave," Grandfather told his son-in-law. "It would be a real shame to see it go to waste, and the table in the dining room is already laid for sixteen."

"What a wonderful idea, Father," Mother took over when her husband failed to take the hint. "Of course the staff should share Christmas dinner with us."

There were cheers from many, protests from our footman Halfpenny – who saw such mixing of the social strata as tantamount to immorality – but everyone soon got used to the idea, and we all (except for my Granny, of course – she has her limits!) did what we could to help get ready for lunch.

When everything was prepared, Grandfather took me to one side to have a word.

"Christopher, if I haven't already done so, I must say thank you." He put one finger to his chin and clearly needed to consider how to phrase what he wanted to say. "You saved me from embarrassment last night because I'd become focused on identifying the cleverest solution to the crime rather than the most likely."

His manner was so genuine that, in a moment, I felt terribly grateful for all he'd done for me. I would have responded, but he held up one hand to make me wait.

"You have often criticised me for treating our investigations as games that must be won. And although I may forget this lesson before long, you are quite right. Our work together is my favourite hobby, even more than painting or fishing or tying flies. I adore clashing heads with worthy opponents, and that is why I was so keen on the idea of the scheming mayor being behind the killings – despite the fact that Maude Evans's death would have done him no good, and he was locked up in a cell at the time his wife was murdered."

"You have no reason to apologise," I told him. "You only did what I've done countless times myself. You got carried away with the emotion of the investigation and said something that you hadn't taken the time to consider carefully enough."

He hid his lips within his mouth for a moment, as though to conceal just how angry he was with himself. "That's exactly it, Christopher. I failed to live up to the example I've tried to set you. I ignored precedent and best practice, and I should have known better."

We were standing in front of the window in the dining room and, just before I spoke, a rush of snow tipped down from the roof above. "You don't have to be perfect, Grandfather. You're already very close."

I could see that he had never considered this a possibility before, and I felt he would have liked me to elaborate when Todd called us all into the dining room. The other members of our party arrived in their best attire, and Grandfather took his place at the top of the table.

We ate Sussex dumplings in lamb's broth, roast widgeon in a redcurrant sauce, quail, venison, goose and pheasant cutlets. Of course, I was very reasonable with all of those rich dishes, because I knew what we were having for dessert. When our two cooks pulled the Christmas plum pudding up to us on the dish lift, a great cheer went up around the room, and my tummy rumbled.

After the main part of the meal was complete, my favourite lordly sleuth decided to make a toast. "Not aiming for perfection, eh?" he whispered to me before he began. "You know, I rather like that idea."

"Get on with it, Edgington," my actually very lovely but equally outspoken grandmother ribbed him. "If you're not careful, the New Year will arrive before we can retire to the sitting room."

"Thank you, Loelia." He peered down his nose ever so snootily, and she would say nothing more. "You will be pleased to know that I plan to keep this speech short. But as this may be the last Christmas we all spend together for some time, I feel there is something I should say."

He took a deep, solemn breath through his nostrils before continuing. "Christmas is a time for family... but not the whole family. In fact, it's really only for the relatives we genuinely like – and, when there aren't enough of them, loyal staff and beloved friends make a highly suitable alternative. Ahh, I seem to have contradicted myself. Perhaps I should start again." He raised his glass and, with his wicked smile on display, he winked across the table at me. "This is the time of year not to suffer fools or put up with terrible bores. So Happy Christmas, everyone. Let's make the very most of it."

The End (For Now...)

And a very Happy Christmas, whoever and wherever you are,
From Benedict, Marion, Amelie and Osian

Get another

LORD EDGINGTON ADVENTURE

absolutely **free**…

Download your free novella at
www.benedictbrown.net

"LORD EDGINGTON INVESTIGATES **ABROAD**"

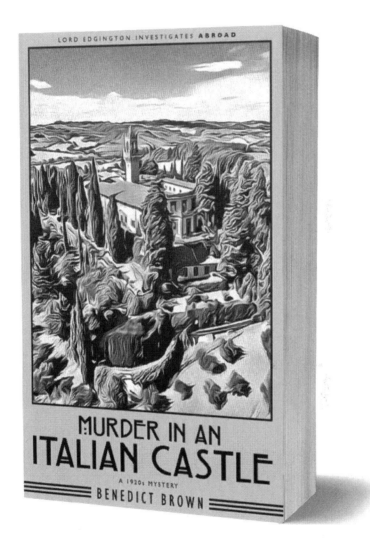

The story continues in book one of "Lord Edgington Investigates **Abroad**", available **spring 2025**. Follow me on Amazon to find out when it goes on sale.

ABOUT THIS BOOK

Another Christmas, another Benedict Brown Christmas book. I must admit, as this is now my fifth (plus a novella), I worry about running out of nostalgic memories upon which I can draw, but I've still got plenty for the moment. All of Chrissy's traditions are, of course, mine and my family's, and a love for this time of year remains strong within both of us.

Unlike Chrissy, I do understand that not everyone loves or even celebrates Christmas, but some of my regular readers have told me that they still appreciate these books despite that. I hope that is the case, even if I have cranked the Christmassiness up to eleven in this book. By taking Christopher home to Kilston Down – a fictional village which has been mentioned regularly since the first book in this series – I could have him reflect more on why the season is so important to him and view it from his increasingly adult perspective. Like most of us when we reach adulthood, he is coming to see that the simple things he has enjoyed throughout his life really aren't so simple after all.

A particular influence for me in this book was the year when I tried to make a perfect Christmas even though no one else seemed too bothered about it. I came home from university a few days before the twenty-fifth only to find that no one in my family had thought to buy the tree or get decorations down from our barely accessible loft. Like Albert, I hardly slept for decorating and wrapping presents but managed to get everything done in time. When I descended from my bedroom on Christmas morning, our front lounge provided that magical glow that I remembered from my childhood, and it was all worthwhile.

I have tried to create special Christmases for my two children, Amelie and Osian, to provide them with future sources of nostalgia. Of course, Amelie is far too cerebral to truly embrace my childlike wonder. By the age of three, she was expressing her doubt about the existence of Father Christmas, mainly because she felt it would be too difficult to hide in the North Pole, but the flying reindeer and near-omnipotence also presented problems.

I dress up as the jolly red man for a party we have every year and, though I don't consider myself a particularly convincing Father Christmas, I still try my best to inject some wonder into the performance for my friends' kids' sake. To this end, a few years ago, I slunk off to get changed when no one was looking and then went around the house to knock on the back door, near where everyone was assembled. As I entered in my elaborate costume, a couple of the older kids stared at me wide-eyed, whereas then two-year-old Amelie shouted, "It's just Daddy!" I hope to have better luck with her little brother.

With this book, I did want to show the trickier side of Christmas and the effort that goes into making this immense production a reality – even if the Cranley-Prentiss family have the luxury of an inordinate number of employees to do the hard work. I recently heard someone describe preparations for Christmas as a piece of collective theatre into which a large part of the population enter, and it is certainly a curious phenomenon. I'm sure that a lot of weddings require less organisation than Christmastime in Britain, America and many homes across the world. That's probably why the build-up to the twenty-fifth of December is often the most treasured part. With all the effort and excitement that goes before, it is hard for the far-too-short day itself to live up to expectations.

Like Chrissy, I must be very difficult to buy for as I almost always end up with socks – I just had a quick look, and I have at least a hundred pairs. In defence of my beloved wife, she also got me a lot of plain t-shirts last year, so that was fun. As it happens, I could do with some slippers this time around, but as I insist on my gifts being a surprise, and no one ever knows what I want, I'm resigned to the fact that I'll have to buy some myself in January. Coincidentally, just after I'd written the joke about Chrissy always getting slippers, I searched for an unrelated term in the British Newspaper Archive and immediately came across a large advert from 1926 which says, "The Perfect Gift is Slippers". I'm not sure Christopher would agree.

I'm happy to say that I don't have such awful relatives as those on Christopher's father's side. I know plenty of people who cannot say this, and one of the true wonders of Christmas is that, more often than not, people manage to put aside their differences to get along. I'm not

240

saying that my brother Daniel and I never had screaming arguments on Christmas morning, but by the time dinner was ready, we'd normally patched things up – and I'm happy to admit that we now get on much better than when we were kids. In fact, my favourite Christmas ever was the time that we had a large party of my cousins, aunts and uncles from Wales there to celebrate with us.

Partly because of my connection to the Land of Song, another thing that had a big influence on this book was Dylan Thomas's beautiful short story "A Child's Christmas in Wales". If you don't already know it, you can find this evocative and lyrical text to read for free online. It's another gift I have received often over the years, and I believe I had four different copies of it until I started subtly regifting them. It is a nostalgic look back at childhood by Wales's most famous poet. I was particularly drawn to it as Thomas was born in 1914, just a few years after Chrissy, so his recollections fit very closely with the imagery I wanted to have in this book. It is also interesting to me as my grandmother Gwen was born just a year later, and thirty-five miles away from him, so reading the book is like having a peek into Christmas as my Nana would have experienced it.

The short story is full of the scents and scenes of a 1920s Christmas. I think the closest similar account I've come across must be Jean Shepherd's writing that inspired the movie "A Christmas Story", as both accurately capture the perspective of a child and our nostalgia for times past. There are other important Welsh influences in the book, which I'll go into in the next chapter, but I also wanted to ground the story in the place where it's set.

Over the course of the twentieth century, the celebration of Christmas has become quite homogenised in the western world. Even the name Father Christmas, which was more common when I was a child, has been overtaken by Santa Claus, but it wasn't so long ago that every region in Britain would have had its own traditions. Surrey was no different, and a lot of the customs that I included were still common in the twenties. The exceedingly odd mummers' play was already old-fashioned by that time and would soon die out, but it added a curious extra touch to the final scenes.

Groups of mummers would go from town to town over the twelve days of Christmas to perform long-established pieces of theatre, always with the same stock characters such as doctors, knights and judges. Father Christmas, St George and Robin Hood also frequently appeared, and such plays helped maintain their myths through the course of the centuries. The tradition can be traced right back to 1296 and, though it almost died out in the mid-twentieth century, it has since been revived by local groups in various areas. Interestingly, the players were known as mummers in the north of Surrey and tiptearers in the south. Kilston Down is in the middle, so I used both!

One thing I noticed when looking at forgotten English traditions is that many of them revolved around begging. There was St Thomas's Day on the 21st of December, when children could go "Thomasing" around the houses to ask for food, drink or coins. Gooding was a similar practice, and across England there were different words for it including, Mumping, Corning, Doleing, Washaeling, Christmasing and Gathering. And of course, in addition to all that, the one that continues is carolling. As we've seen before in these pages, many carols from the time were really pleas for a treat in exchange for a song. I searched out carols that were local to Surrey and found an excellent book from 1911 called "Old Christmas Carols of the Southern Counties", and many of the lesser-known songs included this time around are found there.

Under several of them, I found the attribution "Surrey Gypsies' Carol", and it's interesting that many of these songs were maintained by traveller communities before academics came to collect and collate them. In fact, Alice E. Gillington, the folklorist who wrote that book, bought a caravan and lived among gypsies for much of her life in order to write about their songs and customs. I also found it interesting that one of the songs in the book, which is described as a Surrey Girls' Carol, begins, "We are not daily beggars,/That beg from door to door!/We are but little children/Whom you have seen before!" So clearly this behaviour was not tolerated all year, just as we would now find it strange to open the door to trick-or-treaters in June.

Kilston Down doesn't actually exist, but if you look on a map of Surrey, you'll see where it's supposed to be. It's just next to the real hamlet of Friday Street, right on the edge of the Surrey Hills. I've used some of the real geography of the place, but Kilston Down itself is made to my specifications. The scene of Chrissy sledging and the frozen river was inspired by the picture at the front of this book, which shows a scene from Hampstead in London in 1926 when locals made the most of the frozen river. As an excellent skater, it is my wife's dream to skate on a frozen lake one day, though I don't think there's much hope of that this year in Spain.

I should probably warn anyone with a fictional time machine to avoid Surrey altogether in 1928. In the space of a year, my books have now described a grand total of fourteen murders in my home county, plus plenty of near misses. Of course, this figure is improbably high. I found in the parliamentary record from 1924 that there were only 105 cases of murder in the whole country that year. Interestingly, just fourteen people were actually sentenced for murder, with a further seventeen deemed insane. That's about a thirty per cent chance of solving a case, so clearly the 1920s were crying out for Lord Edgington. I have a feeling that, if I had him solve a murder only once every few books, you would all stop reading them!

For a more realistic view of a Surrey Christmas in the twenties, search for the video "1922 Christmas Shopping, Godalming" on YouTube. It's a wonderful portrait of a small shopping town from the era, and I loved seeing the incredible windows of stationers, butchers and confectioners chock-full of goods. The packed double-decker omnibus at the end found its way into my story, too.

I can now reveal that, in the new year, Lord Edgington, Christopher and an undoubtedly extensive entourage will be shooting off to the Continent for "Murder in an Italian Castle". I'm calling it the first book in the new "Lord Edgington Investigates **Abroad**" series, but it will be a direct continuation of this one. I'm just hoping that new readers are more likely to give book number one a try over book number sixteen, and at the same time crossing my fingers that none of my existing readers think they can now abandon me!

I should finish by mentioning that Dylan Thomas's father studied a degree in English literature at Aberystwyth university, just like a certain murder mystery novelist that you all know. So perhaps one of my children will go on to write a seminal Christmas text. "A Child's Christmas in Burgos" has a certain ring to it. Now all I have to do is provide the timeless festive memories to inspire such literary endeavours. Best of luck with that, Ben.

SPOILER! Skip this if you haven't read the book! Right, now that those weirdos have gone, I can discuss the murder weapon. If I wanted to hide it, I probably shouldn't have called this book "The Christmas Candle Murders" but we learn from our mistakes. There don't seem to have been any cases in which people have been killed by candle, but this M.O. has featured in a Sherlock Holmes and an Edgar Allen Poe story, which I hadn't read until I wrote this book. There are also cases of people being accidentally poisoned by candle because they included lead wicks. Arsenic is definitely lethal in gas form, so the key factor to an arsenic candle would be the space and ventilation in the room. Assuming that the victim drifted off and so wasn't alarmed by the smell or toxicity, I think it's fairly realistic. And, if not, then, oops!

As it is tasteless and odourless, thus easy to administer, arsenic is really known as the king of poisons. It has a fascinating history, and I'd once more recommend Kathryn Harkup's excellent "A is for Arsenic: The Poisons of Agatha Christie" for a good overview. What I found most surprising was that, having been used by the rich for centuries – especially by Italian nobility like the Borgias – an easy way of extracting the poison was discovered by scraping chimneys of metal factories. This meant that the dastardly poison was suddenly available to all, and as arsenic was still difficult to detect, there were famous cases where people literally got away with murder. Which is not a pleasant thought.

If you loved the story and have the time, please write a review at Amazon. Most books get one review per thousand readers so I would be infinitely appreciative if you could help me out.

THE MOST INTERESTING THINGS I DISCOVERED WHEN RESEARCHING THIS BOOK...

No faffing about this time. It'll take me a day to write this and just as long to record and edit it for the audiobook, so let's get down to work.

I've already described the research I did on the county of Surrey where the book takes place, but I found out a lot of other interesting things about Christmas in days of yore. The festivity we recognise today would have been very different before the nineteenth century, when Queen Victoria's husband Prince Albert imported the German-style celebration to Britain. While there would not have been trees, decorations, cards and the like before then, if we jump back another two hundred years, there was a period when Christmas was forbidden altogether.

It wasn't Oliver Cromwell himself who did this, but it was the Puritanical movement of which he was a part that moved to restrict a festival which they saw as hedonistic and Catholic. Cromwell became the Lord Protector of the Commonwealth of England, Scotland and Ireland in 1653, but already a decade before that, shops were forced to remain open in London at Christmas and soldiers could confiscate food from anyone they believed to have been preparing a feast of celebration.

In 1643, an ordinance recommended that the not-so-festive time of year should be spent in "remembrance (of) our sins, and the sins of our forefathers, who have turned this feast, pretending the memory of Christ, into an extreme forgetfulness of him, by giving liberty to carnal and sensual delights'. The following year also saw a ban placed on celebrating Easter and Whitsun. Perhaps unsurprisingly, these measures did not go down well. Over the course of the 1640s, the rules became increasingly draconian and the resistance more creative. People took issue with shopkeepers who opened on the no-longer-a holiday. Despite the ban, brave souls would decorate public places and, on Christmas Eve, the night before parliament was to sit, carollers gathered outside the houses of politicians to keep them up all night with their songs.

In 1647, this festive rebellion turned deadly. Riots broke out in Bury and Norwich and, in Ipswich, things got so violent that a man, coincidentally called Mr Christmas, was killed in a fight. Meanwhile, protestors in Canterbury managed to take control of the whole city. This rebellion was a forerunner to the hostilities of the second English Civil War, which preceded the execution of Charles I.

Although some people continued to celebrate in secret, and there is a pamphlet from 1652 called "The Vindication of Christmas" which describes how a ferryman on the Thames maintained the tradition, Christmas was not reinstated until 1660 when Charles I's imaginatively named son Charles II returned to England and the throne.

"The Vindication of Christmas" is also interesting as it describes already ancient traditions such as roasting apples, feasting, carolling, dances, games and Old Father Christmas, who had been around long before the myth became connected with Saint Nicholas and then Santa Claus. I'm tempted to mount a protest to restore some of these typically British traditions, but I'm far too busy writing whodunits for that.

Funnily enough, Christmas was not officially restored in Scotland until 1958, but Hogmanay was a bigger deal there anyway. Something that was never un-forbidden was eating Christmas pie on Christmas Day. Puritans banned the pie because it often featured pastry depictions of the baby Jesus, and apparently the rule was never taken off the books in England.

Hold the press! According to most other sources, this is just an urban myth. Internet! You've let me down again!

One of the most significant parts of a modern Christmas – that of gift-giving – was originally more common at New Year. With the shift to focusing on the family, as promoted not just by Queen Victoria's picture-perfect example but books like "A Christmas Carol", presents became more popular at Christmas. It wasn't until the 1870s that wrapping paper was used and, if you look at any Christmas card before this period, you'll see unwrapped rocking horses, skipping ropes, and tin soldiers under the tree, which does take some of the mystery away. On one museum website I looked at, they listed beer as a popular present for children, and I have to hope they didn't get carried away.

I've looked into the history of Christmas crackers in a previous book, but one thing I didn't know about them was that they were also known as "cosaques" because the noise they made was said to sound like a Russian Cossack's whip. As for electric Christmas lights, they first appeared as a replacement for candles in the late nineteenth century. The vice president of the Edison Electric Light Company had special lights made for his tree at home on Fifth Avenue in New York in 1882. This caught the attention of the national press and other businesses copied his example. However, it wasn't until half a century later that the lights would spread to homes, as until then they were too pricy for the average person to afford.

The world's two most famous trees at Rockefeller Center and Trafalgar Square have had electric lights since 1954 and 1947 respectively. The London Daily News that first year explained, "When the lights go up in Trafalgar Square at Christmas, London children will have a glimpse of fairy tale glamour. They will see, against the background of Nelson's Column, a Christmas tree, 45 feet high, ablaze with coloured fairy lamps." I was surprised to discover that the expression *fairy lights* dates back to 1722. That was long before electrical appliances, of course, and originally referred to phosphorescent light, much like Will-o'-the-wisp, which can be found hovering over marshes. By 1839 it had come to be used for decorations, though presumably referred to candles at this point. There is an entry in the OED from 1857 which even describes them hanging on a Christmas tree: "The Lilliputian fir-tree, with its fairy lights, its glittering gifts, its joyous circle of visitants, all have, of late years, become so familiar to us in our own land..."

Another key element of the season, Old Mr Kringle himself, hasn't changed too much since the nineteenth century, however, I wanted to know what Father Christmas would have looked like to Children in the twenties. It's accepted that a lot of our imagery of the figure comes from the 1823 poem "The Night Before Christmas" by Clement Clarke Moore and the drawings of the illustrator Thomas Nast sixty years later. Until Nast came along, he was as likely to be green – the more traditional colour of the English folk character "Old Father Christmas – as red, which is why Old Miss Evans pictures him in green. Of course, it's hard to say how quickly the drawings of the American journalist had much impact in Britain, but by 1921 there is a full-colour advert for Twink soap and dye, which describes the "traditional scarlet robe of Father Christmas", and all public appearances of the big man from the time describe him in red. So the idea that we only have a red Santa because of Coca Cola – who started using him for adverts in the thirties – is something of an urban myth.

I mentioned that there is a marked Welsh influence in this book, and I looked into Christmas customs in my mother('s)land in quite some depth. My grandparents, who lived in a mining valley, did not speak much Welsh and perhaps didn't have the most traditional upbringing, so it's possible they wouldn't have known anything of *plygain*. Dating back to at least the thirteenth century, this practice continues in some places today and refers to the procession to church and a service held between three and six in the morning on Christmas Day. This was perhaps a continuation of a Latin tradition known as Mass at Cockcrow, and here in Spain, the midnight mass is still called (very similarly) "Misa de gallo". There are a large number of carols associated with *plygain*, and they are interesting for referring not just to the birth, but the death and resurrection of Christ.

As Maude and Lillibet (named after one of my readers who won a competition that I didn't actually tell anyone about) have the surname Evans, there is a good chance that they can trace their family to Wales (or Cornwall). That idea is reinforced in the prologue when Old Miss Evans is so moved by a Welsh carol. I wanted to include one of the plygain ones, but I couldn't find any with a translation in English, so I went for another popular carol called 'O Deued Pob Cristion'. The English translation from 1928 isn't literal, and the original version is a call to admire the baby Jesus and his heavenly connection. What's particularly interesting is that it was written by someone called Jane Ellis, who, in 1816, was apparently the first woman in Wales to publish a book. That sounds like a joke from a silly comedy, but no, you didn't read it wrong; no women had published books in Wales until just over two hundred years ago. Bravo, Jane.

Other traditions that are connected with plygain include (that old classic) decorating with holly and mistletoe, the production of a delicious toffee called *cyflaith,* and decoration of the church with

248

specially designed candles. It sounds lovely, though I'm already tired by the end of midnight mass and can imagine there must be a lot of very sleepy heads after a three-hour service that finishes just before dawn.

We'll come back to music later, but I have one more thing to say about Surrey before we move on to some completely unrelated topics. There are many famous (and not-so-famous) rivalries in sport, but possibly the oldest (as I could find no close contender) is between the Surrey and Kent cricket teams. They first played one another over three hundred years ago and have, on average, played once a year ever since. It's probably not surprising that these were the first counties in England to lock horns, seeing as the sport is thought to have evolved in that part of the world.

The first match was played for a then no-doubt unfathomable prize of £50 (or £7,500 in modern money), and the result has been lost to the annals of time. Twenty-two years later, Surrey won with a team of men all called Mr Wood. By 1762, when playing in the small town of Carshalton where I was born, the two teams ended up brawling. A decade later, the pot had increased to a mindboggling modern equivalent of £128,000. The normally good-spirited rivalry continues to this day and, though I couldn't find the overall stats, as a proud child of Surrey I am happy to tell you that Kent have lost or drawn all but twenty of the 138 matches they've played at their rivals' home ground.

Speaking of rivalries, I bet I know a cricket groundskeeper's greatest enemy: moles! Yes, I did have to read about the funny little subterranean creatures because of a very minor reference. And, yes, I did find out some amazing things about them. Get ready for this…

Despite the irritating mounds they leave behind, moles, much like their wormy prey, do great work for the soil and the ecosystem in which they live. Their blood is specially adapted to breathe in low-oxygen/high-carbon-dioxide environments. They have two thumbs on each paw! Their long runs are designed to trap earth worms, and as soon as one falls inside, the mole will hear it and run along to paralyse it, before storing excess food in a specially burrowed-out larder. Moles eat approximately half their body weight in food each day! Despite the widely held belief that they are blind, moles do react to light and movement, presumably in order to detect predators who have infiltrated their burrows. Boom! Now you know more about moles. You're welcome.

Staying with the natural world: Willow trees! *Salix babylonica*, the Babylon or weeping willow, came to Europe from China via the Silk Road and had made it to England by 1730. It is now entirely naturalised and common to see there and, were it not for my mother's blue and white china, I might not have known of the eastern connection. The name comes from a mistake by "the father of taxonomy" Carl Linnaeus, as he believed these were the trees mentioned in Psalm 137 in the Bible as growing along the banks of the rivers of Babylon. More recent translations have corrected this to identify the poplar trees that actually grew there.

There is a legend which says that all of England's willows were descended from a tree planted by the poet Alexander Pope. He apparently noticed that a parcel sent from Spain to his friend the Countess of Suffolk was tied with willow branches and, as the tree is so easy to cultivate from cuttings, he was able to plant one of the twigs. In English folklore, willows are seen as malevolent and capable of uprooting themselves to follow passersby, whereas, in Japan, it is believed that ghosts can appear wherever a willow has been planted. Oh, and one last fact: what wood are cricket bats traditionally made from? You guessed it: willow!

Now, what connects willow trees and a 1920s' dance craze? Urmmm… not very much. Either way, the lindy hop first got a mention in print in 1927. It was named for Charles Lindbergh, after his successful flight (or "hop") across the Atlantic. As quoted in the OED, a newspaper in Reno, Nevada, rightly said of this early incarnation… "Obviously the first dance to be named for the Lindbergh flight was the 'Lindy Hop'. Another will be called the 'nonstop' and a third the 'French jump'. Like all trick dances, they will be done in a few theatres and dance halls… and that will be that."

The writer was correct, and the dance soon disappeared. However, an entirely different dance with the same name emerged a year later in the African American community in New York. By 1931 there was an "all-Harlem Lindy Hop contest" which "drew rounds of applause nightly". The dance is thought to have developed accidentally when the dancers

George Snowden and Mattie Purnell got separated in the middle of a step and had to improvise, much to the crowd's enjoyment. The term isn't used in this book, as there's little chance Chrissy would have recognised the dance, but it's the kind of move that would fit with the music that Gareth Heywood and his friends were playing.

It feels right to jump off in another direction now, as that's what happened to me when I started reading about the time Loelia's brothers were young men in the 1870s. So here's a bunch of interesting stuff I discovered from the period of Lord Edgington and the uncles' youth.

The first human cannonball act was performed at the Royal Aquarium in 1877 using a specially built canon to launch a seventeen-year-old acrobat known as Zazel. There was such fear for her safety that politicians tried to change the law to protect circus performers. Zazel, or Rossa Matilda Richter as she was christened, simply took her act to the Barnum and Bailey circus in the US, but perhaps she should have heeded the warning, as she suffered several accidents and eventually broke her back. She ended up in a full-body cast after a high-wire act went wrong. This was particularly ironic as she had spent a good part of her career campaigning for the use of safety nets. However, having recovered and retired, she lived to the not too shabby age of seventy-seven.

Her cannon was designed by a tight-rope walker called "The Great Farini". He was another remarkable character who claimed to have crossed the Kalahari desert and discovered a lost city there with his adopted, female-impersonating, acrobat son. What is far more credible is that Farini traversed Niagara Falls in all sorts of interesting ways in order to best his great rival Charles Blondin, who had been the first to cross it on a tight-rope the year before. Farini did this by turning somersaults, hanging upside down and navigating the wire whilst covered in a sack. However, I think Blondin was the ultimate winner. He crossed the falls whilst cooking and eating an omelette! Have you ever heard of such a feat?

Farini, or William Leonard Hunt, as he was actually called, certainly had an incredible life. He almost died whilst crossing another waterfall on stilts. He served in the American Civil War, during which time he showed his invention of "pontoon shoes" to Abraham Lincoln, and then sadly lost his wife to an accident when she fell from his shoulders off a tightrope and plunged sixty feet to her death. By the late 1870s, he'd taken up a post programming the entertainment at the London Aquarium, which was a wonderful-sounding venue in Westminster which was built as a high-end palace of science and entertainment but quickly came to cater for whatever would sell tickets.

Despite its name, it became well known for *not* having aquatic exhibits, as they were too expensive to keep. It did develop a reputation for itself as a rather scandalous place where young ladies in want of a husband were known to walk about unchaperoned. One such woman caught the eye of a notorious, though well-dressed gentleman. He promised that he would provide for her and, in the meantime gave her some capsules to keep her well. Luckily for her, they did not contain strychnine, but the man, Thomas Neil Cream, poisoned ten other people across three countries. He was even considered to be a Ripper suspect, as he apparently confessed just before he was hanged for his crimes. The fact he was in prison in America at the time of the Whitechapel killings pretty much rules this out, though.

You'll be happy to know that I'm not going to go into what I discovered about the Russo-Turkish war or the Great Game of simmering hostilities between Britain and Russia. I'm not even going to mention the lawsuit brought by the artist James McNeill Whistler against the critic John Ruskin, who accused him of "flinging a pot of paint in the public's face". No, I'm going to change to bullet points!

- Bird's custard – the market-leader custard powder in Britain – isn't actually custard as it doesn't contain eggs. It was developed by a chemist in 1837 for his wife who was allergic to them. It is also a non-Newtonian liquid, which is to say that it does not hold to Newton's law of viscosity, and that means… well, I tried to understand what that means, but I'm not very science-y and the most important thing I took from it is that (wait for it!) you can walk on Bird's custard! Essentially, the more stress you put on it, the more viscous it becomes, and there is a funny program you can find online in which they fill a swimming pool with custard and get someone to walk across it. When the presenter stops walking, he slowly sinks, but he is able to walk round and around without dropping beneath the surface – which is lucky as death by custard is not a good way to go.

- I came across a reference to "Mother Carey's chickens" in a newspaper from the twenties and had to find out what they were. It turns out that it is a nickname for storm petrels, a small, dark sea bird which sailors believed represented the souls of their fallen colleagues. Mother Carey herself is a traditional personification of the sea. She is a witch-like figure who controls the storms and, in one John Masefield poem, she is married to the male symbol of the ocean, Davy Jones. Incidentally, giant petrels are known as "Mother Carey's geese". So now I know.

- I'd never heard the term melisma before, but it refers to the technique of singing several notes for one syllable of a song. 'Ding Dong Merrily on High' is an obvious example of this. There are apparently thirty-one notes for the 'o' of Gloria – or rather, Glo-o-o-o-o-o or o-o-o-o-o or etc...

- As Chrissy described, there really was a hot-chocolate spill when a biscuit van set on fire and streams of molten goodness leaked out of it. It was being pulled by a goods train which had come to a stop at Brentwood Station in Essex in September 1927. I particularly like the part of the article about it which says, "Vigorous but unavailing efforts were made to retrieve the contents of the burning van, and finally the crowd concentrated on the streams of liquid chocolate which streamed out of it." I can just imagine the volunteers looking about between each other, saying, *Well, we have vigorously tried to save the contents. Can we stick our faces in this delicious chocolate now?*

- The two lesser-known books mentioned in this one are real. "Bad Girl" by Viña Delmar really was banned in Boston by The New England Watch and Ward Society, who had a reputation for knee-jerk censorship. Publishers were only too happy to be able to boast of such a fact as it sent sales skyrocketing. So, for a brief time in 1928, its twenty-three-year-old author was big news, and the book was a bestseller across America (outside of Boston, at least). The fact it was actually a very sensible tale about a young mother dealing with parenthood was less important, and there would be a film made of it three years later. Delmar used this exposure to get herself and her husband screenwriting jobs in Hollywood. They wrote two very successful Leo McCarey films, including the still brilliant "The Awful Truth" with Cary Grant. Unusually, their careers there didn't simply peter out after that; they decided to quit films to work in the theatre. Delmar never achieved such success again, but being an Oscar-nominated screenwriter and a bestselling author is good going by most people's standards.

- Mrs Baillie Reynolds, meanwhile, had a much longer career as a novelist and wrote fifty books between 1886 and her death in 1939. This sounds like an insane number until I remember that I'm about to start work on my thirtieth in five years. She wrote crime, mystery and gothic novels with titles like "A Dull Girl's Destiny" and "The Terrible Baron and Other Stories", but she was also a prominent suffragette, a mother of three, and was a big enough author to have her name featured prominently on the poster of a film adaptation of one of her books from 1920. I chose her for this story as I came across her in the newspaper and thought that the title "The Innocent Accomplice" fitted with an element of my plot.

- Some of my early readers were surprised that John Logie Baird is implied by Chrissy to be the inventor of the television. While other scientists refined his invention, I think this is an accurate claim. Technically, according to Wikipedia at least, he designed and "demonstrated the world's first live working television system" and would go on to invent the first colour television (way back in 1928) and transmit the first transatlantic television signals. One of the most amazing things about him is that he built that first mechanical television using bits and pieces that he found at home including scissors, knitting needles, and a used tea chest. In the course of his experiments he received a 1000-volt shock but lived to tell the tale, and when he did just that at the offices of the Daily Express, the editor told his staff "go down to reception and get rid of a lunatic who's down there. He says he's got a machine for seeing by wireless!" He demonstrated his invention in 1925 in Selfridges department store on Oxford Street (where my mum used to work).

He would go on to have a host of firsts and was instrumental in launching the BBC's early television broadcasts.

- I was also curious about how Halloween was perceived in Britain in the twenties, way before the American-style tradition had spread to Europe. Most newspaper articles from the time refer to it as an outdated tradition, but there is also plenty of talk of costume parties and even adverts for bananas mentioning the holiday. Here's a typical article from the Accrington Observer and Times from 1928 "Halloween is rarely celebrated in England to-day, but in olden times many counties had their own quaint ways of keeping up Halloween. In Lancashire it was generally believed that witches gathered on this night at an old tower in the Forest of Pendle to brew trouble for humans during the forthcoming year. Hence Halloween saw the quaint ceremony of *Leeting the Witches*. It was believed that if a lighted candle were carried about the fells from 11 p.m.-12 p.m., and it burned steadily during that hour, it would frighten away the witches, who, however, would do their best to extinguish the light. If the candle blew out, trouble would come to its holder. In Scotland there was generally a torch-light procession of country folk to an open space where a huge bonfire was set on fire. Then a number of people dressed as goblins would appear, carrying the effigy of a witch, which they cast into the flames. As the flames burnt the effigy the company danced round the bonfire." Spooooky stuff!

A little bit more food and drink, and then it's music time! In addition to Todd's main drink which you can read about on the cocktail page, we get mentions of both elderberry and parsnip wine. Elderberry wine was a speciality in Surrey and was often drunk at Christmas. Whereas I found a recipe for parsnip wine having read about it in a classic Christmas book the name of which I will not mention here.

Double Gloucester cheese is possibly the second-most common in Britain after standard cheddar, but that wasn't always the case. As the name might suggest, there is also a single Gloucester, but it was only in the 1970s that this lost British cheese was revived. At that point, there were only about fifty Gloucester cows in the country, but a man called Charles Martell bought a few of them and began to produce the cheese that had gone extinct. He managed to bring back both varieties and, since then, the cheese has gone from strength to strength and remains incredibly popular. Single Gloucester is less common and is protected, so it can only be made in the county of Gloucester. As a result, there are apparently only six farms producing it, and I don't think I've ever eaten any.

And now to something with a bit more rhythm. It both surprised me and didn't surprise me at all that the expression "music soothes the savage beast" has been misquoted for centuries. The actual line is "Music has charms to soothe a savage **breast**, to soften rocks, or bend a knotted oak", and it comes from the first line of the play The Mourning Bride by William Congreve. Appropriately enough, the phrase is not just misquoted, but often mis-attributed to William Shakespeare. Congreve was born a century after the Bard and became known for his comedies of manners in the period just after the restoration of the monarchy that I mentioned earlier.

Not only did he forge a short but successful career for himself with five plays that are still relatively well-known today, he had a wicked turn of phrase and also gave us "Heav'n has no rage, like love to hatred turn'd, Nor hell a fury, like a woman scorned", and the expression "kiss and tell". In addition to this, he likely had an affair and fathered a child with the 2nd Duchess of Marlborough, is buried at Poets' Corner, and sported a rather impressive wig.

This is my first Christmas book in which the musical selection hasn't only relied on well-known standards. I've already spoken a little about how I found some less famous carols, but here are the details... "Past Three o'Clock" was written by George Ratcliffe Woodward (who also wrote "Ding Dong Merrily on High") and refers to the calls of the London Waits – men who would patrol the city playing instruments at night for… some reason. They were essentially night watchmen, and they would call out the time on the hour – I'm sure they were popular with their neighbours.

Both "God Bless the Master of this House" and "Here Comes Poor Jack" are Surrey carols. The first is labelled as a "gypsy's carol" and the second as a "boys' carol" which I assume means it was sung in boys' schools or perhaps by groups of them going door to door. Both can be seen as wassailing songs, as they include requests for blessings and payment for the song. It's interesting that the first of those is also associated with yet another begging tradition known as *souling*. Around Halloween, people would make and distribute soul cakes – a small, round cake with fruit and spices. This may have been a forerunner of modern-day trick-or-treating.

Right, that's your lot. I've probably forgotten plenty of references, but I'm tired, and I haven't had any dinner. Nighty night for now!

ACKNOWLEDGEMENTS

This book feels as if it was written very quickly, though, according to my files, I started it two long months ago. I should probably thank all the writers of Christmas fiction who came before me and helped me get into the festive spirit while it was still thirty degrees outside. I'll thank my audiobook team, too, as they just recorded last year's book **"The Christmas Bell Mystery"** and listening to it in the middle of writing this one really pepped me up. Once again, it sounds as though I'm thanking myself, but the actor George Blagden makes those audiobooks his own, and the producer Leo is an absolute star.

Thank you, too, to my always kind and generous early readers, Bridget Hogg and the Martins. To Lisa Bjornstad, and Jayne Kirk for arduous close editing. And to my fellow writers who are always there for me, especially Catherine, Suzanne and Lucy. Oh, and also to my daughter Amelie for talking about Christmas all the time for some weeks already.

And, of course, a massive thank you to my ARC team… Rebecca Brooks, Ferne Miller, Melinda Kimlinger, Emma James, Mindy Denkin, Namoi Lamont, Katharine Reibig, Linsey Neale, Terri Roller, Margaret Liddle, Lori Willis, Anja Peerdeman, Marion Davis, Sarah Turner, Sandra Hoff, Mary Nickell, Vanessa Rivington, Helena George, Anne Kavcic, Nancy Roberts, Pat Hathaway, Peggy Craddock, Cathleen Brickhouse, Susan Reddington, Sonya Elizabeth Richards, John Presler, Mary Harmon, Beth Weldon, Karen Quinn, Karen Alexander, Mindy Wygonik, Jacquie Erwin, Janet Rutherford, Ila Patlogan, Randy Hartselle, Carol Vani, June Techtow, M.P. Smith and Keryn De Maria.

READ MORE LORD EDGINGTON MYSTERIES TODAY_

- **Murder at the Spring Ball**
- **Death From High Places** (free e-novella available exclusively at benedictbrown.net. Paperback and audiobook are available at Amazon)
- **A Body at a Boarding School**
- **Death on a Summer's Day**
- **The Mystery of Mistletoe Hall**
- **The Tangled Treasure Trail**
- **The Curious Case of the Templeton-Swifts**
- **The Crimes of Clearwell Castle**
- **A Novel Way to Kill** (novella available at Amazon)
- **The Snows of Weston Moor**
- **What the Vicar Saw**
- **Blood on the Banister**
- **A Killer in the Wings**
- **The Christmas Bell Mystery**
- **The Puzzle of Parham House**
- **Death at Silent Pool**
- **The Christmas Candle Murders**
- **Murder in an Italian Castle** (Spring 2025)

Check out the complete Lord Edgington Collection at Amazon

The first fourteen Lord Edgington audiobooks, narrated by the actor George Blagden, are available now on all major audiobook platforms. There will be more coming soon.

"THE CHRISTMAS CANDLE MURDERS" COCKTAIL

This book already contains all I knew about the Smoking Bishop when I set out to write it. It is mentioned in Dickens's "A Christmas Carol" and is a bit like mulled wine. Luckily, I have books and the internet to find out more about it. The main difference between the two drinks is that The Bishop (as no one calls it) includes port wine and you have to roast the citrus fruit to caramelise them. It is believed that the name comes from the shape of the bowl in which it is traditionally drunk resembling a bishop's mitre. There are a number of similar drinks which take ecclesiastical names, such as beadle, cardinal and pope, and all have slight variations in the recipe.

Chrissy explained how to make it pretty well, but here's a reminder (serves 10-12)...

750 ml of port

750 ml red wine

4 oranges (Seville, if possible as they are a little more bitter)

20 cloves

250ml/1 cup of water

Cinnamon, nutmeg, mace, and allspice, with a race of ginger (that's the root, but I'm sure powder would be fine).

90g / ½ cup dark brown sugar

I've come across several different recipes and here is an aggregate of them. Insert the cloves in the oranges (or in lemons if you prefer) and roast the fruit until blackened (though *starting to brown* is another option). One person who has tested this suggests putting them in the oven for 25 minutes at 200°c (another recipe says 60 minutes). Leave them to cool, then heat the alcohol with the water, sugar and spices to your taste (around ¼ a teaspoon of each maybe) until it is lightly simmering. Finally, cut the oranges in half, squeeze them out into the mixture, scrape out all the pulp and juiciness and keep everything on the heat for twenty minutes. Then pour it down your throat (but don't burn yourself)!

You can get our official cocktail expert François Monti's brilliant book "101 Cocktails to Try Before you Die" at Amazon.

WORDS AND REFERENCES YOU MIGHT NOT KNOW

Sandboys – I heard my mother use this expression last year and thought it was surely something you aren't supposed to say anymore. It turns out, though, that sandboys were the cheery individuals who delivered sand to pubs to spread over the floor. Rumour has it that they were happy as they were often paid in beer!

Holloing – to cry out or holler.

Ear-catching – similar to catchy, for music that gets stuck in your head.

Illuminated globe – There's nothing to explain here, I just wanted to say that I checked, and they did exist in the twenties. My brother got one for Christmas when we were kids, and I love them.

Earlily – we don't use the adverb of early anymore, but it is a word, though my early readers all thought it was a mistake, so I removed it!

Dish lift – similar to a dumb waiter, a platform on a pulley for bringing up food from the kitchen below.

John Logie Baird's recent experiments – the inventor of the television was starting to make big strides with his invention. He demonstrated the first transatlantic transmission in 1928 which went from London to New York.

Bee-bonneted – she has a bee in her bonnet.

Thomasing – what children did on St Thomas's Day (the day before this bit in the book) going from house to house, asking for money or food.

Unrufflable – I doubted it would be a word, but it was. Someone who cannot be ruffled.

Spill – a piece of paper or long thin stick for lighting a fire.

Ice cake – I found a reference to this in an old book. I don't know if it's an ice cream cake or something different.

Keep mum – stay quiet about something. Interestingly, the word mummers – which we will see later – is not thought to derive from this, but a Latin word for disguising oneself.

Uncheering – grim and gloomy

Danseur noble – the male version of a prima ballerina. I googled "primo ballerino" but apparently that isn't a thing.

Bramble jelly – a conserve made of blackberries. It's odd that, while we normally use the word jam in English and, though I'm used to most American vocabulary, "strawberry jelly" sounds a little mad, there are a few conserves which take the name jelly in Britain yet don't have gelatine. I do not know why that is.

Sapheaded – not very clever.

Talpa genus – the genus made up of true moles.

Head-hugger – this isn't actually a common term for a woolly hat, but I couldn't find a good one, so I/Chrissy made up our own.

Peroxided – I didn't expect it to be a real word, but it is!

Tantalean – referring to the myth of Tantalus who was punished by the gods by being made to stand in a pool of water which retreats as he tries to drink it, below a fruit tree that is just out of his reach. This is where we get the word tantalising.

Whoopee – a party.

Sororicide – sister murder!

Swine-hound – a rotter!

Snow-logged – not a word, Benedict, but it kind of makes sense.

"As a Porcupine Pines for its Pork" – a real novelty song from 1925.

Brave in ribbons – with lots of ribbons. It might be a reference to a particular book.

264

Stay-at-homeative – an old adjective which can refer to a homebody.

Wantwit – someone not very clever.

Stripling – a young fellow between childhood and adulthood.

Old Father Christmas – looking back at stuff from the 17th century, this seems to be the common name for him.

Hobbledehoy – a clumsy, awkward young person.

Childermas – the day which marks the massacre of the innocents – 28th December.

Of the first water – of the highest standard.

Hypochondriacals – hypochondriacs. Neither word was particularly common at the time, but the former seems to have been used a tiny bit more.

Crackbrain – a not very clever person.

Gooding – similar to Thomasing – begging from door to door around Christmas time.

Smellfungi – grumbly grumpy people. Admittedly, it's a rare word and would already have been largely obsolete in the twenties, but it was too good not to use.

Tiptearers – the northern Surrey word for people who put on mummers' plays.

Mumping – similar to Thomasing and gooding – begging from door to door around Christmas time.

Beeswax – this is a reference to the Odyssey, as Odysseus wanted to know what the sirens sounded like, so he told his men to put beeswax in their ears and tie him to the mast as they sailed past the charmingly monstrous creatures. These days he'd probably just Google it.

Deraisme – a French make of binoculars that were top notch back in the day.

THE IZZY PALMER MYSTERIES

If you're looking for a modern murder mystery series with just as many off-the-wall characters, try **"The Izzy Palmer Mysteries"** for your next whodunit fix.

Check out the complete Izzy Palmer Collection in ebook, paperback and Kindle Unlimited at Amazon.

THE MARIUS QUIN MYSTERIES

There's a new detective in town. Marius first appeared in the Lord Edgington novel **"A Killer in the Wings"**, and now he has his own series...

 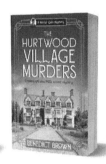  

Check out the complete Marius Quin Collection in ebook, paperback and Kindle Unlimited at Amazon.

ABOUT ME

Writing has always been my passion. It was my favourite half-an-hour a week at primary school, and I started on my first, truly abysmal book as a teenager. So it wasn't a difficult decision to study literature at university which led to a master's in creative writing.

I'm a Welsh-Irish-Englishman originally from **South London** but now living with my French/Spanish wife and our two presumably quite confused young children in **Burgos**, a beautiful mediaeval city in the north of Spain. I write overlooking the Castilian countryside, trying not to be distracted by the vultures, eagles and red kites that fly past my window each day.

When Covid-19 hit in 2020, the language school where I worked as an English teacher closed down, and I became a full-time writer. I have three murder mystery series. My first was **"The Izzy Palmer Mysteries"** which is a more modern, zany take on the genre, and my newest is the 1920s set **"Marius Quin Mysteries"** which features a mystery writer as the main character – I wonder where I got that idea from.

I previously spent years focusing on kids' books and wrote everything from fairy tales to environmental dystopian fantasies, right through to issue-based teen fiction. My book **"The Princess and The Peach"** was long-listed for the Chicken House prize in The Times and an American producer even talked about adapting it into a film.

"Death at Silent Pool" is the fourteenth novel in the "Lord Edgington Investigates…" series. The next book will be out in November 2024 and there's a novella available free if you sign up to my **readers' club**. Should you wish to tell me what you think about Chrissy and his grandfather, my writing or the world at large, I'd love to hear from you, so feel free to get in touch via…

www.benedictbrown.net

CHARACTER LIST

New Characters

Maude Evans – a grumpy, bitter woman who doesn't make it past the prologue.

Great Uncle Terry and Thomas – Chrissy's paternal grandmother's boring, smug and bigoted brothers. They are accompanied by a group of equally distasteful relatives including Aldrich, Peter, Philippa, Paul, and greedy Gerard.

Gareth Heywood – a cheery young gent who has recently moved to Kilston Down.

Alisha Steele – Chrissy's former teacher and a real sweetheart.

Dr Rodrick Steele – her dashing doctor husband.

Lillibet Evans – Maude's equally cantankerous sister.

Mayor Perkins – a nervous, superficial sort of person who is also the mayor for some reason.

Mrs Ethel Perkins – his glamorous and gossipy wife.

Mr Nigel Tibbs – the grocer and (it's no secret to tell you) Ethel's lover.

Mrs Nora Tibbs – the grocer who actually does any work.

Sergeant Keel – your cheery local bobby.

Maggie – the Kilston Down cook. Ooh, she's an angry one.

Jessop – Chrissy's beloved childhood butler.

Regular Characters

Lord Edgington – the man, the myth, the Marquess himself. He is a former Metropolitan police superintendent and the owner of a palatial estate in Surrey.

Christopher Prentiss – his well-meaning grandson and assistant in training, who is coming along rather nicely.

Albert Prentiss – Chrissy's brother, who is going through something of a crisis and is determined to get the upstairs cloakroom decorated in time for Christmas.

Violet Prentiss – Lord Edgington's daughter – Chrissy's mum. A good egg!

Walter Prentiss – Chrissy's father. He is rather set in his ways, but can you really blame him, considering…

Loelia Prentiss – Walter's mother, Chrissy's grandmother, and a real tough cookie (possibly with a soft centre).

Halfpenny – Cranley Hall's aged footman.

Henrietta ('Cook') – the Cranley Hall cook.

Todd – Lord Edgington's factotum and right-hand man. He acts as a chauffeur, barman, stand-in butler, and all-round great guy.

Alice – the Irish maid. **Driscoll** – her gardener husband. **Dorie** – a former pickpocket turned maid. **Timothy** – the Cranley Hall page boy.

Made in United States
Orlando, FL
22 December 2024